Alix found district nursing in Edinburgh very different from hospital nursing in London. The small, often poverty-stricken homes of her patients contrasted strikingly with the well-equipped wards of a modern general hospital. But the patients themselves were like people everywhere; and so were the doctors who cared for them.

It wasn't long before Alix realised that Robert Ross, the registrar, was taking more than a casual interest in her welfare. But she wasn't sure of her feelings about him . . .

Also by Lucilla Andrews

THE SECRET ARMOUR
THE FIRST YEAR
NURSE ERRANT
THE YOUNG DOCTORS DOWNSTAIRS
A HOSPITAL SUMMER
THE NEW SISTER THEATRE
FLOWERS FROM THE DOCTOR
A HOUSE FOR SISTER MARY
THE HEALING TIME
HOSPITAL CIRCLES
MY FRIEND THE PROFESSOR
THE PRINT PETTICOAT
THE QUIET WARDS
RING O'ROSES
HIGHLAND INTERLUDE
THE LIGHT IN THE WARD

and published by Corgi Books

Lucilla Andrews

Edinburgh Excursion

CORGI BOOKS
A DIVISION OF TRANSWORLD PUBLISHERS LTD

EDINBURGH EXCURSION

A CORGI BOOK 0 552 09567 2

Originally published in Great Britain
by George G. Harrap & Co. Ltd.

PRINTING HISTORY

George G. Harrap edition published 1970
Corgi edition published 1971
Corgi edition reissued 1974

This book is set in Pilgrim 10/10½ pt.

Corgi books are published by Transworld Publishers, Ltd.
Cavendish House, 57–59 Uxbridge Road, Ealing,
London, W.5.

Made and Printed in Great Britain by
Richard Clay (The Chaucer Press), Ltd., Bungay, Suffolk.

AUTHOR'S NOTE

I do thank most sincerely the late Professor R. W. Johnstone and the nursing authorities in Edinburgh for the help, advice, and kindness I received when seeking the technical background for this novel. The City of Edinburgh exquisitely exists and has its own admirable Health and Welfare Services, but all the characters and events in *Edinburgh Excursion* are fictitious.

LUCILLA ANDREWS

CHAPTER ONE

I noticed him at Waverley Station that first day. He was waiting on the platform a few feet from my carriage door, and as he was about John's age and height I wondered which would have appalled John more—his short back-and-sides haircut or his trouser turn-ups. I did not remember noticing his face, yet I recognized him instantly when I saw him again. I didn't even remember seeing Edinburgh Castle when my taxi took me for my first drive down Princes Street. My body was in a new city, bound for a new job and a new life, but my mind was still in London.

The one person I knew in Edinburgh that day was my only brother, Bassy. Bassy was twenty-one, in his second year at the University, two years younger and eight inches taller than myself. He shared a flat with three other boys over some second-hand bookshop near the Royal Mile, and when not protesting was reading History. When we last met at home in January his hair and beard had needed a hedge-cutter. Our parents had not minded as they thought Socrates would have approved. Socrates was one of their pin-ups. They were both archaeologists and at present on a dig in Jordan. We all got along very well and kept in touch on picture postcards.

I had sent Bassy a card with the dates of my District Nurse's Training Course and had one back from him a few days ago. He had a heavy date on this evening, but wanted me to have supper at his flat tomorrow. 'Chaps eager,' he wrote, 'and sex-starved as bird-shortage nearly as acute as in deep south. All expecting swinging London dolly. Kindly recall my image and oblige. Turn right at sweet-shop. Love, B.' He had not asked why I had suddenly decided to move north after my telling him in January nothing would persuade me to work out of London. Beneath all the yellow hair Bassy had a kind streak as well as quite a good brain.

It was odd to think January was only four months back. It seemed to belong in another lifetime and to another girl—a complete girl, with mind and body in absolute co-ordination.

The taxi stopped. 'Here we are, miss!'

There were six girls in my new set—three English and three Scottish. Four of us had come up in the same train, but we only discovered this when sorting ourselves out at the flats after our Superintendent's welcoming lecture.

Our Superintendent, Miss Bruce, was a slim, youngish woman with a serene face and calm, clever eyes. She took us through the four months' syllabus—working hours, rest-days, the general conditions we could expect to meet on the district, the extraordinary conditions we would almost certainly meet when least expected—and then dealt with our apparently unusual living arrangements. 'As extensive structural alterations are presently being made to the District Students' Home, two furnished flats in a private block only a short walk from here have been rented as temporary accommodation. In all probability you will remain there throughout your course.' Miss Bruce paused to look us over with a faint smile. 'I trust you've no objections to living out, Nurses?'

The girl sitting on my right had a Grecian profile and the very white skin that occasionally, and in her case wonderfully, accompanies bright red hair. She joined in the 'None, Miss Bruce,' with so much less enthusiasm than the rest of us that I looked at her curiously. She did not notice as she was giving all her concentration to her right hand's attempts to remove her left fingers from the knuckle.

Miss Bruce was glad we approved and hoped we would find our flats comfortable. She knew she need not request six highly recommended and carefully chosen State Registered Nurses to show consideration for their fellow-tenants, but she thought we might be interested to learn the tenants of the two lower flats were quiet, retired business people. The top flat was occupied by a professional man. 'He owns the building,' added Miss Bruce in her quiet and faintly lilting voice.

The chubby-faced girl on my left had wide-set brown eyes that tilted upwards slightly at the outer corners. She caught my eye and murmured without moving her lips, 'You reckon Big Brother's got the whole joint bugged?'

I could not answer as Miss Bruce had glanced our way. The girl's name was Gemmie Downs and she was from Liverpool. Later, when we found she, Redhead, and I had been alloted to Flat 4, Gemmie asked if I thought Miss Bruce had overheard.

'Doubt it. I only just got you.' I turned to the red-haired girl. 'Did you?'

She was Catriona Ferguson from Sutherland. 'I'm afraid I don't follow you, Alix. Did I what?'

Gemmie explained. 'So you're Scotch then, Catriona? How come I saw you on the train? Train in England?'

As Catriona was almost overpoweringly well-mannered she only looked momentarily pained. 'I've spent this last week visiting a schoolfriend in London. I trained in Glasgow.'

I said, 'Seeing we're fellow-aliens, Gemmie, mind if I give you a tip my brother gave me once? Unless one wants to wreck the Act of Union for good, one drinks Scotch but everything else is Scottish.' Catriona was blushing. 'Isn't that right?'

'I—er—wouldn't have put it so strongly, but Scottish is the correct term.'

Gemmie grinned. 'Get away! Hey, Alix, your brother up here? How's that? Where you from then?'

'London. I did general and midder at Martha's.'

'Done your midder then? Why aren't you on the three months' course?'

'I'm not an S.C.M.; just Part One. How about you?'

Gemmie had trained in Liverpool. She was a gay, amiable extrovert and inside of an hour gave us her life's history and main motive for moving out of her own patch. His name was Wilf Hawkins, he was a fitter working on the same shop-floor as her Dad, and he had been asking her to marry him for the past three years.

'I'd to get the hell out of it. Nowt else to be done.'

Catriona was sympathetic. 'Your parents don't approve?'

'That's the bloody rub! My Mam thinks he's a lovely lad—and my grannies—and my aunties! My Dad reckons I could do a packet worse. They've kept on and on. "When you going to wed him, then?" I'd to come away!'

I asked, 'How'd Wilf take that?'

'Right nicely! That's his trouble! He's such a bloody nice bastard! Get this, then! Three years—three years—and not once—not the once—one touch below the waist! What can a lass do with a lad like that?'

Catriona consulted her hands. I said, 'Tough going.'

'I'll say! And when I says, "Right, then, I've had enough, I'm off up to Edinburgh!" what does he say? "Right, then, give us a shout when you get back and we'll down the disco." There's hot-blooded passion for you! It's that mucky Mersey air!'

Catriona raised her eyes. 'I think the Mersey's fascinating. I took a trip there once with my brother.'

Gemmie and I looked at each other quickly, and as quickly away. That was the first of the many similar glances we exchanged that evening. When Catriona was in the bath Gemmie came into my bedroom and closed the door. 'You reckon that Catriona's for real, Alix?'

'You mean her freaky good manners? Yes, I think they're as real as her hair. The roots are the same red.'

'I spotted that.' She examined the family photo on my dressing-table. My life's history, if not my main motive, had followed hers. 'What bugs me is how such a soft sugar-plum with all those right fancy lah-di-dahs could've lasted out her general in Glasgow. I've not heard as Glasgow's a cushy patch. But she makes out like she doesn't know how many beans make five.'

'Maybe she's just crippled with shyness. Gets some that way.'

'Aye? You reckon that's why she's told us nowt about herself?'

'Either that, or as we've not let her get a word in and she's too polite to shout us down.'

'I'll not say as you're wrong, there.' She laughed and examined my Martha's badge. 'Think you'll miss your old firm?'

'I enjoyed Martha's.' I hesitated. 'But I don't think so. I'd been there long enough. Time to move on.'

'Oh, aye?' She eyed me keenly. 'What's his name, then?'

'John.'

'Doesn't he fancy getting wed?'

'Yep. Not to me. He's married now.'

'Sorry,' she said, 'sorry. Shouldn't have asked.'

'That's all right. So's your Wilf from the sound. Think you will marry him eventually?'

'Not knowing, love, can't say. Always wear your hair up?'

'Only when in uniform or trying to impress authority with my stability of character.'

'Right pseud, eh?'

'That's me, even if I've never taken a trip, with or without my brother.'

She grinned. 'That's the one that bloody threw me! She must've run into pot, L.S.D., the lot!'

'They may put it another way, up here. I'll ask Bassy tomorrow evening.'

'Reckon you'll be strong enough for visiting after our first day's work?'

'Hell, yes! We don't start till eight-fifteen, finish five-fifteen, and Miss Bruce said that for the first few days we'd be driven round by our high-powered escorts. After the nightmarish hours we still work on midder in Martha's, district work,' I added blithely and ignorantly, 'sounds like a sinecure.'

I remembered that idiotic remark more than once next day. The experienced district sister acting as my escort and teacher was a Mrs Duncan. She watched sympathetically as I heaved myself out of her official Mini that evening. 'All feet, Miss Hurst?'

I smiled. 'Sister, they haven't felt like this since my first day out of P.T.S. five years ago!'

'How well I recollect the sensation, though my own first day on district was twenty years back! The district nurse taking me round—and we then called them nurses not sisters—was a stout old body and I but a slip of a girl like yourself. She didn't pant and puff half as much as I did, and though Edinburgh born, bred, and trained, till then I'd no idea of the number of steps in this city of steps. I thought you managed the lands well today.'

'Lands? Oh, yes—those apartment houses. Thanks, but coming straight on from midder helps.'

'There's nothing to touch midwifery for keeping one in trim for a good scamper.' She was a pretty woman with a fresh, unlined complexion and short, curly grey hair. 'Apart from your feet dropping off, how do you feel about your first day's nursing far from the security of hospital walls?'

I thought back over the day. I thought of all those unlatched front doors in new council estates, old terraced houses, new privately owned houses, new flats, old, towering apartment houses. Mr MacThis, Mrs MacThat, rows and rows of Mac's and Mc's—old, young, less often middle-aged; some chronic, some accidents, some just home from hospital, some dying. At every front door Mrs Duncan's 'Good day to you!' had met with the same undercurrent of relief in the different voices replying, 'It'll be the Nurse! Come on in, Nurse!'

I said, 'It's even more different than I expected. I think I'm going to like that difference a lot, though I do now find it rather unnerving.'

'If you lacked the wee shivers down your spine you'd be lacking in imagination, my dear. To move into a different world is always an unnerving experience at first. That's what you've done. The well-equipped wards of any large general hospital are in one world; the wee beds in the wee homes of ordinary folk, in quite another. And when making the change the greatest change of all has to take place to the nurse, herself. The student has to alter her whole hospital-formed attitude to nursing when working on the district. In hospital, on her own territory, the nurse is the hostess, the patients her guests. On the district, Miss Hurst' —she raised a finger to mark her point—'from the first day to the last, the nurse is the guest in her patients' homes. Never, ever, lose sight of that fact. You are now the guest, and whether you will prove welcome or otherwise in your patients' homes depends only on yourself. We've all suffered unwelcome guests in our time, but can you imagine anything worse when you're feeling poorly and maybe elderly and alone? But this blethering'll not get you away to your student brother, nor me to my cooking before her man gets home from his work.' She checked her reflection in the driving-mirror. 'Mercy! Age may not have withered Cleopatra, but it's doing a grand job on me.' She hitched forward her hat-brim. 'What can't be repaired must be camouflaged. See you at eight-fifteen. Cheerio just now!'

She had given me a lift home from our headquarters. I waved her off from the pavement outside the tall, grey, flat-faced building that had once, according to Mrs Duncan, been a private house. The houses on either side and across the road were much the same size. Mrs Duncan said they had mostly been converted into flats and that our road and its immediate vicinity were generally considered one of the best residential areas in Edinburgh. When she told me this on the drive home I had intended taking a good look at our classy road, but was halfway up the four flights before I remembered.

Gemmie was stretched on the sitting-room sofa, her shoes off and hat on her chest. She opened her eyes as I limped in. 'Just a bloody sinecure, eh?'

I kicked off my shoes. 'That'll teach me to open my big mouth. How'd you make out?'

'Not so bad, though I'm a wreck of me former self. You?'

'Same.' I took off my coat and unbuttoned my apron. 'Where's Catriona?'

'Gone to sup with some auntie she's got living over what she calls t'other side. Reckon we're wrong side of the tracks?'

I told her what Mrs Duncan had said, then suggested she came with me to Bassy's. 'You'll be doing a favour. Seems there's a bird-shortage.'

'Thanks, love, but some other time. I'd a letter from my Wilf by afternoon post down headquarters. He says he's fixed his landlady and will I ring him reverse at seven for a chat.'

'Round one to Wilf!' I went off to change with Bassy's image in mind. The result got Gemmie off the sofa.

'Groovy! Where's your placard?'

'Bassy'll provide.'

She circled me. 'I fancy that black cord pinny. It looks great over that blue rollneck. Mind, there's two things wrong. Though your hair's down, I can still see your face, and your yards of legs should be in thigh boots.'

'Not the way my feet are tonight, they shouldn't! I bought these slip-ons second-hand from a girl at Martha's. They're half a size too big and right now sheer bliss.' I took Bassy's card out of my shoulder-bag. 'How do you suppose I get to the Royal Mile? I meant to ask Catriona.'

'Search me.'

'I'll find a cop. See you.'

'Have a good knees-up!'

The only long mirror in our flat was on a wall in the hall. I stopped to look at myself on the way out and wished I hadn't. Though I had intentionally dressed to boost Bassy's image, the ego I was really trying to please was John's. He had always said that with my colouring I should only wear black or blue, and that if he ever saw me in a maxi or with my hair up after we were married he'd divorce me. He said it all during those eleven months. And then after five weeks' deafening silence he rang me. 'Darling,' he said, 'you do understand the last thing I'd ever want to do is hurt you?'

I had to say something. I said I understood.

I nearly went back to my room to change the lot. I tried to kid myself it was lack of energy and not moral courage that prevented me; then immediately proved myself a cowardly liar by charging down the stairs as if the house were on fire. It was just possible nothing would have happened had my shoes been a better fit. Only just, as I was tired, moving carelessly, and wallowing in self-pity. When my left shoe shot off on the last flight I pitched forward after it. If the man coming in through the front door had reacted less quickly I could have had the nasty accident I was asking for.

He seemed to grab me in mid-air, and though slightly built and only about three inches taller than myself, somehow he withstood the momentum of my five-seven and

14

nine stones. We rocked dangerously, but remained on our feet. I recognized him as the man I had seen at the station while I was still in his arms. I was too winded to wonder what he was doing in our hall, though not to appreciate what he had just done for me.

'Thanks,' I said breathlessly, 'thanks very much. I could've killed myself.'

'Possibly, if not probably.' He was as breathless as myself, which was hardly surprising since I had landed on his chest. 'Are you hurt?'

'Just shook up.' I moved back and sat on the stairs. 'I hope I haven't cracked your ribs. Are you all right?'

'Quite, thank you.' He straightened his tie and smoothed his lamentable hair-cut. 'Did your ankle turn over? Was that why you slipped?'

I showed him my shoeless foot. 'You didn't see my shoe beating me to it?'

'I was aware the air was suddenly filled with flying objects, but being a trifle surprised, I'm afraid I forgot to observe the finer details.' His voice was deep and very precise. 'You're sure you're not hurt?' He looked beyond me up the stairs. 'Are you staying or visiting here? Is there anyone you would like me to fetch to you?'

'No thanks. I'm fine. I'm just off to visit my brother when I get my breath back.'

'Sit there,' he said, 'while I retrieve your possessions.'

My bag had fallen with me and emptied itself all over the hall floor. I watched him collecting my lipstick, eyeshadow, compact, keys, scissors, postcards, through a haze of self-fury and self-disgust. I thought of the patients I had seen all day, of accident wards in Martha's, and how very easily I could now have been en route for one with a broken back or fractured skull. So the man I loved had stopped loving me? So that was tough. And so was real illness, or accidents caused by other people's carelessness. An accident caused by one's own childish carelessness was only excusable if one was a child.

'This seems to be all. Would you care to check?'

I blinked and discovered he was offering me my bag. 'Sorry. I was in coma. Thanks.' I gave my bag a cursory glance. 'Seems all here. Oh!' I had seen Bassy's card. 'Do you have any idea how I can get from here to the Royal Mile?'

He had a long, sensitive mouth that was contradicted by the toughness of his jaw and in his face. Seeing him close to having now had a good look at him, I understood why my subconscious had bothered to register his face without my realizing it. Pre-John, all my boyfriends had had light-brown hair, rather plain, solid faces, and outsize jaws. For other reasons Bassy had always referred to them as my 'Untouchables'.

His mouth twitched upward at one corner, but whether that was a nervous tic or he was fighting the frivolous urge to smile I could not tell as his slightly hooded hazel eyes were impassive. They were also by far his most attractive feature. 'I believe I can direct you. Where precisely do you wish to go?'

I gave him Bassy's address. 'Only one sweet-shop?'

He smiled rather attractively. 'I'll jot it down for you.'

A couple of minutes later we went outside together. There was a largish blue car parked by the front door, and getting out of the front passenger door a girl in a silk coat the exact shade of my sweater. She could not have been my sister, but as we had the same colouring, we could have got by as second cousins. 'What's the hold up, Charlie?' She glanced at me curiously, but pleasantly. 'You haven't forgotten we're late as it is?'

'No. I'm sorry to delay you like this, Josephine. Merely a minor mishap.' He nodded at me. 'All well, now?'

'Fine, thanks very much.'

'Not at all.' He turned back to the girl. 'I'll just go up and see if he's left a message.'

'Can't you ring from my place, sweetie?'

My bus arrived immediately I reached the stop he had marked on the map drawn on the torn-off back of an envelope. Jogging in my seat on the top deck, I wondered about his exact relationship with 'Josephine'. From her voice and skirt-length she was English. That 'my place' showed they were not married. Sister? His educated voice held only a faint Scottish intonation, but he wasn't English.

16

Mistress? Not him. Even without that hair-cut and those turn-ups he'd respectable citizen stamped all over him. Official fiancée or about to be, or nothing.

Then I found my purse was missing.

A forgotten two bob in the bottom of my bag took care of my fare, if it did not solve the other question. I tossed it around. Not a man like that! Either he hadn't noticed it on the hall floor or it was still in my room. A man like what? Where did I get the big idea I knew anything about men? Remember John?

Suddenly I was damned if I'd remember John. I hadn't a death-wish, but only by the grace of God and Charlie was I now in one piece. My map showed the next stop was mine. I got off the bus belligerently and breathed deeply. I had been in Edinburgh over twenty-four hours, but that was when I first saw it.

Across the cobbles the lines of High Kirk of St Giles were uncompromisingly grim and strangely impressive. Everywhere I looked were tall, cramped buildings, grey as the cobbles, grey as the thick clouds hurtling inland from the Firth of Forth over a paler grey sky. The total, and to me unexpected, effect in face of all that grey was one of austere beauty. I forgot my purse and walked up the hill in the wrong direction before drifting back reluctantly towards the right turning I wanted. Drifting with me were quiet posses of elderly American couples, the husbands in neat light suits with very white hair and their expensively dowdy wives with tired feet. The evening rush-hour traffic raced as wildly over the cobbles as the traffic in London, but the drivers had much nicer manners. The two that nearly mowed me down when I crossed to the sweet-shop both raised their hats when they missed me.

The second-hand bookshop was locked for the night. A door at the side was open and led straight on to steep stone stairs. I went up. Another door, and Bassy's name heading the three others on the card. I rang twice, then tried the door. It was unlocked. 'Bassy? Anyone home?'

That door opened into a large room that looked as if it were the stockroom of the shop below, and stocked by a drunk. A note was fixed to the mirror above the book-piled hearth. 'Alix, sorry had to go to meeting. Food in kitchen.

Make yourself at home. Back around seven. Bassy.'

I shifted enough books off the sofa to get my feet up, kicked off my shoes, and closed my eyes. It could have been five minutes, five hours, or five days later that someone shook me and a man's voice asked me to please wake up.

I surfaced slowly through waves of sleep and was just remembering where I was when I was shaken again. 'Relax, Bassy! I'm awake!' I reached up with my eyes still shut, flung my arms round his neck, and kissed his cheek. 'Thank God you've taken off that repulsive beard!' I opened my eyes and nearly had a coronary when I saw who I was embracing. 'My God!' I leapt off the sofa. 'What are you doing here?'

'Returning your purse. I found it on the hall floor after you'd gone. As you'd mentioned this address, it seemed sensible to try and deliver it in person. Had you not been here I'd have taken it to the police.' He was smoothing his hair again and looking much more like a Charles than a Charlie. Charlie was human. His present expression was reminding me more than a little of St Giles. 'I must apologize for walking in unannounced. I rang several times. Excuse me.' He shifted the sofa and handed me the shoe I had been trying to reach with one foot.

'Thanks.' I sat down to replace both. 'I'm sorry I kissed you like that. Traumatic experience for you. I thought you were my brother.'

After a deep and rather peculiar silence he said he quite understood and produced my purse. 'Do you know how much money this contains?'

'Roughly, four pounds fifteen.'

'Would you mind checking that?'

I hesitated, then saw his point. 'Sure. Yes. All here, and thanks again . . .'

'Alix, my angel!' Bassy was in the doorway. He wore a psychedelic donkey-jacket, faded yellow cords, and his hair and beard were longer and tattier than ever. 'Sorry about that something meeting.' Then he noticed Charlie, did a double-take at his suit, and switched to his alter and reasonably civilized ego. 'I say, do forgive me. Long time no see Alix and so forth. You'll be a friend of hers. How do you

18

do? Sebastian Hurst. London, England.'

'Charles Linsey. Edinburgh, Scotland.' They shook hands. And Charles Linsey explained why he had come.

'I should've guessed,' said Bassy. 'That girl's a menace. Takes after our old man. He's left travellers' cheques and passports all over Europe and the Middle East. Great problem to my mother. Can I offer you a beer? I think we've got some somewhere. If not, milk? We always have milk. Hold it! We may have some gin. Gin?'

'Thank you, but I should be on my way.' The room was now packed with Bassy's equally colourful and hairy chums. 'Goodnight, Miss Hurst, Mr Hurst, gentlemen.'

There was silence until Bassy checked the stairs. He shut the door. 'You lot thinking what I'm thinking?' They all nodded. 'Don't know his face. You?'

A small, dark-haired boy with sideboards, chin-fringe, and bad acne said, 'Like it reads blurred, man.'

'He's a don or whatever they get called here?' I thought of our parents' academic friends. 'So clean and neat?'

Five Englishmen and one Welshman agreed sadly it could happen in Edinburgh.

Later, Bassy walked me home and we talked of John. He said, 'I knew you were hung-up on the creep, but I always thought he'd ditch you the moment a better proposition turned up. Something thrown you?'

'Something.'

The girls were still up, and he came in to meet them. We told them about Charles Linsey. Gemmie was very amused and Catriona very shocked. 'What if he wasn't merely calling here? He could be'—she looked upwards nervously —'Big Brother. And you kissed him!'

Gemmie clasped her hands. 'Ten bob a week off the rent for a start, eh, Alix? Seeing what we get paid, get cracking, lass! Get up them stairs!'

Catriona's face matched her hair. 'It is quite amusing in its way.'

I said, 'If he is.'

Bassy went into our hall and returned with the telephone directory. 'He is.'

CHAPTER TWO

Mrs Duncan drove past on her way back from lunch and drew up ahead. 'What's the problem?'

I hitched my bike more securely against the kerb and went over to her. It was the last day of our first week and we were now making selected calls unescorted. We had been given our separate areas, and Mrs Duncan worked the one adjoining mine. 'Have I got this address wrong? This new man back from hospital.' I handed her a blue card. 'How can a burn be a street?'

'This is right. The burn dried up years ago, but they kept the name when they built the street over the bed. So old Donald Fleming's back? Ah, I know him well, and so will you if you've this area long. He's no equal as an unhandy man about the house.'

'That how he cracked his knee?'

'Aye. Dropping off a ladder, painting the outside of his house. He put a nail through his hand when mending the kitchen chair, and the time before his fist through the window he'd just glazed. And that's but this year! Still, it keeps him happy in his retirement, so one can but hope he'll not kill himself in the process. Which reminds me——' She sorted through my cards and took out a pink one. (Male, blue; female, pink.) 'When you get to giving young Mrs MacRae her anti-anaemic injection this afternoon, will you ask her to oblige me by remembering those twins she's carrying are due in seven weeks? I'd a word with her mother this morning. Yesterday the daft lassie was up top of a table distempering her spare-bedroom ceiling. At her size!' She read my mind, despite my blank expression. 'Yes, my dear,' she added drily, 'I'm aware that aside from this anaemia she's a strong lassie, the right age for child-bearing, and that birth is a natural function. So is death. You've seen

20

a baby die?' I winced, involuntarily. 'You tell her to watch herself, Miss Hurst. Cheerio just now!'

Mr Fleming was a sturdy little man with bushy iron-grey hair and a static expression that reminded me briefly of Charles Linsey. He was sitting by a blazing open fire with his injured leg propped on the piano-stool. The sitting-room was very warm, highly polished, and all the geraniums in the row of pots on the bay windowsill were in bloom.

Mrs Fleming was very thin, very neat, and directly I opened my mouth very apprehensive. She hovered at my elbow and checked with an experienced eye the contents of my sterile-dressing pack and my surgical technique as I dressed her husband's leg. 'Mind you don't throw out those wee tongs with the rest, lassie. They've to return to the Department for re-sterilizing. The dirty dressings may go in my kitchen boiler, but you'll have to put the tinfoil dishes in my dustbin.'

The kitchen was as highly polished as the best room. The dustbin gleamed like my tinfoil.

I had my coat on again when she said, 'You'll be from England, Nurse?'

'Yes.' I smiled. 'London.'

'Do you hear that, Donald?'

'Aye,' said Mr Fleming, 'I do.'

I waited, expectantly, but they did not say anything else. They just looked at me. 'Well,' I said, 'goodbye for now. See you on Sunday, Mr Fleming.'

'Cheerio,' they said.

About forty minutes later I cycled along an old engrimed row of two-up, two-down terraced houses. The MacRaes' was third on the left and their front-door unlatched. I called, 'Good afternoon, Mrs MacRae. May I come in? It's Nurse Hurst.'

'I knew that from your voice! You talk awful quaint, but I like it fine, Nurse! I'll be down!' Mrs MacRae's voice was drowsy, and when she appeared at the top of the steep, narrow stairs her smock was crumpled. 'I was taking a wee nap.'

'Don't bother to come down. I'll come up.'

She was nineteen and chubby, with cropped dark hair and dark eyes. She never had much colour, but seemed much paler than usual. She blamed the dumplings she had eaten for lunch. 'Hamish was home as he'd to deliver a load up the way, so I'd a hot dinner ready. I've an awful weakness for dumplings, but they've no use for me.' She caught her breath. 'You see that? Heartburn! Terrible!'

I watched her, clinically. It could only be indigestion. 'Why not go back to bed for your injection?'

'You'll think me awful lazy—och! No more dumplings for me! Worse than the wee devils having a rave-up.' Suddenly she clutched the stair-rail with both hands. It was not a long pain, but while it lasted her stance and breathing were unmistakable. 'Nurse? Och away!' She clutched me. 'Nurse!'

There was only time to get her on her double-bed, put on my mask and an emergency pair of sterile gloves. The minute baby boy literally landed in my hands. His very red, wrinkled face was covered with fine down and grease, he flayed the air with arms no thicker and much shorter than my fountain-pen, and though his cry was a high, premature croak, it was a very good croak.

'The two, Nurse?'

'At the moment, just one perfect little boy. All right your end, duckie? Good girl. Lie still.' I tore the wrapping off an entire roll of cotton-wool and enveloped the baby, keeping the wool well back from his face and making sure he had enough room beneath to expand his lungs. I added another ligature to his cord, and he tried to kick me in the face with microscopic legs. He was still shouting his head off. 'Junior now looks more like a little Eskimo than a little Scotsman. I don't think he approves of this world.'

'He's a terribly noisy wee devil! Nurse, you said he was all right?' She insisted as every newly delivered woman I had ever known did at this particular moment.

'Outwardly, perfect! Congratulations,' I said slowly, as I was thinking fast. The baby needed an oxygenated incubator as soon as one could get here, but the house had no phone and the second twin might be about to appear. The first baby's placenta had shot out after him and seemed intact, though I had not yet had time for a proper look. Mrs MacRae was not losing more than was normal, but at this stage after such a rapid delivery anything could happen. 'Got any shawls handy? That drawer? Thanks.' I tested the shawls against my face. They were dry. I swathed the baby. 'How about a basket? Shopping or laundry? One with a flat bottom. Got one?'

'On my kitchen table, Nurse.' She was a very sensible girl. 'I've my boiler going there.'

I tore for the basket, lined it with an unread newspaper and another shawl, laid the baby on top and the basket on the kitchen table. I opened up the boiler and plugged into the kettle's socket the strongest electric fire in the house. The heat in the kitchen made me sweat before I ran back up. 'I'm sorry I couldn't let you hold him or have more than that quick look, Mrs MacRae, but he's so little the less handling right now the better.'

She was smiling wonderfully. 'A wee peep was enough, just now. I've a son! Me!' Her voice rose in triumph and amazement. 'Hamish'll be that pleased! He's been awful set on the one being a laddie. Can you hear the other heart? Is it coming away? I can't feel it.'

'The heart's fine, and I don't think he's shifting.' I hitched forward a hard chair with my foot. 'I'm just going to shift the foot of your bed up on this.'

'Och, not alone! You'll do yourself a terrible mischief— you've done it! You must be awful strong, Nurse!'

'Awful worried' was more like it. 'Any of your neighbours have phones? No? Where's the nearest box? Right.' I checked her pulse again. It was now back to normal and excellent. 'I'll be very quick, but while I'm gone, whatever happens don't move. Promise? Even if you feel a bit damp below, just lie like a statue. All right? That's the girl!'

I ran to the phone-box. Mercifully, it was empty and in order. I rang Miss Bruce, as that was the official rule for any nurse with any major problem on district.

'Very well, Miss Hurst,' said Miss Bruce calmly, 'I'll inform the Obstetric Flying Squad. Stay till they take over. Her husband's employer? Good. I'll contact him. Thank you.'

I ran back. No one else was panting. Mrs MacRae was relaxed and smiling. The baby was a good colour, breathing well, and fast asleep.

The nearest Maternity Hospital was some distance away, but the O.F.S. arrived within minutes. The ambulance brakes were barely on when a huge dark-haired man in a white coat leapt out of the back. In one hand he carried a large sterile-dressing tin and in the other a portable infusion set. He was immediately followed by a smaller man in white carrying a portable anaesthetic machine, and a staff midwife with a portable incubator.

I flattened myself against the wall by the open front door. 'Mother, first right, up. Baby, first left, down.'

The big man was an obstetrical registrar and his colleague an anaesthetist. 'As the second bairn appears content to wait, Nurse,' said the registrar a couple of minutes later, 'we won't.'

The baby was already in the ambulance with his incubator re-plugged into the special heating system with which the vehicle was equipped. The incubator had been heated up on the outward journey and remained warm during its brief period of disconnection. The staff midwife was as worried as I was about the baby's size. If he was more than two pounds the difference was in half-ounces.

'All aboard?' The registrar took an appraising look round. 'Thanks, Nurse—wait, now! Mrs MacRae wants a word with you.'

I stuck my head in. 'Don't worry, Mrs MacRae, I'll tidy round and lock up.'

'It's not that!' she raised her head, still smiling. 'Have you a first name that'll do for a laddie?'

'Alexia.'

'That takes care of wee Alex! Let's away before we've to find another name.' The registar whistled piercingly and slammed the doors. I looked at my watch. They had come and gone in five minutes.

Inevitably, I finished much later than the others that evening. We had now organized a flat chore-rota. Gemmie was in the kitchen, cooking supper, Catriona and the one

English girl from below, Sandra, were in our sitting-room.

Sandra came from Sussex and had trained in London. She was a quite pretty brunette with a trim figure and thick legs. On her own admission, she was apparently incapable of posting a letter without escaping rape by inches. 'I just don't know what there is about me,' she was telling Catriona. 'Somehow men can't keep their hands off me.'

'Dear me,' said Catriona, 'how exhausting!'

'Utterly fragmenting!' exclaimed Sandra. 'Alix! My dear, what do you think happened to me this evening? Old Mother Kinloch on the ground floor was chatting me up when I got back, and then this man came in, and—my dear—the way he looked at me!' She flapped the false eye-lashes she invariably slapped on within five minutes of coming off duty. 'He simply refused to move until Mrs Kinloch introduced me, and I must say I think it's going to be rather fun having him as a landlord. Did you know he's a medic?'

'Big Brother? He's a medic? Then why hasn't he got his qualifications in the phone-book?'

Catriona shrugged. 'Possibly as he's neither a G.P. nor a consultant.'

Gemmie joined us. 'Seeing the lad's got himself a blonde bird, Sandra, I reckon you'll have to wait in the queue.'

'Are they actually engaged?' Sandra wanted to know. 'Not that being married really makes all that difference to some men when I'm around—don't ask me why.'

Gemmie disappointed her by assuring her we wouldn't. 'Nosh up, girls! You going to stay and watch us eat, Sandra? Sorry, but only enough for three.'

'Can't stay. I've got a date.' Sandra paused on her way out. 'And who kept you so late, Alix? What's his name? Tell, tell!'

'Alex MacRae. A dolly of a Scotsman, even if seven weeks prem. I fancy 'em young!'

Sandra did not wait for the other details. Gemmie and Catriona had them over supper. We were clearing when Gemmie said, 'Our Sandra fancies Big Brother.'

I said, 'He's quite attractive despite his deplorable clobber. Turn-ups and a jacket the wrong length—and as for his hair-do—ugh!' I filled the sink with hot water. 'If he's a medic., what's he doing being our landlord?'

Gemmie suggested he might have won a football pool and bought the house with the money, or inherited it. 'If he's not a G.P. or a pundit he'll have to be a hospital resident. He'd not buy this on their salary.'

Catriona flushed slightly. 'He could work for the University. It—er—is quite a big university. Did this O.F.S. really come and go in five minutes, Alix? Which Mat. Hospital?'

The next day was my first day off. The others were on duty and left without waking me. I slept through my alarm and did not open my eyes till five to ten. At ten-thirty Bassy was arriving to take me sightseeing. I leapt in and out of a bath and was eating toast and making coffee when our front-door bell rang.

'On the latch. Come in, Bassy!' I called, but the bell rang again. I opened the door. 'Gone deaf—oh!' I smiled. 'Sorry, Doctor, I was expecting my brother. Good morning.'

My caller was the large obstetrical registrar. He had on a very snazzy double-breasted navy jacket, elegant grey cords, a pale-blue shirt, and dark-blue tie. He looked very tired and slightly nervous. 'Good morning, Miss Hurst. Mrs Duncan told me you lived here and were off today, and as I'm off for an hour, I—I thought you'd like to know Mrs MacRae and wee Alex are doing nicely.'

It was as good an opening gambit as any, and though, from the shadows under his eyes, he had forgotten the sensation of an uninterrupted night's sleep, he had climbed four flights of stairs to use it. I offered him coffee. 'My brother'll be here . . .' and the phone rang. 'Do come in.'

'If you're sure I won't be in the way?'

I smiled and reached for the phone. 'This'll be my brother to say he's overslept.'

It was Bassy. He had not overslept as he had not been to bed last night. 'I have this problem, Alix. I'm in Dunfermline.'

'Why Dunfermline?'

'Birthplace of Andrew Carnegie. Bruce is buried in the Abbey here.'

'So?'

26

'So when I drove this bird Melanie home after the party last night we got talking, and I mean talking, and then her mother said why didn't I stay to breakfast and Melly says why don't I stay to lunch? Sorry and all that, but I think I should. Got to remember Anglo-Scottish relations and so forth. Mind?'

I glanced at the registrar. He had propped himself against a wall. He was darker and taller than John, but he had the same type of very regular features and very well-set, dark eyes. In theory I would have expected that to put me off him. I was interested to find it worked the other way round. 'No. Thanks for ringing. See you some other time.'

The registrar was a Robert Ross. He said he got called Robbie. He was on his third cup before he surfaced sufficiently even to talk shop. Last night he had delivered eight babies and two in a moving ambulance. 'The second mobile mother had a P.P.H. (post partum haemorrhage). We'd her group and had taken some whole blood with us.' He drained his cup. 'Messy.'

'And dodgy, getting a needle into a collapsed vein on the move.'

'I have to get the bloody wee needle in. That's what I'm paid for.'

'I've known O.R.s draw their pay and still miss. You didn't?' He shook his head. 'How is she today?'

'Great.' He smiled gloomily. 'They all are. It's just the staff that are nervous wrecks. A night like last night's enough to put one off sex for life. No place like a labour ward for appreciating the virtues of eternal chastity.' He had a strong Scottish accent and rattled out his 'r's' and 't's'. 'Or wasn't that your impression of midder?'

'In spasms. So many of our London mums seemed so swamped by matrimonial problems.'

' "Ach, Doctor, would that I were free again." '

'You get that too?'

'Constantly.'

'How do you answer that?'

'A placebo. A woman in labour needs comfort, not the truth.' He watched me over the rim of his cup. 'You make very good coffee.'

'I've a superb talent for pouring on the boiling water. This is instant.'

His eyes smiled very pleasantly. 'Not only hospitable, but honest! Where did you train?'

We talked awhile about Martha's, and then his teaching hospital in Glasgow. He was a Glaswegian and had come to Edinburgh last year. 'Doesn't Catriona Ferguson share with you? She trained at my hospital.'

'You know Catriona?' I was surprised, as she had not mentioned this last night. Though I had not then known his name, I had described him in some detail. Once seen, he was a man most girls would remember, and not only for his great height.

'We saw each other around. You know how it is in any big hospital. You can see faces around for years before you can put names to them.'

'That's very true.' I glanced upwards, then asked if he knew anything about our landlord.

'Charles Linsey? What do you want to know of him?'

'What can you tell me?'

'He's a pathologist on the research side of the University.'

'Catriona was right!'

He looked up from his cup. 'In what way?' When I told him what she'd said he added, 'We've a different system up here. The Medical Faculty is a direct arm of the University of Edinburgh instead of being a Medical School attached to a teaching hospital, as, I believe, you've in London. You've met Charles Linsey?'

'I've bumped into him, literally.' I explained how. 'He was rather sweet. How does he come to own this house?'

He shrugged. 'That I'm in no position to answer. I barely know the man. I see him occasionally—and occasionally with a decorative English blonde.'

'Josephine!'

For some odd reason a dull flush crept up his face. 'You know Josephine Astley?'

'No. I just saw her once with Charles Linsey. He called her Josephine. This is the first time I've heard her surname.'

'But it's a name you recognize?'

'No. Should I?'

His flush had faded and he was now looking bellicose. 'Seeing you're English, I'd have thought so. Daddy's the industrialist. She's the only child.'

'And you know her?' I asked, guessing the answer explained his belligerence and, quite possibly, his presence. I was a little surprised to find that did not bother me at all, and much more so to learn I'd guessed wrong.

'Of course I don't know her! I'm neither in her social nor financial class, and, frankly, I've little use for either. Such upper-class circles are not for me, and not merely as I wouldn't know which fork to use first, being but a laddie up from the working classes.'

I shouldn't have been so surprised after seven years in a co-ed grammar. 'Come the revolution, Robbie,' I said, 'you're going to have quite a time explaining away all the protein, vitamins, and education you somehow acquired in your humble working-class home. You didn't grow to your size on bread and scrape, though it's as well you did. You need the shoulders of an ox to carry your chip. And, incidentally, since you're so anti the upper classes, how are you going to cope when you're an obstetrical specialist and move into their ranks?'

He was puce. 'You extraordinary gurrrl!' Then he laughed. 'I'm not turning pundit. Once I've obstetrics taped I'm moving right up north as a G.P. Do you know Caithness?'

'Only from the map.' I was not yet sure if I liked him, but I liked the way he had taken this. John would have sulked for hours. 'Boots and a deer-stalker?' He nodded. 'I hope you get what you want.'

'I hope so too, though I don't expect it to drop in my lap. I'm a great believer in getting up off my backside and going out to get what I want. That's why I'm here—as if you haven't guessed. I've to work from noon today, but I'm off next weekend. As I too have a weakness for decorative English blondes, what're you doing next Saturday, Sunday, or preferably both?'

CHAPTER THREE

'In future,' said Mrs Duncan, 'remember to sit only on a hard chair. Did you drown many in your wee basin of water?'

'About six.' I scratched my neck.

'Take a bath and wash your hair directly you get in. That'll wash them off you.' She moved into the near-side lane as we ran into Waterloo Place. 'Hop out fast as I can't stop here. I hope your bus comes soon. There's a drop of rain about to fall.'

'That'll drown a few more fleas. Thanks for the lift. See you in the morning.'

The rain started as I dodged between the newspaper-sellers. The little man walking until eternity or a power-failure was glowing greenly in both crossings I wanted, but as I turned onto the North Bridge in the shelter of the post-office water was pouring off my hat-brim.

Through the curtains of water the towering, close-packed grey tiers of the old city on the far side seemed not built, but carved out of a long ridge on a high hill. The massive carving swept up to the glorious climax of the Castle, half crouching, half floating on its great black rock, as if it were the work of one pair of hands. An architectural Beethoven, I decided, with the inspiration and courage for grand ges-tures and the genius to use them to perfection.

More than the rain was obscuring my view. I blinked impatiently and found I was on the edge of the pavement. A blue car was hovering by me to the resigned despair of the lorry-driver directly behind.

Charles Linsey opened the front passenger door with one hand, holding onto the wheel with the other. 'If you want a lift, get in. I can't wait here.'

I jumped in. 'Thanks. Sorry about the mess on the floor.

I'm rather damp.'

'It'll dry.' He glanced sideways as we were stopped at lights. 'Why didn't you use the bus shelter?'

'Forgot.'

'In this rain?'

The lights changed. I studied his profile as we drove on and wondered why, since he was exuding disapproval, he had bothered to pick me up. His disapproval did not worry me. As I had first discovered with Robbie Ross, one of my unexpected post-John bonuses was the total loss of my former instinctive desire to hit every mildly attractive new man I met between the eyes. Not giving a damn made life much easier, as one could be honest. I told him exactly what I had been thinking.

'Beethoven?' he queried, frowning. 'Surely Wagner?'

'God, no! Wagner would goldplate the Castle and re-do the Royal Mile in black marble and swans.'

'You think so? Mozart?'

'Not this side. Across, yes. Those enchanting Georgian streets and squares are pure Mozart. But from Holyrood to the Castle, Beethoven. You know the last movement of his Seventh? How it carries one up, up, up?'

'Yes,' he said, 'yes. I know what you mean. I agree. Beethoven.' He looked at me again. 'That safety-belt the wrong fit?'

I realized I had been wriggling my shoulders. 'I'm sorry about this,' I said and explained. 'The old boy's bedding looked quite clean, but the bed was in a wall recess, and they kept hopping out. Do you know the type of bed?'

'Oh, yes,' he said, evenly, 'very well. Difficult for nursing purposes.'

'Not too bad today, as I could sit him out while I made his bed. My escorting sister said if I couldn't the only way to make the bed properly would be to take off my shoes and stand on it.'

'It would be so.' We were stopped by more red lights. 'You must find all this very strange after hospital nursing.'

'In most ways, but not on the livestock count. I've met far worse than fleas in Cas. at Martha's. Bugs. Ugh! They really make me creep.' He was touching the back of his neck. 'Bitten already? I'm terribly sorry! I shouldn't have accepted this lift.'

He smiled very nicely. 'Only a sympathetic itch. Even if not, you can scarcely be held responsible for providing temporary sanctuary for a flea with strong nationalistic tendencies.'

It was Sandra's day off, and she came out of her flat in an unbuttoned shortie housecoat as I reached her landing. 'What were you doing in Charlie's car?' She backed when I explained. 'Picked you up? Huh! If that's your story you stick to it, though you're wasting your time. His girfriend was showing Ma Kinloch her ring this afternoon. I needed shades! What do you say to that?'

'Love is a beautiful thing, and I need a bath. Coming up?'

'Can't. I'm dressing for a date. Do you think I'll need a pantie-girdle as well as tights?'

Gemmie had come up the stairs. 'Tights, pantie-girdle, and bloomers, love. Give the lad a good run for it.'

Sandra said it was all very well for Gemmie to be coarse, but frankly she thought a girl couldn't be too careful, as she knew what men were.

Gemmie nodded gravely. 'Randy lot, these Scots lads.'

Sandra looked put out. Her date was Welsh.

Gemmie and I went up. I asked, 'You find 'em randy?'

'No more so than the lads back home. Sometimes less. You?'

'Same.'

It was Catriona's cooking evening. She was in the kitchen when I joined Gemmie to dry my hair in front of the sitting-room fire. Gemmie was reading the National Health Act and knitting a sweater for Wilf. As we always pooled information acquired independently, I told her about my lift and Josephine Astley's ring. She told me Catriona would be twenty-four on Thursday week. 'But when Miss Bruce asked her if she wanted the day off she said not as she's nowt special on. Imagine? With that face!'

Catriona had become our favourite enigma. She was easily the prettiest district-student, and ours was not the only set; she was the only girl among us to start our course with the ready-made social advantages of an aunt on the spot and her training hospital an easy car- and train-ride away. Yet so far she had not had one date and the only person to ring her at the flat was Mrs Ferguson who was her aunt. And she was a very nice girl.

We decided she needed a birthday-party. When she came in to say the macaroni cheese was ready we were working on the stuffed olives.

Catriona mangled her hands. 'It's sweet of you, girls, but I couldn't—I mean, Miss Bruce mightn't approve—anyway, who'd come?'

'Wilf, if he can get up. Bassy'll give him floor-room and provide more men than we can possibly accommodate. The girls below, their dates, Robbie Ross—anyone you say.'

'I—I can't think of anyone.'

Gemmie lowered her knitting. 'Let's have it straight, love. You just don't fancy it?'

'It's not that, but . . .'

'So you do? Right! That's fixed! Where's this macaroni cheese, then?'

At the weekend I asked Robbie.

'Thursday? Catriona Ferguson's birthday? I doubt I can get off, Alix.'

'Fair enough. I warned her you'd probably have to work.'

'What did she say to that?'

' "What a pity". So you can't make it?'

He flushed faintly and fingered his tie. 'Do you want me to come?'

'Don't be thick, duckie. Why else would I ask you?'

'Don't expect a poor bloody accoucheur to fathom the workings of the female mind.' His 'r's' spat out like bullets. 'When did any girl mean what she says?'

I looked at him curiously. Till now our date had been going nice and smoothly. 'Does this corn mean you don't like parties? That your feet are hurting too much after all our sightseeing? Or that you want me to spell out if my invitation includes bed without board?'

He stopped looking peeved. 'Going to spell it out?'

'Sorry, no. Just one jolly party that, we've promised Miss Bruce, will end at eleven-thirty, won't disturb the neighbours, and will avoid ribaldry on the stairs. Kids' stuff.'

'By Thursday night, my level. I'll make it if I can.' He kissed me then as it was the right moment for that. He kissed well, even if his mind was not wholly on the job. Nor was mine, so I noticed.

Having a driving licence, I sometimes worked on my own in a car. I had one most of that week. Mrs Duncan's escort was now more the exception than the rule during the day, but most mornings after the early briefing the whole staff had from Miss Bruce, Mrs Duncan took a look at my call-list. 'Who've you new today? Ah, Mackenzie, Mac-Nabs, Brown—all the same building. Remember those lands we did your first day?'

'I thought I'd heard those were being demolished?'

'Not these. The lands opposite. Once that's done, they'll do this lot. They'll be re-housed in that new estate going up beyond Mrs MacRae's.'

'Those cute little houses? Very nice for them!'

'You may think so,' said Mrs Duncan, 'but not as many as you'd imagine'll agree with you. Folk grow attached to the cramped wee homes and neighbours they've known and maybe fought with for years—and particularly. the older folk. So don't you be thinking to put in a wise word on the advantages of moving. Folk need time to think these things out for themselves without being bothered by unwelcome advice from guests. You've not forgotten what I said about always remembering you're a guest?'

'No.' I did not add Miss Bruce stressed this as often as herself, since Mrs Duncan already knew it.

'Another thing you must remember is never to pass adverse comments on domestic matters such as the arrangement of the furniture. If it inconveniences you and you've to climb over a chest to get at your patient, well, a wee climb doesn't hurt a healthy lassie. Unless some alteration is essential for the patient's welfare, but not to make the nursing easier, leave things be. Oddly,' she added, 'if you think only from the patient's angle, it's amazing what a nurse can get used to without harm to patient—or nurse.'

The row of high, narrow, nineteenth-century apartment

houses lay at the end of a long, shabby street, made shabbier by the dust from the buildings being demolished. A little group of infants watched me through the iron stair-railings. My 'Hallo!' made them laugh immoderately.

A young woman in hair-curlers and a floral wrapover apron came out of a doorway. 'Old Mr Mackenzie? Aye, I heard he'd the doctor after taking a fall. He's away round the other side. Through the arch, up the stairs, right, third door second floor, left.'

Mrs Mackenzie was at her door. She had been married forty-seven years, and her husband had been blinded in the First World War and never seen her face. Once she had been beautiful. Now she was old, tired, and anxious, but neat and clean. She carried herself with pride. 'He will take his wee stroll whatever the weather, and yesterday the ground was awful slippery after the rain. His back's that stiff and black and blue.'

Mr Mackenzie had a splendid head of white hair and a strong, serene face. He was delighted to hear I was from London. He said he'd a great affection for London. He minded well the grand time he'd had in London when he went for a soldier. 'I wasna married then, ye'll ken, Nurse, and I was a bit of a laddie——'

'Hush, Davie! The nurse is but a slip of a lassie!'

The smile on the old man's closed face was like a smile in sleep. 'There was that laddie fra London that time we'd that trip to Perth. You mind him, Bella? You mind the way he'd take me walking when he got home to the house from his work in the evening? He'd a way of describing everything —aye, I mind him well—he'd the right touch had that young laddie.'

I asked when they had made this trip to Perth. They had to think. 'It would be forty years back,' said Mrs Mackenzie.

'Forty-two, Bella. Forty-two. I mind it well, just now.'

Their small apartment was crammed with heavy, worn furniture and smelt of furniture polish and stove blacking. The MacNab flat, directly above, had a different smell.

Mr MacNab was in bed. 'I'd the terrible stomach complaint again this morning, Nurse. I couldna be away to my work. It'll be best when I'm out the way for good.' He was in the forties, thin and dark haired, and his face and voice were querulous. 'I'm nothing but a burden,' he said, over and over again, as burdensome people do. 'Best out the way.' He pulled the bedclothes over his shoulders. The flannel sheets and blankets were so grey with dirt that it was impossible to guess their original colour. 'The tablets the doctor left have settled my stomach, but the discomfort'll be back. The way I suffer—terrible.'

His wife was forty-two. She could have been sixty-two. She was past everything but resignation. She needed an injection for her anaemia.

I gave this in the kitchen. 'Mrs MacNab, can you get a bit of rest today? Just put you feet up for a while? You do look a little tired.'

She said simply, 'If I sit he'll have me up. Maybe he'll drop off. Maybe, then.'

Mr MacNab's medical history was on his card. There was nothing organically wrong with his stomach or anything else. Mrs MacNab had medical reasons for looking ready to drop. There was so much I wanted to say, my unspoken words stifled me nearly as much as the smell. When I left their flat I walked to the nearest fire-escape opening and stood ostensibly admiring the view as I breathed out. The air was clean, but that smell hung on at the back of my nose and throat.

Mr Brown had been sent home from hospital yesterday. He was thirty-three, and his great blue eyes stared out of a yellowing skeleton's face. It was two years since he had been able to work regularly, and his wife was bread-winner. She was twenty-seven, small, and very fair. She was a waitress. 'I'm lucky,' she said, 'as shift work lets me see so much more of Archie.' They had no children.

Mr Brown opened the door to me. He lay on his bed while I did his dressing. He called it 'my abscess'. The pink candlewick bedspreads were soft with washing, the white curtains crisp, and despite the open windows and demolition across the road the flat was dustless.

Mrs Brown sat with her hands in her lap. 'Being English, do you know Cornwall, Nurse?'

'I'm afraid not. You do?'

Mr Brown was face downwards. He twisted his head over one shoulder. 'We borrowed the wife's brother's van to go there for our honeymoon four years back. It was spring and all the flowers were out.'

Mrs Brown said, 'It was just the way it looks in a travel poster. The daffodils, the violets, the rocks black, and the sun on the sea. Two whole weeks we'd there, and every day the sun shone. Can you believe that!' She was trying not to watch the dressing. 'I've told my brother, directly Archie's better, we'll be having his van.'

'No doubt of that,' said Mr Brown. 'Much coming away today, Nurse?'

'Not much, Mr Brown. How's that feel now?'

'Grand, thanks. I'm doing fine.'

We were all lying, and we all knew it. They hadn't been lying about Cornwall. I asked more about their visit. Their faces lit up as they told me. I remembered my father saying once in every lifetime everyone should reach Samarkand. I was very, very glad they had.

By Catriona's birthday Mr Mackenzie had returned to his daily stroll, Mr MacNab, reluctantly, to his job, and Mr Brown remained one of my regular, twice-daily calls. The infants on the stairs greeted me. 'Hallo, Nurrsie!' and introduced themselves. 'Meggy, Fiona, Alistair, Donal, Mary, Stevie, Tommy, and here'—a fat toddler was thrust forward—'is wee Jaimie, and he's but two though he talks fine! Say hallo to the Nurrrsie fra England, Jaimie!'

The first post arrived at the flat after we had left in the morning. On Thursday as we were leaving a florist's van-man delivered two dozen long-stemmed roses for Catriona.

'Hey, those cost a bomb!' Gemmie hastily filled our largest jug with water. 'Who're they from?'

Catriona was puce. 'Just—er—an old chum.'

Gemmie and I exchanged glances, but waited till we met at lunch. 'Chummy saying it with a few quids'-worth of early roses explains why no local lad's got to first base, eh, Alix?'

'Why stop at roses? Why not date her?'

'Like he's married?' she murmured as Catriona joined us.

The last patient on my list that afternoon was a Miss Lees. She was a retired schoolmistress living in her own semi-detached at the southern end of the very long road that was the boundary between my own and Mrs Duncan's areas. It was Mrs Duncan's day off. Miss Lees had a phone. I was with her when Miss Bruce rang me.

'You appear anxious, Miss Hurst. Urgent call?'

'Fairly, Miss Lees. I'm afraid I must go now.'

'You'll take a cup of tea first? No? Oh, dear! Have you far to go?'

'Just the other end of this road.'

'The flats?' She pressed her pale lips together. 'You'll not credit this now, Miss Hurst, but when my late father purchased this house thirty odd years ago this was a very good residential area.' She patted the corrugated grey waves of her old-fashioned set. 'The rot started with those flats. Not that I allow such matters to disturb me. As I used to say to my girls, when a particular aspect displeases turn your eyes in another direction.'

From what Miss Bruce had said it seemed as well one Mrs Baker had never been Miss Lee's pupil.

Mrs Baker was a stout woman with dyed black hair, red dangling earrings, and a tough, sensible face. She detached herself from the little group of women outside the main entrance. 'What could a body do but call the doctor, Nurse?' She panted up the stairs with me. 'Seeing she'd not taken in her milk and I've never known her leave it out, not in the fifteen years I've bided here. And when there was no answer to my knock, or ringing her bell, or my wee shout—what could I do but walk in to see for myself? And when I saw her there lying in her bed that white and still, I'm telling you, Nurse, I thought she'd gone! Aye, the turn I took! I was that sure she'd gone. The doctor said I did right to call him! Is it right she's refused to be away to the hospital?'

It was, though I evaded saying so. 'I've not yet seen Dr MacDonald. Thank you very much, Mrs Baker. You've been a great help.'

She gave a grim nod at the door we had now reached. 'I'll get no thanks there. I ken well Mrs Thompson'll be out for my blood. She's aye been that anxious to preserve her privacy. It's no use your ringing, Nurse. There's none but her to answer.'

According to Miss Bruce, the Home-help should have arrived by now. 'The Home-help hasn't come, yet?'

'Aye. And been sent packing.' Mrs Baker stepped back a foot or two, folded her arms, and waited.

I took a long mental breath and opened the door. 'Good afternoon, Mrs Thompson. I'm Nurse Hurst. Please may I come in?'

The silence was first broken by a rustle of paper. Then, 'If you must, but you'll be wasting your time, Nurse.' The voice was old, tight, and breathless. 'Mind you shut my door after you! I've no use for peepers!'

Mrs Baker smiled dourly. 'What'd I tell ye?'

It was a cool afternoon, but the tiny flat had the clammy chill of a building unheated for months. It was as clean as the Browns', and the flannel sheets and blankets on Mrs Thompson's bed were so worn with age and scrubbing they had no warmth left. The newspapers she had removed from between her blankets were just visible under the bed.

She was a widow of seventy-one and roughly five foot six. She now weighed about five stones.

Miss Bruce had said, 'I've seldom heard Dr MacDonald so distressed. Acute malnutrition, plus angina. But though she requires instant hospitalization for both, since she's refused his advice, he's convinced to force matters at this stage will bring on another, and possibly fatal, attack. In his opinion that can happen at any time. He's ordered oxygen and all the essentials for home-nursing, but says she may well refuse them. She insists she's treated these attacks success-fully on her own and that all she requires is a little rest. Do whatever she will let you to help her and, if you can, try and persuade her to change her mind about hospitalization. Dr MacDonald'll return to her shortly, and if she insists on remaining at home tonight, the night duty-sister will call and arrange for her to have a special nurse all night.'

Mrs Thomspon refused to let me make her bed, wash her

face and hands, re-do her long, neatly plaited, thinning white hair. 'I've aye preferred to fend for myself, Nurse. I can manage well.' Her hooded, sunken eyes were cold as her bedroom air. 'No doubt you've others to attend to.'

'Not today. You're my last call.' I rubbed my back. It was not aching. 'Been a long day. May I sit down?'

'If you wish.'

'Thank you.' I smiled at her. 'Though I think your city the most beautiful I've ever seen, Mrs Thompson, it does have a lot of steps and stairs. Being a stranger, my feet aren't used to them yet.'

As I hoped, that roused her sense of hospitality to strangers, whether welcome or otherwise. I had noticed that particular characteristic was shared by the overwhelming majority of my Edinburgh patients. 'You're welcome to rest your feet. You'll be from England?'

'London. Ever been there?'

She had not, but she seemed faintly interested. I talked of London for a good half-hour before I risked suggesting tea. I knew Dr MacDonald had done some immediate shopping. 'May I use your kitchen and make us both a cup? I don't know about you, Mrs Thompson, but I'm parched!'

She hesitated, then took a purse from under her pillow. 'You'll need this coin for the meter. I'll not have it said I turned an English lassie from my door empty-handed. If you wish'—she had to stop for breath—'a wee bit bread and marge, help yourself.'

'Just tea, thanks. I'm only thirsty.'

I put her shilling in a saucer on the kitchen dresser and used one of mine. The G.P.'s shopping was on the table. I put the tea, sugar, eggs, and milk in a larder that took me by the throat. One could have eaten off the shelves and floor, but the total original contents might just have made an elevenses snack, if one was not hungry.

Over tea I chatted on.

Mrs Thompson's smile was stiff and unused. 'You're an awful lassie for blethering, but I'll say this, Nurse'—another pause for another gasping breath—'you make good tea.'

The medical equipment arrived. She began by ordering the lot out of her flat. I plugged my greatest assets. 'Please,

Mrs Thompson, don't for my sake! I'm so new to this job and Edinburgh. It'll do me, personally, a packet of harm,' I lied. 'It'll look as if I'm not nursing you properly. If not the oxygen just yet, these blankets? Bless you! How about a hot-water bottle? Nothing like a hottie to keep one's feet warm—and isn't it freezing, today? Or is that just because I haven't yet got used to your bracing northern climate?'

She allowed her feet were a wee bit chilled. 'Maybe I'll use that bottle for now. I'd not have you in trouble with your superiors, seeing you're but a lassie and I've eyes in my head to see you mean well. But just for the now, you'll understand. I've aye paid my way, and I'll take no charity.'

I tried to explain no charity was involved. I did not succeed, but did get her to accept two eggs beaten-up in milk and sugar.

There were two photographs of young men in Army uniform on her cane bedside table. Different uniforms. 'My man and my boy. The two wars took the two.' Her pinched, grey face assumed a fierce dignity. 'I've none to greet for me. I've been a burden to none. I'll be a burden to none.'

Dr MacDonald returned. He was a solid man in his fifties, and he carried an air of patient impatience as tangible as his black bag. 'My dear, we but wish to help you. Why not come to the hospital for a day or two?'

'I'm obliged to the two of you, Doctor. You mean well, but I prefer to fend for myself. I've aye done that—and that Mrs Baker had no call to go sticking her nose in——' and suddenly her voice stopped. Her hooded eyes remained open, staring, and still.

A very little later I closed her eyes.

Considerably later, Miss Bruce said she would put away my car. 'At least she did not die alone.'

I walked back home very slowly and took the long road up the hill and then round, instead of the usual short cut through the grounds of one hospital. I was about halfway before I remembered the party. I stopped walking.

CHAPTER FOUR

I had stopped in a square almost entirely taken over by various departments of the University. The majority looked closed for the night, but there were a few students ambling around, and occasionally a youngish to middle-aged man or woman came down front steps jangling car-keys. One grey-haired woman in a shapeless tweed coat had had rickets as a child. No welfare orange-juice or cod-liver oil on hand in her infancy. Nor Mrs Thompson's.

'Waiting for your brother, Miss Hurst?'

The voice was behind me. I glanced incuriously over my shoulder. Charles Linsey had come out of the front door nearest to me. 'No.'

He came down the few steps. 'Returning from work? Aren't you very late?'

'Yes.'

'Isn't this the evening Miss Bruce mentioned something to me about some birthday-party in your flat?' His brief smile was faintly self-derisive, I noticed, without wondering why. 'Would you care for a lift back? Or are you waiting for someone else?'

'I'm not waiting for anyone. And thanks, but I don't want a lift back. Not yet.'

He looked at me more closely. 'You're very pale. Are you all right?'

I had lied enough for one day. I needed to explode, and he was there. He got it all, and then I said, 'She had her pride.'

He had listened in an impassive silence. He said as un-emotionally, 'One can only be grateful the poor woman had that one consolation.'

'Grateful? For the unnecessary misery that damned pride cost her? The welfare services mayn't provide luxury, but

42

if only she'd tapped them, as she was fully entitled, she could've had enough bedding, warmth, food, clothes, and someone to chat her up and keep an eye on her regularly.'

'Of course. I understand that and deeply regret her not asking for help and consequently living and dying in such tragic circumstances. But, if you'll forgive me, I think you're seriously underestimating the importance she'll have placed in her pride.'

Impatiently I shook my head. 'I saw her larder. I saw what she looked like. She's not the first Edwardian I've met—and not only from her social background—who's been incapable of understanding what the Welfare State is actually about and throttled from asking by the same tragically stupid pride. "What'll people think? What'll the neighbours say?" What the hell does it matter,' I demanded, 'on an empty stomach?'

He said, simply, 'Though tragic and misplaced, it mattered more to Mrs Thompson than a full stomach.'

'You sound as if you approve?'

'Not the consequences.' He hesitated, as if speaking in one language and thinking in another. 'But I have to admire her pride.'

'Admire?' The word nearly choked me. 'You're not serious? Think what it did to her!'

'I'm also thinking it was more than probably the one factor that kept her alive so long.'

Suddenly the invisible wall between us was as thick as the Castle rock. I said, 'We aren't speaking the same language.'

'Since you find that surprising, I assume you're having that not uncommon English difficulty in recalling England stops at Berwick and Shropshire.'

'Does it really make much difference if I am?'

For a few seconds he stared at me as if I were a foolish and peculiarly unattractive child. He slapped himself. 'I need a cigarette and haven't any on me. I've some in my car. Let's sit down and sort this out.'

I went with him only as I hadn't the energy for thinking up a good objection.

'Do you smoke, Miss Hurst?'

'Not since my first lung carcinoma ward.'

'Sensible girl. I'll have to stop. Not now.' He inhaled deeply. 'Does it really make much difference? Yes, Miss Hurst, it does. This isn't England. This is Scotland. Another country, another people, with their own history, laws, culture, national characteristics. Yet none of that has occurred to you?'

'Yes, but——'

'But you still expect Mrs Thompson of Edinburgh to react identically with Mrs Smith of London? Or possibly Mrs Jones of Swansea? All being part of the same? And if the Scots and the Welsh have their own varieties of accents, so do the indigenous inhabitants of most English counties. Consequently, that larger bit at the top and smaller bit at the side are merely extensions of England? Am I right?'

'I guess so. And that's wrong?'

'If you'd worked in Paris the length you've worked here, and spoke good French, would you still expect to understand Madame Dubois as well as you believe you understand—understood—Mrs Thompson?'

I sighed. 'No. You do?'

'Naturally. I'm another Lowland Scot. I know social backgrounds may alter certain superficial traits, but fundamentally we're a dour, suspicious, proud race. You're a practical, intelligent, modern English girl. Your common sense insists a full stomach comes before pride. We're the same generation and my intellect agrees with you, but national characters go much deeper than that. In consequence, I know very well that had I to make the straight choice, absurd or not, I'd keep my pride, and on my empty stomach I'd feel I'd kept the one thing that mattered.' He was briefly silent. 'That's why I know it will have proved a genuine comfort to Mrs Thompson. For that only, I'm grateful. God knows that poor, brave, lonely old woman needed the one comfort.'

'I see what you mean. I didn't understand. I thought I did. I still wish——' I broke off. 'What's the use now?'

He did not seem to be listening. He was sitting sideways, facing me, but looking beyond me. 'I think she had another

44

comfort at the end. You were with her and she'd taken a liking to you——'

I blushed. 'I wouldn't say that——'

'You wouldn't,' he agreed quietly. 'I do. I think she'd have been very touched to see how deeply her life and death have distressed you. Not that anything would have forced her to admit the fact. Could she've been here with us now'—his precise voice switched into broad Scots—'she'd have ye ken she saw no call for a grown lassie to be too sad for greetin' o'er a wee bit grief.'

I looked at my hands in my lap. 'You knew her.'

He said nothing, and it was a very long time before we spoke again.

In the long lingering northern twilight the street lamps were pale amber, the tall houses were more black than grey, and their outlines merged gently into the slowly darkening sky.

It grew much darker as we sat there, sometimes talking, sometimes silent. He did most of the talking—about his present job and then the three years he had spent in London as an assistant pathologist at St Benedict's Hospital. He was interesting, as people talking about the jobs that interest them invariably are, and I was very grateful to sit listening and occasionally putting in a word. I was even more grateful for the strangely undemanding quality of his attitude towards me. I thought not only of John's, but of so many other men's constant demands on one's emotions and attention. Generally, I did not much mind that, but now I was too emotionally drained to have anything left to give.

It was dark enough for him to need the dashboard light to see the clock. It was ten-thirty. 'You don't want to return till the party's over, do you?'

I hesitated for obvious reasons. 'Well——'

'Yes or no?'

'No, but I've held you up ages.'

'That's unimportant as I'm in no hurry. When did you last eat? Would you care for some food?'

'God forbid!' It had slipped out. 'I'm sorry. I expect you're starving by now.'

'I'd eaten before I saw you. Shall we stay here or shall

we have a change of scene? Have you seen the city by night?'

'From the top of a bus.' He was shooting up in my estimation. Not only undemanding, but he managed to be kind without giving me a guilt-complex.

'I'll show you another view. It's only a wee drive.' He switched on the engine. 'Do up your safety-belt.'

We did not speak again until he narrowly avoided killing a youngish woman in Princes Street. She had long, brassily dyed hair and was very drunk. She did not turn her head our way when his swerve cleared her by about three inches.

He breathed out. 'Thought I'd got her. She get over?'

'Yes. The traffic the other side had time to brake. Wouldn't have been your fault if you'd hit her. She just stepped off the pavement into us.'

'But had I killed her, my hands on this wheel . . .'

I glanced at his hands. I had not noticed them before, but he had very good, very sensitive hands. Blood would not easily be washed off them. 'If you had killed her the fundamental responsibility would be mine.'

'Did you start the First and Second World Wars? Even if you did, by what right do you overrule my right to use my own free will as I see fit?'

'You sound like my father.' There was enough light to see the sudden rigidity in his face. 'Dr Linsey, that was a compliment, not a crack. I like my father very much. He's very wise and very kind, and I don't think I only think that as I'm his daughter and love him a lot. But I can't argue with him, either. As I haven't a logical mind and he has, he can make verbal rings round me. I start off thinking I'm on solid rock, and by the end of the first round, as now, I'm floundering in quicksand. I hope you don't mind my explaining?'

'On the contrary. You don't mind the quicksand?'

'Too used to it.' He had taken a sharp left turn off the main road into a dark and narrow lane running up a hill. 'Where's the city gone? We could be in the wilds of the country.'

'You'll see directly.'

The lane appeared to end in an open space on a flattened hilltop. He drew up by a bulky, unlighted building. I asked what it was.

'An observatory. There's another over there hiding the crest.' He reached into the back for a leather jacket. 'Put this over your coat and we'll take a walk.'

It was now properly dark, and the air was surprisingly cold on my face. I recognized the forlorn elegance of the grecian pillars against the sky, some small distance from where we stood. 'I've been wanting to come up here.'

'I'd not advise you or any other woman to walk up here alone, and certainly not after dark, though, if possible, the view's even better by night. There's a path running round that other observatory. Come and look down.'

We walked across the rough, open ground. On the path he stopped and stood back. He said, 'There's the city of Edinburgh.'

Not a city, but a gigantic jewelled carpet of moving as well as stationary jewels and constantly enlarging as more and more lights came on. Unlighted St Giles was a sombre patch of black velvet. The Princes Street Gardens were dark green velvet, and above the green and the invisible Castle Rock the floodlit Castle and the Governor's House were golden galleons sailing towards the long double rope of yellow diamonds that was Princes Street.

I had no idea how long we stood there or when we moved on slowly and sat on a bench overlooking the Leith side. In Leith Walk directly below the old buildings were pure fairy-tale gothic and must have housed Hans Andersen's characters. Leith was another, smaller glittering mosaic; Portobello and Joppa a beringed finger pointing into the dark, quiet water of the Forth. There was even a sickle-moon over the midnight-blue mirror of the distant sea. Beneath the moon a star hung like a dropped pearl.

He lit another cigarette. The flame caricatured the height of his brow, the length of his lashes, and the angles of his high cheekbones. 'I thought you'd like to see this.'

I glanced at him reflectively. He sat about a foot from me, leaning back, and moving only the hand holding his cigarette. Nothing in his manner or tone suggested his

47

awareness of the healing qualities of peace, beauty, and kindness, or that any generosity was involved in his sharing what was plainly a deeply personal pleasure with a stranger. For a very little while I wondered why he was doing this for me, but without any real interest in the answer. It was so much more restful to sit and stare and appreciate in ignorance.

Walking back along the path, I asked if he had seen Athens. 'I haven't. Can it possibly beat this?'

'Athens is beautiful, but'—he paused apologetically— 'I'm an Edinburgh man.'

I smiled. '*Civis Romanus sum.*'

He stiffened, and then, realizing I was not sending him up, smiled back. 'Precisely.'

Driving home, we discussed our families. He had a mother, stepfather, and two younger half-sisters. I had the impression he was very fond of his family, though his strongest expression of approval was, 'I like seeing them.'

'That's a break.'

'I'm afraid I don't follow you?'

'It's a break to hear of another family not constantly at each other's throats. After hearing so many of our friends' horror stories of parental antipathy and deprived chilhood Bassy and I often feel downright deprived ourselves over our lack of those currently groovy chips.'

He smiled quietly. 'I think that bothers my youngest sister more than a little. The poor child's sixteen, enjoys her boarding-school, loves the Highlands. Now my stepfather's retired, being a Highlander he's moved back to the hills.'

'Aching to rebel without cause for rebellion? The poor kid! Pathetic!'

'Isn't it? However, as she's aiming for some, and preferably English, university, is fairly intelligent, and very strong-minded, I've no doubt she'll be happy on the barricades in a few years' time.'

'Why's she aiming for England?'

'She says that's where it's all happening.'

I smiled. 'Will her parents mind?' He shook his head. 'Will you?'

'No. Not that it would signify if I did. My younger—in

48

fact both my sisters, have minds of their own.'

'Is your other sister at University?'

'No.' We were back in Princes Street. 'Let me know if you see any more suicidal drunks.'

'Sure.' I intended asking more about his second sister, but sneezed instead. Forgetting I still had on his leather coat, I reached for a handkerchief and had used it before discovering it was not mine. Nor was it his, unless he used Miss Dior.

It then seemed incredible, but it was a fact that till then I had forgotten he had a fiancée. I wondered where she was right now, if he would tell her about this, and if so, if she'd have the sense to believe him. Some would. Most wouldn't. I could hear John's shout of laughter. 'Up on that lonely hill in the dark and not a finger on you? Not queer? Then you, my sweet, are a lying bitch.'

Once my father said, 'As most people are only capable of judging by their own standards, it's useful to remember their judgments will tell you far more about themselves than the judged.'

I wished I had remembered that when I first met John and been amused by what I had assumed to be only a moddy, cynical pose. It was no pose. John did not trust anyone, including himself. I wondered how his wife was handling that, and then discovered I was thinking of her without wincing. I thought of John and breathed very deeply. It was like coming unexpectedly to the end of a long, dark tunnel. Just a man I had once known and loved enough to leave me with an emotional scar. And dead scared of being hurt again.

It was twenty to twelve when we got in. The hall and stairs were as quiet as the street outside.

He looked up the stairs. 'Would you like to come up in my lift and walk down one flight rather than up four?'

Mrs Kinloch had told us there was a private lift to the top flat beyond the door at the back of the hall, but I had yet to see it in use. Had John, or most Englishmen of my acquaintance in Charles Linsey's age-group, made this suggestion at this hour in London it would have been for the most obvious reason. I was instinctively convinced that was not his, nor was it mine for accepting. If the party had not ended it would at any moment. His fiancée might not get the wrong impression if she heard we had walked into the parting guests. Sandra certainly would.

He unlocked the door. 'I have to keep this locked to satisfy my insurance company. As you'll see, this lift opens into my front hall. The elderly relative from whom I inherited this building had it put in as he liked living above and found the stairs too much.' The lift stopped. He opened the gates for me and immediately unlocked his flat front door. 'I'll see you down.'

'Don't bother, please. Thanks for everything. You've been,' I said, 'incredibly kind.'

'And what were you to Mrs Thompson?'

We looked at each other as if we were very old friends, and both forgot to say goodnight. I went down quickly and let myself in. I did not hear his door close.

The flat was empty and only the hall light was on. A note on the hall table said Miss Bruce had rung earlier to explain why I would be late. At ten-thirty, when Robbie had been called back on duty, the party had moved en masse to Bassy's flat. 'Ring if you feel up to coming on, and Wilf'll collect you in his car. If not, please leave chain off door. G. and C.'

I took the note, a sandwich, and milk into my bedroom, put out clean uniform, set my alarm, then sat for ages on the side of my bed, looking at the ceiling.

'A wee bit grief' was exactly how she would have put it.

CHAPTER FIVE

Wilf Hawkins had some time off owing, and stayed on till Sunday night. He was twenty-five, thickset, dark as Robbie, very good-natured, but no pushover. He seldom took his eyes off Gemmie and, on the rare occasions when he spoke, sounded like an early Beatle. He called us Cat, Al, and Gem.

In confidence, Catriona and I told Gemmie that if she did not fancy him we did. Gemmie handed this on to Wilf in our presence.

'Oh aye?' Wilf smiled slowly. 'Who's first then? I'm not fussy.'

The party had gone very well. The girls gave me every detail without asking for mine in return. They were too accustomed to death for morbid curiosity, and I knew if I wanted to talk I would. I didn't.

Mrs Duncan said, 'I'm sorry you'd that disturbing experience,' and left it at that. This was not from callousness, but because to encourage any nurse or doctor to remain over-involved in the death of any patient is to encourage that person straight into a bed in a psychiatric ward. Sooner or later, for a little while, most nurses and doctors do become over-involved with some patient. Then, consciously, one has to move out of the shadows as there are always more shadows ahead. Old Mrs Thompson was dead, young Mr Brown was dying. Not that I found Mrs Thompson easy to forget, but for sanity and my other patients' sake I had to make the effort. As Charles Linsey had been so involved in her death, I preferred not to think of him.

Wilf's visit disrupted our chore-rota. On Monday evening Catriona and I cooked supper together. It had been her day at the antenatal clinic; she had seen Robbie and he had asked after me. 'I don't think he really enjoyed the party without you, Alix.'

'Sandra says he had a ball!'

She cracked an egg with elegant disapproval. 'Sandra is a bletherer and a troublemaker!'

'You don't want to take her so seriously.' I guessed what was wrong, having had the inside story over the phone from Bassy. 'So she made a pass at Robbie? Making passes is a reflex action for her.'

'That's no escuse! He was your date. You'd think she'd have more pride.'

Pride was not a subject on which I cared to dwell. 'Robbie's not my personal property. We're just casual dates.'

She shot me a rather peculiar glance. 'He hadn't a reputation for casual dating in Glasgow. He may be more serious than you appreciate.'

'I'm sure he's not!'

'Time will tell,' she said, tritely and firmly. As time had already told Gemmie and me that beneath Catriona's gentle and ultra-polite exterior lay a very strong and sometimes maddeningly stubborn character, I let it go. If I argued all night I would still lose out. In any clash between the three of us in the flat to date Catriona had always won. If she gave way, as over her party, it was because she had wanted to give way.

Occasionally, and invariably without warning, Miss Bruce or another very senior sister escorted us on our rounds. The following day Miss Bruce came out with me.

There were eleven calls on my morning list. The first was on Mr Brown. The front door was unlatched as his wife was at work and he was now having to spend nearly all his time in bed. If possible, his yellow face was even thinner and, in his wife's absence, his huge, too-aware eyes had a dull glaze. He was reading a paperback thriller with a pornographic cover and on recognizing my companion pushed it into his bed. I didn't think Miss Bruce had noticed. I should have remembered she was a very experienced District Supervisor.

'The poor man,' she said, when we were back in the car.

'If any writer is capable of taking his mind off his ebbing health for a wee while I'm only too thankful.' She read my immediate notes. 'That was the usual amount of discharge? Dear me. Yes, yes, I agree he's best left in his home as long as possible. He's happiest there.'

'He's got a perfectly wonderful wife, Miss Bruce.'

'Very evidently, Miss Hurst.'

My other patients were enchanted by my high-powered escort. 'Ye'll be on yer best behaviour,' they informed me, in audible whispers, 'having the Lady Supervisor herself! Would the lady not wish to sit down?'

Miss Bruce obligingly perched herself on tables, against chests-of-drawers, and in one house, as there was no other seat, on the foot of the patient's bed.

The patient, a Mrs Hunter, was an elderly arthritic, crippled in both arms and legs, but still able to use her hands through sheer will-power. She could crochet awkwardly, but skilfully, and never stopped. She never stopped talking either. While I blanket-bathed her she regaled us with her own and her neighbours' affairs. The couple next door were not speaking again. 'Last year it was the ten months without the one word! Ye'll no' credit that, eh? And what's he done now but bring home his fancy woman and the wife cooking for the three of them and not a word has she to say to her man! The words I'd say—aye, Nurse, the water's fine and hot—and there's Mrs MacDonald the two doors away returning to her own folk in Fife. Did ye not hear her man had passed on? Aye, up the hospital. Wait now, whiles I show you the fine wee words in the paper.' I removed the washing-basin for her to twist round from the waist and rootle in the large plastic shopping-bag she kept by her pillows. She handed a cutting to Miss Bruce. 'Do you see that "dearly loved husband of Mrs Mac-Donald"? Five years she nursed him before he was away up the hospital last month—and a terrible life he led her! Aye, but he was a hard man. He tried to stop her using his pension—and the gas—and she nursing him like her own bairn.'

Miss Bruce said kindly, 'Clearly a most devoted wife.'

'Och no! She'd no use for him at all! Many's the time

she'd be in here. "And when's the old de'il going to go?" she'd say. "I canna last out," she'd say. "There's no pleasing the old bugger, and I'll be glad when he's gone." But she coldna put that in the paper.'

'Scarcely suitable,' agreed Miss Bruce. 'Nevertheless, whatever her late husband's faults, there seems no question that she was a most dutiful wife.'

'That's a fact.' Mrs Hunter thrust her head through the neck of the clean, warmed flannel nightgown I was holding ready and emerged with a cheerful beam. 'There's some awful queer folks about. No doubt of that!'

An administrative sister was waiting at the front door when we got back for lunch. 'Maternity have just rung you, Miss Bruce. It'll be convenient if you could slip up there now.'

'Could you run me up, Miss Hurst? I'll only be a few minutes, and while you're waiting you may be allowed a look at your prem.'

The Lady Superintendent of the maternity hospital handed me over to a young office sister. The office sister walked me briskly down a long polished corridor with pale-pink walls and ceiling, and stopped by the plate-glass window of the Special Care Nursery. 'Alexander MacRae is in the Prem. Room, but if you'll wait here, Miss Hurst, I'll have a word about you with the ward sister.'

I moved closer to the window. The two pupil-midwives sitting in low chairs and bottle-feeding babies glanced at me incuriously. The staff midwife by the weighing-table noticed me and came out. 'Someone looking after you, Nurse?'

'Yes, thanks, Staff. An office sister.'

'That's an English voice I recognize.' Robbie appeared in an office doorway as the midwife returned to her weighing-table. 'What are you doing here?'

'Paying a social call on my prem., I hope.' I nodded at the window. 'How many of those are yours?'

'No more than half and only two called Robert.'

'Losing your touch, Doctor?'

He came closer. 'I've been thinking that myself. I missed you at the party.'

'I couldn't help that——'

'No, but you could've rung to apologize for standing me up. Why didn't you?' He seemed really peeved. 'Seeing it was you that invited me.'

I was tempted to invent, rather than hurt his feelings more, then remembered there was more than one way of doing that job. 'I should've rung you. I'm sorry. Quite honestly, I forgot.'

He smiled reluctantly. 'I'm losing my touch, all right. Not merely neglected, but forgotten. And to make it worse, by a bloody Sassenach.'

'You suffer, Robbie.'

He dug his hands in the pockets of his long, limp white coat and hunched his huge shoulders. 'And you,' he said very quietly, 'have the most beautiful dark-blue eyes I've ever seen. A man could drown in them gladly. Did you know?'

The office sister was advancing down the corridor behind him with a mask and gown over one arm. I said, 'And how is Mrs MacRae doing, Dr Ross?'

The sister had reached us. He answered as if she had spoken, and I was now as transparent as the nursery window. 'Mrs MacRae is getting along very nicely, but we're keeping her in to be safe. I'm sure she'll be pleased to hear Miss Hurst has been in to see wee Alex.'

The sister said, 'I expect Miss Hurst would like you to give Mrs MacRae her good wishes.'

I said, 'Please, Sister. Thank you.'

England and Scotland might be different countries, but hospital etiquette had us on common ground. And after the more relaxed and much more adult inter-staff relationships on the district, this stilted formality I had for so long taken for granted struck me as silly and sad. I suddenly understood why so many senior ward sisters seemed ashamed of their femininity and passionately to resent it in their juniors. Keep up any act long enough and it ceases to become an act.

Alex MacRae was asleep in his incubator. He now weighed three pounds ten ounces. 'He looks wonderful, Staff. Like a baby, rather than a red, wrinkled hippie.'

'He was your bairn?' The Prem. staff midwife looked at me across the top of the incubator. 'You're the girl that uses shopping-baskets? You'll not mind my saying it's a wonder you got away with it?'

'Not just a wonder, but a miracle. He scared the living daylights out of me. His mum thought him indigestion.'

'But she did know she was carrying him. See these four-pounders.' We crossed the tropically heated room to peer through more transparent walls. 'The mother was over eight months gone and the first head presenting before she'd any idea she was pregnant.'

'Two this size!'

'Aye. She said neither she nor her husband had noticed anything unusual, apart from her putting on a wee bit weight round the belly, and as it's eleven years since her last, they thought maybe she was at the change. She's four others, and the lot laddies.'

One of the twins was awake and drowsily blinking blue eyes. Both had delicately boned faces and a faint fuzz of red hair. 'Is she pleased with these?'

'Not yet. Maybe later. Maybe.'

'Pity. These are cute. All complete?'

'Perfect. So often the way with unwanted.' She glanced over my head. 'You're wanted.'

The sister and I were halfway down the corridor when Robbie galloped by, his white coat billowing behind him, and vanished through a door at the far end. I had noticed the door on our way in. It was marked BABY RESUSCITATION UNIT. When we reached it Sister said, 'One moment, Miss Hurst,' and went in. I waited, literally holding my breath. If there was a more disturbing sight than the tiny, terrifyingly limp body of a new-born baby in a state of collapse I hadn't seen it.

The sister reappeared as red in the face as myself. 'They seem to be getting her going again.' We walked on as briskly as before and in silence.

The Dr MacDonald who had attended Mrs Thompson was Mr Brown's G.P. I met him coming out of the buildings one afternoon some days later. 'If I could bottle Archie

Brown's will-power I'd cure enough patients to have time for a game of golf with my wife. You a golfer, Nurse?'

'I'm afraid not.'

'You should learn. Good exercise, better relaxation.' He watched the demolition workers across the road. 'I'll be glad when that job's done and we're rid of this dust. Have you heard it is about to be the object of a research project?'

'The dust? No, Doctor. Why? So many sore throats and eyes?'

'So few. For some unknown reason, the folk in this area are presently enjoying a remarkable freedom from such minor infections. That may well be coincidental, but the possibility of some bug-killing factor in this dust has occurred to learned minds. Any time now, Nurse, we'll have a vanload of pathologists and technicians setting up shop over the way with their test-tubes, wee bags, and slides. I'll be interested in their results.'

'Do you approve of this project, Doctor?'

He smiled lugubriously. 'I always approve of the sight of other men working, Nurse. But, yes. In my opinion, the matter's well worth investigation.' He clicked open his pocket-watch. 'Time I was away to my work and left you to yours. Good day to you.'

I looked after him briefly and thought of Robbie. It was a Martha's maxim that to be a successful G.P. a man needed first, luck; second, a wife; third, a black bag; fourth, patients.

I turned away, had my usual chat with the small gang on the stairs, then on up to the Browns' flat.

Bassy was sitting on our stairs when I got back alone. Gemmie had gone to a movie with Sandra and Catriona had a late dental appointment. It was some time since I had seen Bassy. He wore a scarlet track-suit, white sneakers, sky-blue cravat, and one gold earring.

'In drag, Bassy?'

'Groovy!' He fingered his earring. 'Melly's wearing the other. Any free nosh going? I'm skint.'

'Sure.' I removed my hat, coat, and shoes and took him into the kitchen. 'Another vast book-bill?'

'No. I'll be all right when I draw out tomorrow, but if I do it today I'll be skint two days next week.'

I had a better look at him. 'You've lost weight. Had lunch? Tea? For God's sake, boy, breakfast? What?'

'Milk. Pinta man, that's me.'

'Got a death-wish? Or just settling for tubercle?' I draped the grill with bacon. 'Milk alone's not enough for a growing lad. Where's the money gone? You're generally so crafty at making yours last.'

He sat on the kitchen table. 'Some birds are more expensive than others.'

I had not yet met Melanie. She had been at the party. Catriona described her as a very pretty little brunette, with huge goggle glasses; Gemmie, as one of yer actual female intellectuals. Wilf said, 'Dead sexy.' Aside from the goggles, the picture fitted all Bassy's girlfriends from kindergarten upwards.

'Melly doesn't fancy going Dutch?'

'She fancies it. I won't let her. Her IQ's higher than mine. Soothes my bruised ego to lash out.'

'Won't do your ego much good to have her bring you fruit and flowers when you're smitten by some ugly bug. You will be if you keep this up.' I added another egg to the frying-pan. 'Tubercle's under control, but still around.'

'Take five, Cassandra. My life and my lolly.'

'Don't kid yourself! Taxpayers' plus Dad's allowance.'

'Stuff that!' he retorted with a petulance that was mostly hunger. 'When Dad hands out, how we use it is our business. Nor's the taxpayer handing out bloody charity. My grant's an investment, and a something good investment. I'm the future of this country. Without my brains it probably will fall bloody apart.'

'Which country? Scotland or England?'

'Same thing.'

'Now there,' I said smugly, 'you are wrong.' I repeated most of the conversation I had had on this with Charles Linsey.

'When did he tell you this?'

'The night I missed the party.' I told him about Mrs Thompson. 'I haven't told you before as I didn't feel up to it. I haven't told anyone.'

He moved off the table and drew up a chair for himself. 'Pete saw you in Linsey's car.'

'Which Pete? The big medic. or the little man from Kent with acne who shares with you?'

'Little Pete. He's too sexually inhibited for raves and was working late that night. He's seen Linsey around and knows his car. He says you were both in it hours before driving off. He could see Linsey more clearly than yourself. He says it looked to him as if Linsey was on the make. Is he?'

I was half annoyed, half amused. 'No. He doesn't have to be. He has a very snazzy blonde of his own.'

'So Pete says.'

I handed him his food. 'Too bad little Pete's not twins. They could really groove it, swopping vicarious fantasies.'

'You've got Pete wrong. He's a good guy, and anyway he hasn't enough imagination for a good fantasy. He's a mathematician. He hasn't got a mind. He's got a computer between his ears. He just collects facts, programmes them in, and once in, there for keeps.' He concentrated on his food for a few minutes. 'Seems Linsey's bird is loaded.'

'So Robbie says.'

Bassy nodded absently and went on eating.

I was very puzzled. Though my father and I often had absent-minded moments, Bassy and mother only looked that way when their brains were working overtime on some tricky problem. Yet it could just be hunger.

'Seeing much of Robbie, Alix?'

'Not much.' I made tea and poured myself a cup. 'Why?'

'He seems a nice guy. Mmm—he doesn't seem to like Linsey.'

'So?'

'So this is Robbie's scene. He should know.'

'He might if he could see it clearly. His chip's in the way.' I drank some tea. 'When did Pete tell you he'd seen me with Charlie above?'

He hesitated. 'Yesterday.'

'Wow!' I sat down. 'Bassy, what's going on? You afraid I'm ripe for a rebound or something?'

'It could happen, particularly as Charlie's your type.'

'Ex-type. He's nothing like John.'

'If he had been I'd have been here two minutes flat after that chat with Pete.'

'Why? You never used to be so concerned with my moral welfare.'

'I never thought you a case for concern until I'd my first ugly butcher's at that creep John. Christ, Alix, that——' He broke off. 'Mind you,' he went on more gently, 'it did figure. He was a good-looking bastard, and his voracious technique must've been a traumatic as well as novel experience for you after the old Untouchables. Not surprising it rocked you off balance.' He smiled suddenly. 'Little Pete thinks you the snazziest bird in Edinburgh—which also figures.'

That scar was even more tender than I had thought. 'How'd you make that out?' I asked between my teeth.

'Use your IQ, woman? Pete's too dark and half a foot too short, but otherwise, acne and all, he's a natch for one of your Untouchables. Forgotten how mad you used to get after your dates when you were in sixth form? All that acne, sweat, heavy breathing, and after-shave fumes—and not even your hand held?'

I had to smile faintly. 'Yes. I remember now.'

'And that Henry Whatsit—the house surgeon in your first year—and the one that came next—what was his name? Tom Someone. No relation, but they could've been brothers. I remember once after one or the other came home with you Dad saying he felt so sorry for the wretched youth, as though he'd spent the weekend chasing you round our house and garden, he obviously hadn't the faintest idea what to do if he ever caught you. That's Pete right now,' he added cheerfully, as the food was sending up his blood-sugar, 'and you should see the looks he collects from his poor birds after dates. We've tried to help him. We've given him Fanny Hill, and he knows it by heart, but still can't get started. And though he's short on imagination, he's not thick. At maths, of course, he's a bloody genius. If he goes into industry ten years from now he'll be getting ten thousand a year or more. He'll make the really big league. You'll see.' He looked upwards. 'I have the impression Charlie now has a good bit in common with Pete ten years on. You fancy him at all?'

I could see he was genuinely concerned, and in the circumstances I couldn't blame him. Had our positions been reversed I would probably now be down at his flat trying to pump common sense into him. 'No. I just like him. You know?'

'Yep.' He stretched his arms as if a weight had rolled off. 'Hi, beautiful!' Catriona had come in. 'I'm free-loading, again! How's the tooth?'

'It was just a check-up. Bassy, excuse me, but I'm afraid you've lost an earring,' said Catriona.

After he left I needed to talk. 'I'd rather we kept this between us, Catriona.'

'Yes, indeed!' Oddly, she wasn't shocked. She was angry. 'If Sandra—the neighbours—anyone had seen him taking you up to his flat at midnight! Naturally, I understand it was just to save you the stairs——'

'And, possibly, his fiancée from getting the wrong impression. Like I told you, there didn't seem to be anyone around, but there could've been.'

'In one way that's a relief. But since he's supposed to be an engaged man'—she went scarlet with indignation—'I'm not sure that in another way it doesn't make it look much worse. What could have possessed the man to be so indiscreet?'

'How about common sense and kindness?'

She looked at me fiercely. 'I'm sorry, Alix, but if you still believe in Santa Claus, I don't.'

CHAPTER SIX

Meggy Drummond was the leader of the infant gang on the stairs. Meggy was nearly five and under a pudding-basin haircut had the face of a Victorian china-doll and the instincts of Genghis Khan. She ruled her gang absolutely, partly as she had the strongest personality, partly as she carried the most physical weight. Any hint of rebellion and Meggy jumped on the rebel, literally, but she was a tough and not a bully. After she had decided to accept me, if the gang spat on me or chucked grit at my car, it was just to give us all a good laugh, and no longer xenophobia.

It was releasing wee Jaimie's head from the stair railings that got me in good with Meggy. Jaimie was one of her many brothers, and when I arrived that morning the gang were trying to remove the fat infant's head from his body. The only child not bellowing was Jaimie, as Meggy kept shoving toffees into his mouth. There were no adults about, probably as the children were making such a noise. It was on the very rare occasions when they were silent that the maternal heads popped out of front doors like anxious, berollered jack-in-a-boxes.

'Want any help, kids?'

All but Jaimie looked at Meggy. She looked me up and down. 'Ye canna shift the bluidy bars. Ye're no strong enough.'

'There may be an easier way. Hold my bag, duckie. I may have something inside it to help Jaimie.' I hoped that would save my nursing-bag from being slung down the stairs directly I let it go. It did.

The children breathed heavily down my neck as I measured the greatest width of Jaimie's crown against the width of the bars and then used in reverse the technique required when delivering a normal baby's head in birth. It

62

worked better than I expected. Within seconds Jaimie was sitting in my lap rubbing his red ears and chewing another toffee.

Meggy exploded in relieved fury. 'Ye daft wee ——! Try that again and ye'll no get a sweetie fra me—ye'll get a boot up the backside!'

Jaimie pushed the toffee into his left cheek pouch, spat efficiently at his sister, and smiled at me angelically. 'Bluidy gurrrls!'

I had never heard Meggy's four-letter word. I asked Bassy to translate. He was rather shaken. 'My God! Who've you been mixing it with?'

To Meggy and gang a foreigner was anyone who did not live in their building. The demolition workers had long been targets. The appearance of the van with the dust-researchers was an unexpected and glorious bonus. For a while they abandoned the stairs and haunted the site.

'I'll have ulcers before this job's done, Nurse,' the site foreman told me. 'One good charge and we'd have the lot down and be away, but in this built-up area we've to go slow. Keeping those wee devils off the job is making an old man of me!' He ducked as a chip hit my car roof. 'I'm not a violent man and I've never raised my hand to a bairn in my life, but what I could do to those wee——' He cut himself short and substituted 'those bairns!'

'You have my sympathy, though when they're not heaving missiles they're cute kids.'

'Cute? Huh! Not the word I've in mind, Nurse!' He was a square man in his forties with a craggy, weather-pitted face and very small grey eyes. 'You'll be from England? What brings you up here?'

'I thought I'd like to work in Edinburgh.'

'Aye?' He considered me, dead-pan. 'How do you like it now you're here?'

'Very much, thanks. Missiles and all. It's such a beautiful city for one reason.'

'Taken your fancy, has it? No accounting for tastes.' He allowed himself a very small smile. 'Maybe it's no so bad.'

Archie Brown seemed so much better that morning that I

was worried. I looked for but did not see Dr MacDonald's car anywhere in my area. At lunch I consulted my private oracle.

Mrs Duncan advised me to wait until my afternoon's visit. 'The doctor's aware the grass should've been green over that poor laddie these last two months. No doubt he'll be round there himself later, but being Wednesday and his partner's rest-day, he'll have the double load of visits. It's but bad news that can't wait.'

'Yet, if this is the terminal rally?'

'Will that be news to Dr MacDonald?'

Gemmie was alone at our usual table. I asked her advice, but she had her own problems. She was starting a cold and had had a row with a patient's relative. 'There was this new cardiac asthma on my list. Her old man was a general, but she's a right lovely old bag—nothing toffee-nosed. Then in comes her daughter with the shopping "Ooh, Nurse," she says, looking like I was summat nasty the cat's fetched in, "I'm sorry you've been troubled. I asked the doctor to fetch in a nurse for my mother, but I meant a proper nurse. You do understand?" ' Gemmie was blazing. ' "Oh, aye, missus," I says, "I reckon I do seeing as the language we're speaking is my mother-tongue, even if I'm not good enough for you." I let her have it, Alix? She was that mad! Said she'd report me to "my superiors". Just shopped meself to Miss Bruce.'

'What did she say?'

'She was so right nice I feel bloody awful!'

Catriona arrived. 'Have you two remembered our monthly report has to be in tomorrow? I could shake myself for forgetting! I've promised to have supper with Aunt Elspeth this evening, and this means I'll have to sit up half the night.'

I said, 'Why not ring your aunt and have supper with her another evening?'

'I—I can't. She's—er—asked friends in.'

I tried to catch Gemmie's eye, but she was too deep in her private gloom. I finished my first course wondering why Catriona so often these days looked on the verge of an anxiety state when her aunt's name came up, but by my pudding was back to worrying about Archie Brown.

At four that afternoon Dr MacDonald's empty car was outside the buildings. The infant gang was minus Meggy and Jaimie, grouped in the main entrance and looking strangely subdued. 'Hallo, kids! Where's Meggy?'

The deafening response was mostly incoherent. I caught enough to make me sweat coldly. I had to be careful. The majority were too young for reason, but not for fear, and could easily be frightened into silence. If I had heard right, that could be fatal. 'So Meggy's gone for a drive in a car?' I kept my voice casual. 'How nice! What kind of a car?'

'A fine blue car!'

'Very nice. And with a man?'

'Aye! The man was away with Meggy and the sweetie bottle.'

I felt sick. 'Which man was this? Meggy's dad? Anyone's dad? Any of you know this man? Had you seen him before he gave Meggy the sweeties and asked her to take a drive?'

'He didna give Meggy the sweeties!' protested Fiona. 'They were Meggy's sweeties—wee white sweeties, and she liked them fine! I didna like mine. I spat it out—like this!'

'I spat mine better!' This was Alistair. 'I can spit fine—much better'n Fiona!'

'You're both top spitters, duckies!' I held them apart. 'Tell me more about Meggy. When did this man take her for a ride in his fine blue car?'

'Just now.'

That could be anything from five minutes to five hours back. 'How about Wee Jaimie? He go for a ride? He's up at his auntie's? What about Meggy's mother? Does she know Meggy's gone for a drive? Did Meggy tell her?'

They shuffled uncomfortably, I thought with guilt, until Dr MacDonald's voice answered, 'It's all right, Nurse. Meggy's away up at the hospital with her mother.' He patted a couple of the nearest heads. 'Away now, you bairns. I want a word with the nurse.'

We walked a little way from the entrance, and I breathed as if I had been running.

Dr MacDonald took a medium-sized and empty aspirin bottle from his pocket. 'New yesterday and left on the kitchen dresser. When Meggy was seen offering them round there were ten left. The rest, give or take a couple, she'd eaten. Apparently she liked the taste.'

'Oh no! But she's all right?'

'Thanks to the mercy of Providence and the observant eye of an itinerant pathologist driving up to join his colleagues across the way. I've just come from the hospital. The contents of her stomach have been satisfactorily evacuated, and they're keeping her in under observation for maybe twenty-four hours, but she should do nicely. Naturally, had there been any delay a dose this size could've been quickly lethal on a child her age. Her mother's very shocked. Maybe she'll learn from this, but others...' He shook his head. 'Do you know how many bairns die annually from poison swallowed accidentally in the supposed safety of their own homes?'

'Throughout the U.K.? Over a hundred.'

'Over a hundred.' He looked back and up at the high, narrow, crowded grey building, and it seemed that from every one of the many windows faces looked down. 'But figures are statistics that happen to other people. Not to me and mine. So the bottles of medicine and tablets remain on kitchen dressers or in unlocked cupboards and drawers easily available to small, inquisitive hands. The clearly marked "Poison" labels on the bottles of domestic disinfectant will continue to be ignored, and the bottles will remain on draining-boards and lavatory floors. And since to investigate and taste are natural instincts in normal infants, every year one hundred and maybe more bairns will die unnecessarily.' He sighed with impatient despair. 'In thirty years in general practice I've seen every variety of human grief. There's none worse than the loss of a beloved child, and when that grief is accentuated by the terrible knowledge that one wee bit of forethought could've saved that beloved life, the knife goes in too deep for healing. Yet will the parents learn to think ahead? Not in thirty years,' he said wearily, 'not in thirty years. However, this time we can breathe again, thanks to a certain Dr Linsey's promptness in bundling the mother and bairn in his car and up to the hospital within minutes of spotting the bottle in Meggy's hand. He got in touch with me at the hospital to

66

explain the situation. He'd quite a time contacting me, as I was over the other side attending my partner's patients.'

'Linsey,' I murmured. 'Of course! The car fits. I might have guessed had I not been too busy imagining everything from rape to murder.'

'Unhappily, not without reason these days.' He lifted his bushy eyebrows. 'You're acquainted with this pathologist?'

'If he's the man I think he must be, yes, slightly.' I told him about our flats.

'That's the man.' I thought he seemed about to add more, but was mistaken as he went on to discuss Archie Brown. 'You'll have observed this improvement?'

'Yes. It's been worrying me. Can it be genuine?'

'There's no question that today he's suffering less discomfort, discharge, feverishness, and jaundice.'

'Doctor—the final rally? Or could it last?'

'I wish I could answer that, Nurse.' He shrugged like a Latin. 'According to every textbook and expert opinion I've consulted on his condition, this can't possibly last. But according to them, he should be dead already. In my opinion all that's keeping him alive is his mind—and don't ask me how, as many a more learned man than myself would be unable to provide a satisfactory answer to that question. The human mind is a strange, powerful, and still largely uncharted instrument. Have you seen any apparently spontaneous cures of the incurable?'

'Two—no—three.'

'I've seen a few more. Not many. A few. If Archie Brown's mind can achieve that, though I've to admit, sadly, I doubt that's possible despite today, but once in a wee while the impossible becomes the possible—and if it does I shall rejoice greatly.' He glanced up as the low clouds unleashed a sudden squall. 'Ah, good! A drop of rain'll be welcome after the uncomfortable warmth of this afternoon's sun.'

Having only shivered at half-hourly intervals all afternoon, I agreed the sun had been unusually warm and we went our separate ways, smiling.

The rain had stopped and I was smiling on my way out.

The previously uncomplaining Archie had just admitted himself fed to the back teeth with the view from his bedroom window. Boredom was always one of the first signs of convalescence. At first unintentionally, my smile enveloped the car slowing opposite. Then I recognized car and driver and waved.

Charles Linsey did not smile back at once, which seemed reasonable, as he was not expecting to see me there. When he did it was a little stiffly. I didn't mind. I was much too pleased with him for saving Meggy's life, and over Archie. Also seeing him again reminded me how very nice he had been the night Mrs Thompson died. As his car disappeared behind the plain van on the site I decided Josephine Astley had been born lucky as well as rich. If she could only get him to grow his hair and do something about his suits she really would have it all ways. Then I wondered why she hadn't done something about both already. Though I had only seen her once, that once was enough for me to expect them to worry her. If I loved him they would worry me very seriously as they clearly proved he and I were on different wavelengths.

I remembered a psychiatrist saying that in the most ideal of human relationships a man and a woman could be on the same wavelength 90 per cent of the time, and in consequence 90 per cent honest with each other. He thought the remaining 10 per cent could and should never be shared, since humans were human and over-exposure only illuminated the less attractive elements in human nature.

I was assessing in retrospect my relationship with John as I drove back and had placed it around the 40 mark when I saw Sandra walking along the pavement ahead. I drew up for her. 'What's happened to your bike?'

Sandra and Gemmie were the only two in our set without driving licences. They were having the driving lessons provided by our authorities in these circumstances, but had not yet taken the test. Both had brought their own bikes up with them, and preferred using them to the ones officially provided. Sandra's was a very high-powered semi-racing job.

'The gears have jammed. I've left it at that shop back

there. The man's promised it'll be ready first thing tomorrow. He wanted to bring it up to the flat tonight, but I wasn't having that? I mean! Anyway, I've got a date—and guess who I've just seen driving by?'

My mind was on John. Not painfully, but in that strange pale mental plane in which it is so difficult to sort the dreams from the reality. Did it really happen? Was it really me? And if so, how can the me now be so divorced from the me then that I can't properly remember what he looked like? A little like Robbie? No. Robbie looks like himself. 'What did you say, Sandra?'

She repeated herself.

'Charlie,' I said absently. 'Yes. I've just seen him too.'

'Trust you! No wonder you're in one of your day-dreams! Don't forget he's hooked! Too bad you can drive, isn't it? He might've given you another lift!'

She was so annoyed that it seemed just as well for Charlie's sake that he was engaged. 'When did your gears jam, Sandra?'

She was the only girl I had ever met who could bridle. She did it superbly. 'Don't be bitchy, Alix! Anyway, I've got a date tonight.'

'Don't forget the monthly report's due tomorrow.'

'I've done all but today's!'

Gemmie snorted when she heard this. 'She would! She's so bloody efficient she makes me feel inadequate.'

That was true. Sandra managed to combine the most active social life in our set with extreme efficiency on duty.

Gemmie's cold was so much worse that she made only a token protest when I insisted on taking her temperature and then ringing Miss Bruce.

'Poor Miss Downs,' said Miss Bruce. 'Undoubtedly this is some cold virus she's not as yet encountered. Tell her to stay in bed, and I'll be up to see her in the morning. Thank you, Miss Hurst.'

Gemmie mopped her streaming eyes. 'How many cold viruses are there then? I've forgotten.'

'I think Europe has about one hundred and ninety, and we've roughly fifty-five in England—or thereabouts.'

69

'Right bundle of sunshine you are, love! Sure you don't mind fetching me supper in bed?'

'Call me Miss Nightingale, but not Flo. I do so dislike familiarity from my patients.'

She was half asleep when I removed her supper-tray. 'I'll love you for ever for this, Alix.'

'Oh, duckie, not sure I fancy you.' I turned off her light. 'Sleep well.' When I looked in ten minutes later she was flat out and snoring.

I had to get on with my monthly report, but the prospect of filling in any type of official form invariably reduced me to a dithering wreck. So I had to wash up our supper things, then the kitchen sink obviously had to be scrubbed, and the floor washed. Then I spring-cleaned the bathroom. I had the vacuum-cleaner in the sitting-room before I remembered the noise would wake Gemmie and saw the clock on the bookshelf. Reluctantly I put away the unused machine, swamped the sitting-room table with my patients' notes and cards, and began sorting them.

New patients; old patients; number of visits; visits in my own area; visits on relief-work. Whom had I relieved? That meant another stack. Children one to five; children five to fifteen; patients over sixty-five—oh no! The first two stacks had to be re-sorted.

Infections? Another general post. Injections had to be specified. Streptomycin, antibiotics, insulin, mersalyl, anti-anaemic—Mrs MacRae's second twin was a girl and they were calling her Roberta. Other injections? Had I given any? Yes, several.

How many visits had lasted forty-five minutes and over? Miss Bruce and the city fathers had to know. Again, several, but none to compare with the time against Mrs Thompson's name. Nearly a month back already. Time here went even faster than in London.

'Time, a maniac scattering dust . . .'

No dust, and tonight Meggy could have been dead. I had finished and was trying to summon the energy to make coffee when our front-door bell rang. I answered it quickly to save a second ring's disturbing Gemmie. Robbie was on our doorstep. 'Am I too late to come in, Alix?'

'Shush. Gemmie's asleep.' I kept my voice down. 'Come on in.'

'You're sure it's not too late?'

It was after ten, but still broad daylight. I shook my head, smiling, and jerked a thumb at the sitting-room door. He followed me in silently. I closed the door and told him about Gemmie's cold and that Catriona was still out. 'What are you doing wandering abroad at this hour?'

He had been having a drink with some friend who had offered to lend him a boat over the next weekend. 'He's got a mooring at Cramond. Aren't you off Saturday? Come sailing.'

'Thanks, I'd like that, though I can't sail. Never done any. Will it matter?'

'Not for the type of sailing we'll be doing Saturday.'

I looked at his expression. 'Then why, to quote Mrs Duncan, the Sabbath face?'

'I'm a wee bit surprised you don't sail. I thought sailing and skiing were the "in" outdoor sports of the English upper classes.'

'I'll check on that for you next time I run into one of the English Upper class.'

He froze. 'That, from a girl with your accent, is either patronizing or tactful. For your information, I find both equally offensive.'

I took a closer look at him. He had not been so belligerent since those few minutes the first morning he called round. I wondered how much he had been drinking, though he did not look drunk and if he had to work later he was unlikely to have had more than his usual single whisky, and that slowly. 'On call tonight?'

'From eleven-thirty. Why?'

He hated the world too much for the truth. 'Just wondering if you'd time to join me for coffee.'

That lit a spark in his dark, angry eyes, but it was not laughter. 'I don't have to rush, but why bother making coffee?'

I resisted the urge to explain I was right out of hemlock. 'I need reviving. I've just spent two hours filling in one form, and my blood-sugar's in a bad way.' I smiled to spread sweetness and light. 'For your information, you're now observing my typical post-form syndrome.'

'Which obviously requires instant adrenalin.' He hauled me into his arms and kissed my mouth, my face, my neck, as if he couldn't recall his last meal and didn't know when he would get another. 'Isn't this the right therapy, Alix?' he muttered breathlessly.

I needed breath. 'If you say so.'

He raised his face to scowl at mine. 'What's that supposed to mean?'

'That I'm now being intentionally tactful.'

'Why?'

'Because you're overwhelmingly stronger than I am, and I'm not a masochist.'

His eyes looked darker, his chin bluer, and his very regular features less clear-cut. 'You've never minded my kissing you before.'

'Before was different, and you know it.'

'Maybe.' His hold tightened. 'As you knew what you were doing when you hustled me in here on tiptoe not to wake Gemmie, let me know Catriona's away and we've the place to ourselves.'

'I—Oh, blimey!' I stifled my laugh against his shoulder. 'Robbie, I'm terribly sorry. I honestly am! I only whisked you in behind this closed door as any voices in our hall echo all round the flat. Don't know why. Something's wrong with the hall's acoustics.'

He let go of me so abruptly I nearly fell over backwards and had to steady myself on the back of a chair. He stomped to the other side of the room, put his fists on his hips, and glowered at me. 'That's not all that's wrong! When you're over the best bloody good laugh you've had in years you may as well tell me. What's wrong with my technique?'

I was actually laughing at myself, not him. I was remembering my Untouchables. Had Bassy been present he'd have been hysterical. And John. 'Your wide-eyed-jolly-hockey-sticks technique is so inhibiting, darling, that most men'll read your come-hither as an instant go-forth. But I'm not most men. I'm different. He was.

72

I tried to explain my laughter to Robbie. He took it as more tact. He knew he was a failure. 'If not, would I be sitting here holding a P.M.? Even if I got you wrong I'd you in my arms. Why couldn't I keep you there? Or get a flicker out of you? And that's happened before! What do I do wrong?'

'Robbie dear, I'm not sure I'm the right person——'

'Ach, don't give me that!' He sat astride an arm of the sofa. 'You're a pretty, experienced London girl. You've been around. You could teach me a lot, and I wish you would. I find you very attractive.'

'Well, thanks.' I needed a chair. 'So you think all London girls are swinging, promiscuous chicks, addicted to Pot, L.S.D., and other kinky devices?'

He said sternly, 'I'm not suggesting you're daft enough to be hooked on any drug!'

'That's a break.' I swallowed. 'The rest?'

'I'm not talking about the rest. I'm talking about you. I want you. Why haven't I got you?'

I studied him for a few seconds. He was now more hurt than angry. It was mostly my fault, and I liked him. So I told him the truth.

When I finished he was sitting on the arm of my chair stroking my hair. 'Were I not such an insensitive lecher I'd have worked this out for myself. But when I came in just now I honestly thought'—he hesitated—'no, that's not right! I was in such a bloody black mood I wasn't thinking at all.'

'I saw that. Why were you so mad? Anything to do with me?'

'No.' His face hardened unrecognizably. 'I ran into someone I once knew earlier this evening.'

'Old girlfriend?'

'Aye. Something was said between us that got under my skin.'

'Like "Get back to the Gorbals, laddie"?'

He breathed in sharply. 'Was I that obvious?'

'Yes. Want to talk about her?'

'No. Mind?'

I shook my head. 'Anyway, this seems to be my night on

73

the psychiatric couch. Maybe I needed it. I feel much better for unburdening. I hope you don't mind?'

'Ach, no.' He kissed me, but gently. 'What I need, Alix, is a wife, and not merely as I'll have to have one when I turn G.P. But I want a wife, a home, a family. I wish I didn't just find you physically attractive. I wish I loved you. I'd ask you to marry me tonight if I did.'

'Then I'm glad you don't. The one thing a beautiful friendship can't survive is a rejected proposal of marriage. You know?'

His face hardened again. 'I do, indeed. Mind you,' he added too quickly, 'were I not in my present job I might be fool enough to persuade myself a purely sexual attraction would be a good enough basis for marriage. But in obstetrics one sees so much married hell. I'm not risking that for you or myself, though if you'd have me I think you'd probably make me a very good wife——' He stopped, as Catriona looked in and backed out. 'Is that clock right?' He checked with his watch. 'My God, it's slow. I'm due on wagon call in fifteen minutes, and if I'm not there fifteen minutes from now the first emergency'll call in. Come and see me out.'

On the landing he fixed our front-door latch to close without locking and shut the door. 'If the citizens of Edinburgh had less active sex lives I might have time to attend to my own. Pick you up here, one on Saturday. Can you swim?'

'Not well.'

'No problem. Getting the life-jackets out of the hatches'll leave more room for the skeletons. Thanks for not rattling mine.'

'No trouble.'

He ran one finger gently along my face. 'Maybe I could do a lot worse. So might you. Shall we try and sort this out?'

'It can wait. The baby-wagon won't.'

'You're so right!' He went down three at a time. I heard him talking to someone on the stairs, but was too preoccupied by the many thoughts he sparked off to register more than distant male voices. It was chilly on the landing, but I sat on the nearest stair to think things out.

'Locked yourself out, Miss Hurst?'

I looked up without getting up. Charlie was looming over me and looked a different man in a superbly cut dinner-jacket and very bad temper. 'Hallo! No, I'm just thinking. What's up with your lift?'

'Grounded below since last night, and likely to remain there several days. Some vital part has to be manufactured before it can be replaced.'

'Is that why the front hall was full of mechanics when we got back this evening? Bad luck.' That 'luck' reminded me of Meggy. I thanked him for saving her. 'Dr MacDonald told me.'

He bowed slightly. 'News travels fast.'

I was sorry to see him so glum and gave him a big smile. 'Even good news!'

'Precisely. Goodnight.' He walked round me and took the last flight so fast I wondered if he had run into an old flame, had a row with Josephine, if there was something disturbing about these short, white high-summer nights, or if I had merely said the wrong thing.

I had.

CHAPTER SEVEN

Catriona showed me the 'Forthcoming Marriages' column in yesterday's *Scotsman* at breakfast. I did a double take. 'I suppose this is right?'

'Oh yes. There was quite a bit of talk about it at the dinner-party last night. Not that Aunt Elspeth was surprised. She never thought Josephine Astley would marry Charlie Linsey, and she knows this other man's mother well. He was at school with Charlie.'

'Poor old Charlie!' I wished I had done my thinking elsewhere last night. 'Not that I'm all that surprised, now I think about it. Not with his ghastly turn-ups. But why didn't your aunt think Josephine would marry him? Presumably she knows him. Why haven't you told us?'

She was looking neurotic again. 'I—I don't like—well—gossip. Aunt Elspeth knows so many people, having lived here most of her life. She—er—didn't think them compatible. Is that Gemmie moving?'

'She was still asleep when I looked in five minutes ago.' I reached for the paper. 'Wonder if this'll last?'

'The date's fixed for later this month.'

'Someone's a fast worker,' I said tritely.

'According to Aunt Elspeth, they've been friends years. Charlie must've guessed it was in the air.'

I thought back a few months. 'Not necessarily. I'm really very sorry for Charlie.'

'He'll get over it. Men do. A man can always find another woman. Och, yes, I know they talk all that blah about love, but what they actually mean is lust. That's easily satisfied if you're a man.'

It was some time since either Gemmie or I had made the mistake of believing Catriona's soft, sugar-plum veneer went even skin-deep, but this did surprise me. 'I've gathered you didn't reckon much to men, but not that you reckoned this low. Or are you getting Gemmie's cold? You're rather puffy round the eyes.'

'That's my report. Took me till three.' She cleared the table as I began washing up. 'But apart from my father, brother, and the rare, sweet laddie like Bassy, I've no opinion of men at all!'

'They aren't all creeps. Think of our Wilf——'

'And for every Wilf I can think of cohorts of insensitive lechers I wouldn't trust further than I can spit! And what's more,' added Catriona in her most Scottish manner, 'I never spit!'

'Hey, slaves!' Gemmie's head came round the door. 'Eight-o'clock news is just starting. Thought you'd like to know!'

The morning was half over before I had caught up with it or realized Catriona had rung a mental bell. Briefly, it seemed strange she should have so exactly echoed Robbie. Then I remembered their mutual training hospital. 'Insensitive lecher' must at some time have been top of their hospital's insult pops. Last year, after a particularly lively series of protests in Trafalgar Square, 'fascist imperialist lackey' had echoed round every department in Martha's. I once heard a junior sister hurl it at a male student who had rashly walked round a screen closing a female ward to all male visitors. He had beat it as if the Red Guard were after his blood.

Charlie's car passed mine twice that morning. We met in person on my afternoon visit to Archie. Recalling my supersensitivity immediately after John, I greeted Charlie with a big hallo to prove I was only the passing stranger who knew nothing about anyone's private life. 'Dust keeping you hard at it?'

'Temporarily. I'm sure the patients are doing the same for you. Don't let me keep you.'

It was as clear a brush-off as it was a total reversal of his former amiable attitude towards me. He looked so tight-lipped and tense that twang him and he'd sound a high C. He worried me in the way my patients worried me and made me feel very guilty over the unintentional brush-offs I had probably given casual acquaintances at his present stage. Close friends I had avoided intentionally, having found the patronizing element in pity intolerable, and compassion even more disturbing. The ability of the compassionate to share my feelings having added guilt for upsetting them to my share. That immediate reaction had not lasted long, but while it lasted it had been like swimming under water and not daring to surface, as surfacing meant opening my eyes and seeing my world for what it really was.

Archie was maintaining his improvement and Meggy was back from hospital, slightly pale and very pleased with herself. 'I was that sick, Nurrrsie! I was sick on my wee cot, and the nurrrse and the doctor, and he'd to change his fine white coat and his shirt, and then I was sick on the floor. I was bluidy sick, ye ken?'

'I get the picture, Meggy. You liked the hospital?'

'I liked it fine! I'd a jelly like a rabbit, all red and floppy, and an ice-cream, and a jelly like a wee fish that was yellow but wasna floppy, and more ice-cream, and I wasna sick, not the once!'

I had a new patient that afternoon in one of the newest housing estates. A neighbour directed me. 'Mr Richards? Away over there, two down. Is he poorly with his chest again? It'll be the dust. Aye, it's terrible, the dust.'

For a few seconds I looked round for signs of demolition. The small pinkish-yellow houses were in mint condition; the little gardens were less well cared for and lacked the passionately raised flowers found in English gardens on any comparable estate, but the grass was cut and as dust-free as the clean, salty air. Then I re-read the occupation on the new blue card in my hand. 'I've heard dust is a problem in mines. Thank you, Mrs——'

'Mrs McWilliams. You're welcome.'

Mr Richards was forty-eight, with a fine-boned face that looked ten years older and the powerful shoulders and arms of a much younger man. He had been a miner for thirty-three years, and his hands were scarred with coal. His breathing was laboured and his cough painful. He said, 'I've had it worse.'

He was an ill man, a very good patient, and he did not want to talk. So I worked in silence. When he was in clean pyjamas in a bed remade with clean sheets, he said, 'That's better.'

'Good. Just your injection.' He rolled up his left sleeve. 'I hope that didn't hurt, Mr Richards?'

'No.'

The double bed took up most of the room. The bedstead was old, but the mattress and bedding were newish, thick, and clean. Every inch of furniture and floor had the high polish I had now come to expect in nine out of every ten houses I visited, irrespective of the financial and social background of the occupants.

I discussed this with Catriona, walking home that evening. 'In comparison, we three are slum-bodies. Our floors haven't been polished since Wilf did 'em. Just as well the neighbours don't call. They'd think we're lowering the tone of the house.'

'I shudder to think how they already view us!'

I laughed. 'You're not serious?'

She was. 'Since, to most people, there are only two types of nurses, the sinners and the saints, and we've men calling at all hours, can one wonder if our neighbours think the worst?'

I looked at her pale, composed, and exquisitely etched profile without answering. We both knew the only men to call on us since Wilf were Bassy and Robbie. The neighbours knew Bassy was my younger brother, which presumably let him out. Mrs Kinloch knew Robbie was an R.O., and enough about hospital life from a medical son-in-law to appreciate the long and odd hours worked by all hospital residents. All hospital residents have a tough time in getting away even when officially off duty, but none tougher than the obstetricians. To be any good at that job a man or woman must be genuinely fond of babies and like women. No good obstetrician lightly hands over a woman in labour or a problematical baby, and large city maternity hospitals seldom, if ever, consider employing even a junior obstetrician who is not good at his or her job. Mrs Kinloch might not know for sure, but Catriona certainly did, that Robbie either called on me when he could get off, whatever the hour, or not at all. Her rather childish crack would have been excusable from an outsider, but as she was an intelligent and generally non-childish insider, I found it very thought-provoking.

Gemmie's cold was better, and as Saturday was her day off and tomorrow Friday, Miss Bruce had said she could go home in the morning. For once all three of us were free on Saturday. Catriona asked what I was doing and on hearing said it was time she went home. 'Will you mind being alone for the night, Alix?'

'Not at all, though if Bassy's having his usual Friday-night rave I'll probably stay there. I feel like some air, so I think I'll go down now and find out his plans. Either of you coming for the walk?'

Neither had the energy. Gemmie offered me her bike to use now and while she was away. 'The back tyre's getting a slow but stays up if you pump it.'

The back-tyre did not need pumping that evening. Bassy was at home along with a couple of dozen fellow-students. I hesitated in the doorway at the rows of hairy, hostile faces. 'Should I go away?'

Bassy was holding the floor. 'You can stick around. Only my sister,' he explained. 'Only a nurse. Strictly tech. type.'

A small girl with long, dark hair, white lips, and outsize black-rimmed goggles made room for me on a cupboard. 'Hi, Alix, I'm Melly Drew, Bassy's bird.'

'Hi, Melly.' I climbed up by her and looked round. I had never seen so much hair in one room at a time. Most of the hair needed washing, and all combing. 'What's going on? Bassy on a protest kick?'

'With every reason! We've to back up poor old Tam.'

'Which one's poor old Tam?'

'He's not here. Bassy told him to stay under cover.'

I was very curious. 'What's he done?'

Her reply made me smile. 'He's lucky he's not a Martha's student. For this he wouldn't be under possible suspension,'

I murmured, 'he'd be out.'

Bassy had the hearing of a gun-dog. 'Probably the only system an uneducated medic.'ll understand.'

'Medics. aren't educated?' I queried rashly.

The room fell about with laughter. When Bassy could make himself heard he said that despite the much broadened educational system insisted on by the Scottish universities, he had yet to meet the scientist who was not an illiterate barbarian. Two dozen Arts heads nodded in smug agreement. 'Most of us here,' Bassy went on, 'are over twenty-one. All of us have an intelligence high above average, or we wouldn't be here. To treat highly intelligent adults like irresponsible, low-grade teenagers is something stupid!'

I said, 'Even when a highly intelligent adult behaves like an irresponsible, low-grade teenager?'

The room shouted me down. I shouted back. They won.

Bassy saw me out. 'Don't lose any sleep over this, Alix. We know what we're doing and we'll get what we want.'

'You wouldn't, were I one of "them". I'd tell the lot of you to stop playing the fool and get out! Where do you get this "have to be at university" rubbish? You're here first because you chose to come, then were accepted. If you made the wrong choice, as you're all so bloody intelligent, who's fault is that? If you don't now want your places just step aside and let all those thousands with good "A"s who couldn't get a place move in.'

Bassy smiled indulgently. 'As ever, you're missing the main point. And we didn't just choose to come. We worked something hard to make the right grades.'

'I know that! But what none of you seems to know, or have even a glimmering of suspicion about, is your incredible good luck in have these years——'

'No luck involved! Bloody hard work!'

'No luck?' I turned furiously on the hairy faces watching entranced through the open doorway. 'You lot should come out on district with me any day of the week. You'd see kids younger than yourselves doing adult jobs, running homes, coping with bedridden gran upstairs, mum in a mental hospital from worry and overwork, dad either at work or at the pub, plus three or four younger brothers and sisters —and not just in Edinburgh, but in London or any other city! And some'll have just as good brains as any of yours, but at the right time they weren't in the right place, didn't get the right food, the right teaching—or, if they did they'd to stay home to help out too often to use it—and that takes parental backing. You don't think luck comes into this?' No one answered. 'It's no good trying to make you see sense!'

Bassy said, 'What is "good" and what is "sense"? Define and discuss.'

'You know I can't. Even if I could, it'd be a waste of time when you're on a rabble-rousing kick.'

'This is no kick,' he said quietly. 'A very real principle is involved, though you're too thick to appreciate it.'

'Oh, blimey!' I knew what he was like when a real or imaginary principle stuck in his throat. 'Had I tears to shed I'd shed 'em now for "them".'

Mr Richards' breathing was less laboured in the morning. The sound of his cough continued to appal me. I flagged down Mrs Duncan's car.

She said, 'Even with the improved machines and conditions mining remains a hard and dirty job. His temp's down? That's good.'

'His cough tears me apart. What it must do to him!'

'You've not worked in a mining area before? You'll get used to that cough if you do. That cosy coal-fire on a chilly day can cost a lot more than the money you paid for it.'

'Yet his wife says he's fretting to get back below.'

'I've no doubt she's right. Have you many more before lunch? It's nearly time to return.'

'Only one injection at my post-office.'

The sub-post-office-cum-general-stores lay at the far end of the road and on the same side as the Archie–Meggy buildings. The shop was on a corner, and the road running by at right-angles to 'my' road marked the boundary of Sandra's present area. Charlie's empty car was parked just round the corner and, as there was no other available space, I drew in directly behind it. He came round from the shop as I was locking my car. He was looking slightly more human as the stiffish breeze had untidied his hair, but more a 'Charles' than a 'Charlie'. From its deplorable cut his hand-woven tweed suit was a family heirloom.

We had met earlier up the other end, and, having then dealt with the approaching end of the demolition, only the weather remained. It was a chilly, grey day, with the pale sun just occasionally struggling through the thick overcast, but the breeze had kept the blue-grey rain-clouds moving too fast for a squall, and at that moment the sun broke through again. 'Isn't it a grand morning, Nurse!' every other patient had announced, as always when not actually pelting. A two-hour cloudburst they termed 'a nice wee drop of rain'. A twenty-four hour deluge was 'a good shower'. Having discovered I genuinely preferred this cooler, wetter, but infinitely more bracing climate, my 'Lovely day after a dubious start!' was no act.

Charles gave the sky a dour glance. 'The rain's kept off.'

Close by a bicycle bell was rung with unnecessary vigour. I looked round as Sandra sailed past and returned her wave. 'One of my set. Lives in the flat below ours.'

The impassive silence in which he received this would have disconcerted me two months ago. Messrs MacThis, MacThat, Richards, Brown, and others had taught me such a silence need imply no more than the obvious fact that the man in question considered speech superfluous. 'I must get on,' I said, 'or I'll be late for lunch.'

'You must, if you've shopping in mind. The post-office is about to shut.' His tone was impatient, even hostile. He walked on to his car before I could explain I was paying a professional call. I was not sorry, as I was in a hurry and there was a limit to the sweetness and light I was prepared to shed on such a patently unwilling recipient.

The little shop was still packed with customers. My patient, the sub-postmaster's wife, was helping out behind the stores counter. The counter-flap was weighed down with parcels. 'Can you get under, Nurse?'

I ducked beneath to encouraging clucks from postmaster and customers. 'As well ye're but a slip of a lassie, Nurse!'

We retreated to a back room piled high with boxes of

83

soap powder, tins of sweets and biscuits, cans of every variety, bottles of pickles, ketchup, salad cream, and shampoo, and plastic shopping-baskets. 'My man's that pressed, so you'll not mind giving me the injection in here, dearie? There's a wee sink over the corner for you to wash your hands. Or should we go up?'

'Here's fine, thanks.' I propped my open nursing-bag on a stack of tins, washed my hands, then took out the sterile pack containing all I needed. Cleaning my patient's arm with spirit, I thought momentarily of the countless injections I had given in hospital. I was now using the identical technique, but, as Mrs Duncan once said, 'in two different worlds'.

'That's grand, Nurse! I didna feel it at all! Will you take a sweetie? Maybe a biscuit? Do you never nibble? Ach, small wonder you've that wee waist! Ye'll not mind if we return?'

We raced back to the shop. I ducked again under the flap and straightened my hat. 'See you next week.'

'I'll be looking out for you, Nurse. Cheerio just now!'

'Cheerio just now!' echoed her husband and the remaining customers.

My district had hooked me. 'Cheerio just now!'

During that afternoon I decided a quiet evening alone in the flat would be very pleasant. After one solitary hour I had had enough. I changed out of uniform, stuffed my bag and a raincoat into Gemmie's bike-basket, and, as the wind had dropped, the sky cleared, and by any standards it was a glorious evening, I bounced leisurely over the cobbles in the Royal Mile, hoping Bassy would provide me with some concrete excuse for not staying in and writing up a lecture.

When I reached his flat little Pete was locking up. 'Like you're looking for Bassy? He's making the sit-in scene.'

'There's a sit-in over Tam? That why you're loaded with blankets and food? Hell! This going on all night, Pete?'

'It could happen.' We went down the stairs, and he surveyed my back tyre lugubriously. 'Like it needs air.'

'So it does! I thought the cobbles extra bumpy. Must be a slow slow.'

Pete deposited blankets, milk-bottles, bread, cheese, a bag

of apples, and half a stale cake in a heap on the pavement and pumped up the tyre. 'Does Bassy have the message, Alix?'

Though unhooked on his pop-English, I found it nauseatingly infectious. 'Like why I'm here?'

'You read me good, man.'

I explained having forgotten to tell Bassy last night I was on my own and that I was in the mood for a T.G.I.F. ('Thank God it's Friday') rave. 'This sit-in lasting all week-end?'

'The whole scene's changing. Could be a happening.' He reloaded himself. 'It grieves me, Alix.'

'Not your fault protests are Bassy's own thing, Pete. Thanks for pumping my tyre. You're a dolly.'

He had a very shy and quite delightful smile. He ambled off with the milk-bottles clinking in his pockets and the back of his neck bright red.

The sweet-shop on the corner reminded me of the post-office this morning and then of my first evening. I smiled to myself. If Charles shared Robbie's views on London dollies, that kiss, as Catriona would undoubtedly say, must have confirmed his worst fears. Then I turned upwards into the Royal Mile, and, as on my first evening, the austere beauty of the scene got me by the throat. I pushed uphill very slowly, stopping occasionally to hang over the handlebars and absorb the delicate and infinite variations of greys.

In that evening's light John Knox's house was near-pink, Huntly House had a mauve tinge, the cobbles a pearl-grey sheen, and St Giles loomed ahead like charcoal velvet, and awesomely unostentatious. On either side the high buildings seemed to be still huddling together to keep inside the old Flodden Wall, and I thought how strange it was that that wall had originally been built as a defence against the old enemy, my ancestors. The thought left me vaguely guilty, and feeling as if I had no right to this personal enchantment with this alien city.

Once I had attempted to explain this enchantment to Robbie. He had taken it as a great joke. I remembered that now, and then how well Charles had seemed to understand and how he had shown me that view from the hill. He had understood my remark about Beethoven. I had not mentioned my passion for Beethoven to Robbie, nor would I mention Edinburgh again to him, in this context. I did not mind being laughed at, but I minded very much when people and things I loved were made laughing-points.

I pushed on even more slowly, being in no hurry to exchange enchantment for an empty flat and lecture notes. Even the girls below were out—Sandra on a date and the other two at some hospital dance.

'Nurse Hurst!'

I stopped and looked round vaguely, wondering if I had imagined that woman's voice. Then: 'Nurse Hurst! Up here!' It was Mrs Brown at an upper window of a small restaurant. 'Can you wait, Nurse?' She vanished, to appear in the doorway. 'My boss says I may have a word with you. Are you away anywhere special, or can I ask you a great favour?'

'Hi, Mrs Brown! I'm just pottering. What can I do for you?'

She came out onto the pavement, looking ready to hug me. 'Providence must've sent you, Nurse! I've been that upset, not knowing what to do for the best. You'll know I've an awful good boss, and he's asked me to work late this once as the other waitress is poorly. But Archie's expecting me home by eight, and he'll fret if I'm late. Could you ride over and tell him? You will? Och, Nurse, I'm that grateful! The weight off my mind!'

The ride would have taken only about twenty minutes had the back tyre stayed up. After the first mile it refused to hold air for more than a few yards at a time. Eventually I gave up and walked.

Archie Brown was at the window in his dressing-gown. I called up, but he did not hear, and as I was in a sweater and skirt with my hair down and minus a car did not recognize me. When I rang his doorbell he all but flung the door off its hinges. His hollow face was yellow-grey. 'No bad news, Mr Brown. Your wife's working late. She'll be home at ten.' I explained why.

'Nurse, I'm that obliged. I don't mind telling you, I was getting a wee bit anxious. Will you step inside?'

86

'No, thanks, as I should be getting back to a lecture I haven't written up, and you should be back in bed. All right now?'

'Just fine. Just fine.'

I had left my bike by the main entrance. It was surrounded by Meggy and gang when I got down. 'Ye've a wee flattie, Nurrrsie! Ye canna ride yer bike!'

An older boy was investigating. 'No wonder ye've a flattie!' He gave me a woman-driver-what-can-you-expect scowl. 'The valve-rubber's gone. Have ye no got a spare?'

'I hope so.' I looked in the tool-bag. It contained only one of Gemmie's dirty aprons. 'No. Is there a shop handy?'

'Aye, but it'll be shut just now.'

I shrugged. 'So I have to push back.'

Meggy had shot off while I was looking in the tool-bag. I did not notice where.

'Having a busman's holiday, Miss Hurst?'

I pushed back my hair from my face. Meggy had returned tugging Charles after her by the hand, having apparently produced him out of thin air. There was no sign of the pathologist's van or his car. 'Hi! No. Not so much a holiday as a demonstration of what my grandmother used to describe as the cussedness of inanimate objects. Look at that back tyre!'

'Meggy didn't disclose the precise nature of your problem, though I gathered your cycle had been visited by disaster unparalleled.' He stooped to investigate. 'Ride over a nail?'

'It's no a puncture!' the older boy had answered. 'It's but the valve-rubber that's perished, and she's no spare! Daft! No spares!'

I said firmly, 'It really doesn't matter. I shall enjoy pushing it back on this glorious evening.'

'It'll no last!' Cassandra Junior was at it again. 'There's a haar coming. My dad says.'

'A what? Oh, yes. A sea-mist. Surely,' I appealed to Charles, 'not yet?'

He straightened and dusted his hands. 'I shouldn't wonder.' From his manner the immediate destruction of the world would occasion him no surprise, but considerable relief. 'This is a low-lying area, and the air smells of an incipient haar. I can run you back and your cycle can go on the open boot'—he glanced at Meggy—'as our mutual friend informed me when she again diced with death by leaping in front of my bonnet as I was driving off.' Meggy was now successfully ordering Cassandra Junior to wheel my bike round the far side of the block. 'From that child's determination to raise help for the Nurrrsie fra England, one Scottish Nat. less to ruffle the Union of the Crowns when she grows up.'

Thinking he was joking, I smiled. 'We English are dead crafty. Like they say, "catch 'em young enough and you catch 'em for life".'

That evoked the dourest glance I had collected since crossing the Border. 'Quite.'

I wondered whether to explain I was being facetious, then decided that would be even more tactless. 'Thanks for offering this lift. You're sure it won't take you out of your way?'

'I've finished for the day and was just going back. I usually finish around this time. We live in the same building. No bother.' His tone contradicted his words. 'But to spare yourself this problem in future you might be well advised to invest a couple of bob in valve-rubbers.'

'I'll do that.' I did not explain it was Gemmie's bike or my errand to Archie Brown, partly as I couldn't be bothered, partly as, in his present mood, he'd probably read it as another fiendish English plan to undermine Scotland's right to home rule.

I watched his face as we drove back in silence. His expression was giving nothing away, but he couldn't hide the intelligence, the sensitivity, or the toughness. When it came to a straight choice, I mused, his intellect would always win over his emotions, but not without a great deal of mental trauma. I suspected that was what was really bugging him now. In any affair, if one wanted out, the only intelligent thing was to let him or her go—but it hurt. I was sorry for him, if glad for myself that I had worked this out. Otherwise the atmospheric silence would have wholly convinced me I was personally responsible for the original construction of the Flodden Wall.

CHAPTER EIGHT

We walked up the four flights together as his lift was still broken. My empty flat and lecture notes had become the Promised Land—and then I found I'd forgotten my key. 'What's so maddening,' I said, 'is that I now know where it is—pinned to my uniform dress.'

He stopped studying the landing floor. 'I'm afraid I've no spare. I gave Miss Bruce the only three to this lock.'

'She told us. Hell! I would choose tonight!'

'Something special about tonight?'

I explained. 'The girls below'll put me up when they get in,' I added. 'Could be worse. Could be raining.'

He said, 'Unfortunate your brother should've been involved in this sit-in.'

'Yes.' I smiled involuntarily. 'Inevitable' was the right word, but as he worked for the other side I didn't say so. Had he not been our landlord I would have asked if he knew anything about picking locks. I wanted to try that, which meant getting rid of him. I used the first excuse that occured to me. 'I'll ring Mrs Duncan and ask if I can call in on her.'

'She lives near?'

'Corstorphine. But I'll enjoy the bus-ride out. So all I need is the nearest phone.'

There was a small silence. 'Presumably mine.'

That slip-up made me suddenly aware I was very tired. It had been a normally busy week. The last two hours had been unusually energetic, but what had most exhausted me was this strained atmosphere. I could work all day and dance half the night without feeling tired, but a slack afternoon with a moody ward sister invariably left me, as most people, physically drained with my brain in slow motion. Yet he was trying to be helpful, had driven me back, and, above all, been so nice to me previously. 'That's a break I'd overlooked!' I flogged enthusiasm into my voice. 'Would you mind my using it?'

'Could any neighbour in these circumstances?'

'Maybe not, but thanks.' We went on up. 'One way and another I'm having a rather traumatic evening.'

'So it would seem.'

His flat provided me with another traumatic experience. Had I given it any thought I would have expected to find it serviceable, bookish, slightly impersonal, and much too tidy. I was only right about the books.

The room into which he took me and the dining-room, visible through an open door beyond, were furnished with a discreet, very personal, and very expensive elegance. Most of the furniture was antique, and very good antique. My maternal grandfather had been in that business, and a little of his knowledge had trickled down to me through my mother. One look, and I understood why his insurance company insisted he kept locked the door to the lift below, and why he had just needed two different keys to unlock his front door.

He left me to use the telephone on a flat-topped rose-wood desk. I rang the number twice, then checked. The line was in order and I had the right number. I went out to the hall, a white lie ready.

He said, 'I heard you having trouble. Out?'

That took care of my white lie. 'She may be in her garden.' I spoke slowly and tried to think fast. My mind was mainly on my lock. I had hairpins, scissors, and a nail-file in my bag. 'I think it's worth taking a chance. Even if she's out I like seeing the world from the top of a bus.'

'I assume you haven't looked out of a window in the last few minutes.'

The drawing-room had three windows, and there was one in the hall. The view from the hall must have been great when not blotted out by a grey–white mist. I could have wept. I smiled idiotically. 'As my father would say, "What do you think that is—Scotch mist?" And it is.'

'Surely not the first haar you've experienced?'

'No, but so far the thickest.' I turned from the window.

91

'Thanks for your phone.'

'Anyone else you'd care to ring?'

There was only Robbie, and he was working. 'No, thanks. I can't think of anyone I know well enough to bother——' I broke off, realizing belatedly how that must sound. 'I know what I'll do! I'll go to a movie. I love movies. So restful to the feet.' He was looking at his watch. 'The last house'll have started, but I'll catch most of it.'

'Would you go to the last performance in a London cinema on your own?'

'Well, no—but this isn't London.' I meant that as a compliment. That was not how he took it.

'Edinburgh is a Capital as well as, to you, a provincial city, Miss Hurst. All cities have certain undesirable elements in common.' He gave me a long, thoughtful look. 'I could use a drink. Would you care to join me?'

It was a civilized suggestion. My feet were killing me, and I had a niggling sensation there was some simple solution to this, only I was too weary to remember what it was. Relaxing over a drink might fix that. If not, as it was later than I had thought, I had just to spin out a little time to be able to use Sandra's possible return with her date as a decent excuse for getting away. 'Thanks. I'd love one.'

'I thought you might.'

I had a better look round the drawing-room while he got the drinks. The contents did not match his car, but his car matched his salary. At Martha's it would have been in the senior residents', not the consultants', car-park. But if the drawing-room rugs alone were the genuine Persian they looked to me they were worth more than Martha's S.M.O.'s annual salary. He must have inherited the lot along with the house and that terrible tweed suit.

Over our drinks I made small-talk and he listened. Our roles were the reverse of that night in his car. It was that, and my unbroken neck, that kept me from drying up, though the effort left me wearier than ever. And as I thrashed out the traffic problem, the tourist industry, and the coming Festival, I had constantly to remember I was too accustomed to silent Scotsmen to have the conceit to take his attitude as any kind of a personal reflection on

92

myself. Nor was he the first man I'd seen brooding darkly over a whisky at the end of a heavy week. On Friday nights at home my father frequently sighed over his first drink as if convinced the gods had it in for him.

When I finished my drink I was down to plugging Sandra. 'Very sociable girl, Sandra. She's out on a four-some tonight, and as it's Friday she'll probably bring them back for a snack. Most people get party-minded, Friday night, don't they?'

'Do they?'

'Oh, yes. You don't?'

He shook his head.

(Thank God!) 'It might be worth my nipping down now in case she's back. She may well be.' I glanced again at my watch, and suddenly that niggle emerged as a coherent thought. With difficulty I resisted the urge to give three loud cheers. 'If she's not I've just realized what I can do! I can go down to headquarters. There's always someone there on the switchboard, and I can wait in our rest-room until Sandra or the other two get back. I'll find that out by ringing first, and if they're much later I'll ring for a taxi to bring me up. The mist now doesn't matter as though it's quite late, it's still so light. Anyway, I could do that walk blindfold.' I stood up and made my bread-and-butter speech. 'I'm a nut to forget headquarters. So obvious!'

He had risen slowly. 'Even Homer sometimes nods.' There was a new edge to his voice. 'I'm sure you won't make this mistake again.'

I was puzzled. 'Did you remember headquarters?' He nodded. 'Why didn't you say so?'

He hesitated as if choosing his words. 'Being so obvious, I assumed it must've occurred to you.'

'Then why didn't I say so?'

'Presumably for reasons of your own.'

My brain had gone back into slow motion. I widened my eyes to wake myself up. 'What reasons?'

His tight smile was like a cold hand on my spine. 'Come now, Miss Hurst! Despite that charmingly ingenuous expression, since you're not the naïve teenager you most successfully appear out of uniform, I can't believe you seri-

93

ously wish, much less require, me to answer that.'

I woke up fast. My God, I thought, not again! Doesn't anyone read anything but old copies of *Time* magazine and the colour supplements? I was only faintly amused. The best joke goes off second time round.

'Are you thinking I kept it dark hoping to pressure you into dating me tonight?'

He ignored that and opened the door. 'I'll see you down.'

Later I realized my post-John detachment was then making its final and most effective appearance. It was that, plus my parents' upbringing, that prevented my going through that door like a jet. This wasn't the same again; this was much more complicated. For the man who had been so nice the night Mrs Thompson died to make it so clear I was *persona non grata*, I had to have upset him in depths.

My parents said, 'When you run into unexpected opposition, if possible and safe, try and gauge its strength before running away. If then, or from the start, it seems too tough to handle alone, run like hell.'

'Just a minute, Dr Linsey. If you thought I was trying to twist your arm, why offer me a drink?'

He turned to face me. If he wasn't looking at me with a new respect he was looking at me in a new way. 'Since you press me, had I any alternative?'

It was like thinking one was on rock and discovering it was quicksand. 'That's why you drove me back?'

'One could say that,' he drawled. 'One could add one dislikes disappointing children as much as one dislikes seeing them used.'

'Used?' The absurdity made me smile. 'You can't honestly imagine I briefed Meggy to rustle you up?'

He wasn't amused. 'Regrettably I'm not over-gifted with imagination. If I were we could both have been saved the embarrassment of this present situation.' He paused, but I said nothing. 'As must also be obvious.'

'No.'

'No?' The tight smile reappeared. 'Do I have to speak plainly?'

'Please.'

He lifted his chin as if I had slapped his face. 'As you

insist, very well. I'll tell you plainly, Miss Hurst, that while it's a pity I'm not more imaginative, when even the most unimaginative man is presented with an apparently unending series of unfortunate coincidences, there comes a moment when he finds himself forced to wonder how accurately the term "coincidence" can be applied anywhere in the series. And then to reflect on the fact that coincidence always has to stop somewhere. And after, where in the series did the stop come? Not that that last is now of more than academic importance.' He paused again, but I was too dumbfounded by his conceit for speech. 'Will you forgive my offering you a wee bit of advice? Though you're a very attractive as well as sadly over-accident-prone girl, don't—er—in your own words—try and twist my arm again. I don't like it and won't have it. Try it again, and I'll warn you now—next time, you pick yourself up, walk home, or both. Understand?'

All I properly understood was that I needed a good psychiatrist. I'd liked him. I'd thought we communicated rather well. His ex-girlfriend, John, Robbie, Bassy, Catriona, even Aunt Elspeth, flashed through my mind. 'Yes,' I said absently, 'I get the picture. Thanks for the drink and lift.'

He said, 'I really must congratulate you. Your self-control is as admirable as it is, in my unfortunate experience, unique.'

He had spoken very politely. It was still just about the nastiest crack I had ever received. I smiled very, very sweetly. 'Just my typical English phlegm in the face of defeat, Dr Linsey.'

He wasn't surprised. He knew it all. 'You've got that key with you, haven't you?'

I flapped my eyelashes. 'You've guessed that too? I should've known you would. But I thought it was so safe in my bra, along with the spare valve rubbers for Gemmie's bike—and, of course, the plans.'

He stiffened. 'What's that?'

I repeated myself. 'As you've guessed from seeing how I've brainwashed Meggy, I'm no harmless district student. Among other things I'm England's secret answer to the S.N.P.' I went on to include everything from the post-office this morning to Archie's prognosis and wee Jaimie. 'Meggy's kid brother, only two, but with a fascinating vocabulary. Get his "Up the English!" next time you're trapping dust. I'm afraid he comes out with a "—— off, ye bluidy Sassenach!" more often than not. But give me time. I'm working on the kid. When I'm done and he's your age, if some stray English girl tries to kid him she only used his phone for a call she invented to get rid of him while she tried to pick a door-lock, he'll swallow it! And if for some freaky reason he once did her a good turn and has a busted engagement he may even credit her with way-out feelings like gratitude and sympathy! Can you imagine anyone being so credulous—sorry—you can't, being short on imagination.' I stopped for breath and to look him up and down. 'Far be it from me to contradict my host under his own roof, but on present showing I wouldn't have said there was anything lacking in your imagination. I'd have said it's in great shape. You're must too modest, Doctor! Ever thought of being a writer? You should.'

He was leaning against the closed door looking as if I had spoken exclusively in four-letter words. He had to cough before he could speak. 'If there's any truth in all this non-sense——'

'Truth? From the girl you've diagnosed as a crafty little tart on the make? Perish the thought!'

He went white round the mouth. 'I refuse to allow you to put such terms into my mouth or to use them in connection with yourself in my presence!'

'You refuse? Should that have me on my knees?' I walked up to him, shaking my head. 'Would you mind opening that door, please? Your ego needs more room, and I need fresh air.'

He didn't move. 'Locking yourself out was a genuine error?'

'Do I have to take off my bra to prove my 36B cups hold nothing but me?'

He jerked away and opened the door. I swept into the hall, but could not undo the self-lock on the front door. He did it. 'We've to sort this out seriously. I'll drive you down to your headquarters.'

'Thanks, no! Being chucked out of a man's flat gives me all the masochistic kicks I need for one night.' I ducked under his arm and was halfway down the first flight before I finished speaking or saw Bassy peering through my letter-box. Melanie and two other boys were with him. They all swung round. I reached the landing with Charles just behind me.

Melanie caught Bassy's eye, flicked back her long hair, and without a word removed herself and the two boys.

Charles and I spoke together. He said, 'Good evening, Mr Hurst.' I said, 'Can I use your flat tonight, Bassy? I've locked myself out and the others have gone home. Or have you seen Pete?'

'Yes. I was going to ask you to put up Melly. You can both have our place. It'll take all night driving her home in this mist, and I've got to get back to my sit-in.' He spoke as if he and I were alone. 'Did you come out without your bloody key again? Alix, you're the most god-awful idiot bird I've ever run into! Come on. Let's go!'

'One moment, if you please, Miss Hurst.' Charles stepped between Bassy and myself wearing the bored expression of a sophisticated adult who suddenly strays into a teenage party. 'I still feel we should talk things out. If there has been a lamentable misunderstanding——'

'There has.' I cut him short, tersely. 'But I don't feel like any more talk. I'm tired. I've had enough.'

'I'm sorry, but naturally, after that, I can only offer my apologies for any distresss I may have caused you.'

'I shouldn't bother.' I met his eyes. 'It's not important.'

'I'm afraid I can't agree with you there, Miss Hurst.'

I shrugged and looked at Bassy.

Bassy was the taller man by about five inches but, as he slouched badly and was so thin, even with his full beard he gave the general impression of a gangling schoolboy who'd outgrown his strength. He actually possessed the muscular strength of a professional wrestler, and as he was a passionate advocate of non-violence, he kept in good condition. At his most heated he had never gone beyond threatening to thump an opponent with his 'Make love, not war' placard. So on his many demonstrations he was always posted close to the hooligan fringe. When he went into action his peace-keeping technique very much resembled Meggy's.

He seemed to uncoil inside his crumpled red tracksuit. 'Apparently my sister no longer wishes this conversation to continue—sir! I'd be obliged, sir'—his pompous manner matches Charles'—'if you'd take that as final, sir, because if you don't I'll probably bloody thump you down these stairs —sir!'

'Possibly, rather than probably, Mr Hurst. But I take your point. Goodnight to you both.' Charles calmly walked back up the stairs. As we heard his door close Bassy jerked an urgent thumb downwards. 'Cold as charity at the sit-in,' he remarked, as we went down. 'The bastards have turned off the heating.'

Sandra, her boyfriend, and another couple were on the third landing. Sandra was pink. 'What's going on above, Alix?'

Bassy answered. 'A right rave! Too bad you missed it, Sandra. Sorry we can't wait, but my bird's just taken off with two other guys.' He hurried me on to the front hall and removed his track jacket. He was wearing four sweaters. 'You can have this.'

'Thanks. My mac's in his flat.'

'He knows what he can do with it! Let's get out of the joint. Don't like the smell.'

The mist clung round the street-lamps in orange circles, and the slow traffic made the sound of tearing silk. The high buildings were ominous, jostling ghosts; the pavements could have been oiled. We would have walked as slowly on a clear, dry evening.

I peered round. 'Where's Melly?'

'Making for my place with Bert and Hamish, if she's not there already.'

'How do you know? You didn't tell her.'

'Plan B. You were A. She's got Pete's key. With her IQ one doesn't have to spell it out.' He moved nearer. 'And meanwhile, back at the ranch? ...'

He listened in silence, and remained silent when I finished. 'I know,' I said, 'I need my head examined. Come to that, so does he. I'm not sure yet which he is—psycho or schizoid.'

'Bit more complicated than that. And though you're a bloody moron with men,' said Bassy very slowly, 'and haven't Melly's IQ, it's not all your fault you didn't get the whole picture that night I was skint. I thought I'd given you enough to catch on. That's the snag of having a brain for a bird. One forgets other birds don't have 'em. I couldn't say the lot then as Pete asked me not to. He has this anti-father fixation. Root cause of his inhibitions and his acne.'

I stopped walking. 'What's Pete's Oedipus got to do with Charlie?'

'Dad's a top accountant specializing in company taxa- tion. So he has a mathematical genius for a son and top clients.'

'Charlie's one?' I demanded incredulously. 'On an aca- demic salary? Tell that to the parents!'

'Not on his salary, if he draws it, which he probably doesn't as the lot'd go in tax.'

I propped myself against a dripping wall. 'Why?'

'Pete says he's not in the big league yet, though his mum is. Family property, mostly in London—and quite a bit of London. London property's worth having and the value keeps rising. Pete reckons Charlie's present share as chicken- feed, but as he's the only son—Mum's second husband is in her own league and able to take care of the two girls— Charlie has a rosy future. And safe. Pete says there's the hell of a tight entail on most of Mum's nest-egg.'

'What does Pete reckon chicken-feed?'   \

'Over a half and under a million.'

I took a long, long breath. 'No wonder he runs an inex- pensive car. This explains his flat.' I explained that. 'But not why no one else has told me—Robbie, Catriona. Such chicken-feed is news.'

'But old news. Maybe it hit the headlines when Mum married Charlie's old man. According to Pete's dad, he was an up-and-coming but ordinary medic., son of the manse, loaded with principles and education, with no more than he earned. Seems he insisted they either lived on that, or he wouldn't marry the girl. He sounds a decent guy with a right touch of the old John Knoxes. The marriage didn't last long as he was killed at Dunkirk, but Pete's dad says it seemed surprisingly happy. Pete's dad then reckons Mum came to her senses by remarrying into her own league. Pete says the one thing that really hurts his dad is idle money. Pete's bloody peeved he's not on speaking terms with Dad right now, as he's sure Dad's blowing a gasket over Charlie's being ditched by his loaded bird. Pete thinks it might cure his acne to see his old man sweat.'

'Pete has problems.' I muttered vaguely. 'And Catriona. She doesn't fancy girlish gossip. Think that's why she didn't tell me?'

'Either that or she thinks money too sordid a subject for a nice girl to mention. She went to a good girls' boarding-school. And it shows!' He added feelingly. 'Christ, but it shows! Poor kid!'

'Robbie didn't go to a boarding-school.'

'No, but he wasn't around the Edinburgh social scene thirty-odd years back, doesn't mix in it now, and very likely hasn't heard it around his hospital. Pete said he'd been keeping a big ear out among our medics. and since he told me, so've I. They don't seem to know Charlie as anything but an ordinary, quiet sort of guy—if they know him at all, and not many do.'

I was feeling rather ill. 'What's Charlie's Mum's name?'

'Don't know. All Pete said was that he'd never met her. He'd only met Charlie once, and that was two years ago when his dad was standing him lunch in London for getting three Grade A's for his "A"s. Charlie stopped at their table or something—only for a few minutes—but Pete's computer mind never forgets faces, and as the city pages are his favourite light reading he filled in most of the financial side for himself. He recognized Charlie when he brought back your purse, but only tipped me off after seeing you in his car. Pete may hate his old man's guts, but he wouldn't want to do him dirt. So he asked me to keep this to myself. Also, like he said, why force Charlie to buy up barbed-wire by the ton to keep out the rush of eager birdies switching subjects? Charlie hadn't done him any harm. And Charlie then seemed hooked. Now he's off the line, spread the word, and if you don't think every other student-birdie is suddenly going to develop a passionate interest in pathological research, then you really are out of your tiny mind, Alix! One doesn't have to love the bastard to see he's a sitting duck.'

'No. Charlie has problems.' I was quiet for a few seconds, thinking of all my meetings with Charles, and particularly of those since the day that wedding announcement appeared. 'Makes me want to throw up, but I can see I could've seemed eager to get in on the act now he's free. What I don't see is why he earlier stuck his neck out. Why bring back my purse?'

Bassy said that had foxed him until Pete provided the answer. 'Had Charlie left it on the floor and it had been stolen, and you'd later asked the cops if it had been handed in, they'd ask you for details. That'd involve Charlie. But if he'd taken it to the cops, what if you later claimed some cash was missing? And that's been done before, and though you couldn't make it stick—your word again his—who'd be most hurt by any kind of scandal? Who'd everyone most love to hate? Hard-working, under-paid nursie, or poor old MacRockefeller?'

'No, he wouldn't like mud in those turn-ups. Yet, didn't he risk worse taking me up that hill at night?'

'Pete thinks so, but you're the only nurse Pete knows. Didn't you say you were all apart, and being a medic. Charlie read you right? Haven't you said at such times nurses and medics. get an instant togetherness?'

'Well, yes.' I thought back. 'He was still engaged and I was in uniform. Both'll have worked on us.'

'Chastity belts for two?'

'Roughly.' The mist was very wet, very cold, and I shivered. 'Must've been that, though after tonight I don't really figure it. Yeugh! How could I've thought that pompous, priggish, conceited sod *sweet*! And how do you suppose he thought I knew his bank balance? Pete?'

'Pete doesn't think he spotted him that first evening. Pete hadn't the chin fringe, sideboards, or acne when they met in London. Word just gets round—like now.'

I said, between my teeth, 'Doesn't matter how. Just what he thought! What I could do to the sod!'

'Take five,' said Bassy kindly. 'You did it when you sent him up. No guy enjoys being laughed at by a bird.'

I thought of Charles' expression as he leant against his drawing-room door. I began to feel better. 'No, he didn't like that at all, I'm delighted to say.'

CHAPTER NINE

Melanie sat cross-legged on the floor sipping milkless tea and blinking myopically without her glasses when Robbie rang me back next morning. 'So that's where you are, Alix! I've rung your flat three times.'

'Sorry, what's the crisis?'

'My miserable opposite number's slipped a disc. Today's out, but I can make tomorrow. Any good?'

'Not a chance. Working day. Sorry again.'

He said bitterly, 'Other folk have free weekends and private lives. Do you ever get the impression we're in the wrong business? Hang on.' He was talking his end. 'Alix? I've to go. I hate to do this to you, but what else can I do? I'll be in touch. Right?'

'Fine. Thanks for ringing.'

Melanie went on sipping and blinking as I bemoaned the lot of overworked, underpaid hospital residents. She had tied her hair back in a pony-tail, and without the white lipstick and heavy eye-do she was a very pretty girl.

She said, 'Society always has taken advantage of workers in vocational occupations. It's unfair, but life's unfair. Robbie's only answer, and yours, is to change jobs. Would you do that?'

'No. Nor would he.'

'Then society knows it's got you where it wants you. How about when you marry?'

'God knows. I know I'll hate chucking nursing. Face it when I come to it, I guess. How about you?'

She had a husky voice and a particularly attractive Scottish accent. 'The more I think on marriage, the more convinced I am it's the biggest con-trick ever worked on women. Every unintelligent girl I know can't wait to race up the altar. Every unintelligent boy says marriage is not catching him. But I've observed it's the really bright lads who can't get themselves wives fast enough—and the last thing the bright girls of my acquaintance want to be is the wee wife.' She reached for her glasses and perched them on her nose. 'It's a problem one's hormones'll undoubtedly solve in the wrong way. Did that Pete not even leave an ounce of marge?'

'Nothing but that packet of tea.'

She got off the floor. 'I'll away to the shops. I can't support human rights on an empty stomach.'

While we cooked and ate brunch she delivered a long lecture on those rights that would have impressed me had I been listening properly. What did impress me was the way she never once, directly or indirectly, referred to last night.

'I should do my duty by mankind now, Alix. What'll you do?'

I looked around. 'Spring-clean this slum. I think I should.'

'Why should the fact that you're female make you feel not merely responsible but guilty about the mess left by your brother and his male flatmates? Don't you realize those responses are but conditioned reflexes imposed upon women as second-class citizens by a male-dominated society? St Paul,' said Melanie darkly, 'has a lot to answer for! And the Normans in England. Anglo-Saxon women had considerable rights until William of Normandy swept them away!'

I said, 'I'm sure you're right, Melly, but what you don't realize is that I always clean anything handy when in a filthy temper. The dirtier the better the safety-valve.'

'Oh? Now that's logical.' She smiled. 'Me, I cook.'

I rang to check before going back that evening. Catriona had answered and was still clucking anxiously when she let me in. 'Even your date off! How wretched for you! I know how you feel about Robbie!'

'How the hell can you, as I don't know myself!' My raincoat was hanging in the hall. I held it at arm's length. 'How did this get here?'

'I brought it in. It was in a paper bag on our doorstep. I thought you'd forgotten it. Hadn't you?'

I did not intend coming out with it, but that damned

raincoat had shaken me. Also I had done a great deal of thinking as I spring-cleaned. 'Catriona, you did say Aunt Elspeth knew Charlie slightly?'

Her face closed. 'Yes. Why?'

'Too slightly for him to know you're living here?'

'She may've mentioned it to him. I don't know.'

I said, 'Figures. Auntie know his mother and family background?'

'Er—yes. Why?'

'I wish you'd told me. I know you don't fancy gossip, but wish you had.' I told her all but Pete's side of the story. 'Bassy heard somewhere and put me in the picture later last night. Turn clam on this one, please, as I don't fancy having spread abroad the jolly news that our landlord thinks me the cutest little gold-digging chick in the call business.'

'He can't think you that?'

'You weren't there. I was.'

She was having another attempt at disjointing her fingers. 'I feel so responsible. I've known for—for quite a long time, but I thought you'd have heard before last night.'

'How? This isn't my scene, and though Bassy's been here nearly two years, he only heard recently and by chance.'

'I wasn't thinking of Bassy——' She broke off, looking very troubled. 'But you know how people will talk! People always talk, and as I detest being talked about I try not to talk of others in that way. And if you'd not heard I never thought you'd be interested, but some girls might and—well —living in the same building, it might be difficult.'

'Difficult for whom? Charlie?'

She coloured defensively. 'Whatever the man is or is not, he is one of my fellow-countrymen!'

I smiled wearily. 'Scots, wha hae! You and Charlie should get together, but at least your intentions were good.' I tilted my head. 'Sounds like our Gem on the stairs.'

Gemmie exploded in a minute later, flapping a new engagement ring in our faces. 'You've both got yourselves a date as bridesmaids, first Saturday of our holiday between this lot and our year on district. I'm asking Miss Bruce for a Glasgow vacancy, and my Wilf's asking his boss to shift him to their Glasgow branch. How's that for planning, eh?

Only seven more weeks, so we're going to be right busy. Alix, you're lovely with your needle—you'll help me with my wedding-dress, going-away coat and dress, and your two dresses?'

'Sure! Any time! How about Wilf's suit?'

She laughed. 'You reckon we might, eh? Why not?' She rounded on Catriona. 'Stop standing around like a nervous rice-pudding, love! You're my size, so you'll be model—and hey, Alix! What's all this, then, about your moving up with Charlie last night?'

Catriona said quickly, 'The poor girl locked herself out and he offered her the use of his phone and a drink. Nice of him, wasn't it?'

'Then why's Sandry saying he'd words with Bassy? She says, sounded like a bloody riot!'

'Haven't you heard Bassy's organized a sit-in? Charlie does work for the opposition, and when students get protesting someone's blood usually flows, doesn't it, Alix?'

'I couldn't have put it better myself.'

Gemmie's wedding was the big topic among the district students for several days for more than one reason. Our was not the only set, and the nearness of her wedding day underlined how even nearer were our final exams. Over that weekend the demolition work was finished, and Charles's car disappeared from its usual parking-place behind our house. The electricians working overtime on his private lift had gone by Tuesday evening.

The sit-in was called off. Bassy rang me to say Tam was back in business. Everyone on both sides was slapping everyone else on the back and packing up for the vac. Bassy was staying on alone in his flat to do some work. 'See Charlie?'

'Not a sign.'

'Jolly good. See you when I've surfaced from under the books.'

Mrs Duncan was on holiday that week. There was general post on district, and I was working half in her area, half in my old one. Mr Richards and Archie remained on my list.

Archie was at a standstill. Whenever I saw Dr MacDonald he said, 'If he's not worse he's to be better. You've seen how his blood-count's holding?'

'Yes, Doctor. I've never seen one like it.'

'You're not in a minority of one, Nurse, or even two. Archie's become such a medical curiosity they'd like to have him back in hospital for better observation. How do you think he'd take returning?'

'I think—though, of course, I could be wrong—I think it'd kill him.'

'In my humble but fixed opinion, Nurse—inside of forty-eight hours. Good day to you!'

I was using a bike that day and nearing the Richards' house when the fine drizzle became a downpour. When I propped the bike against the kerb and unstrapped my nursing-bag, the water from my hat-brim cascaded over my hands.

'Nurse, you're that wet!' Mrs Richards looked ready to dry me with her floral apron. 'And you not accustomed to our weather. Away with you into my kitchen to dry, or you'll be as poorly as my man!'

'It does rain quite often in England, Mrs Richards.' I removed coat, hats, and boots, and changed into the spare shoes I carried in a plastic bag. 'How is he this morning?'

'He'd a better night and his cough's easier, but he's awful low in his spirits.' She watched me dry my face with a tissue. 'He'll be better for seeing you. He's taken a liking to you, Nurse. Did you not know that?'

I was disproportionately touched, as my morale had taken more of a beating than I realized at the time, on Friday. 'Your husband is such a good patient, he's a pleasure to nurse, but I thought he might just be as patient with nurses as he is with illness.'

Her eyes creased affectionately. 'My Tom's no man to complain, but if he doesn't like a body, that body knows it well! Not that I'm complaining. He's been a good man to me. Always the money regular, never once has he raised his hand to the bairns—or myself, and though he's aye had an eye for a bonnie lassie, no trouble that way, you'll understand. And what man that's a man doesn't appreciate a bonnie lassie, eh?' She took me into the bedroom. 'Here's your English nurse to help you forget the rain, Tom.'

'It's not the rain that's on my mind, woman! It's my work!' Mr Richards glowered at me. 'Did you get a bit damp in that wee drop just now?'

'Just a bit, Mr Richards.'

He did not talk again until I was closing my nursing-bag. 'Had you a word with the doctor, Nurse?'

'Yes. He said he'd spoken to you last night.'

'Aye.' He gazed at the rain pelting down the window-pane. 'You'll be aware I've to work up top when I return?'

I sat on the end of his bed, as there was no other seat and a standing listener carries such an aura of impatience 'You're going to miss working underground?'

'A man gets used to working with his mates. It's a hard life below, but it's been my life and I've no wish to change I've a good record, Nurse. All these years and not the one bad accident. I know my trade.' He held out his hands 'These are the marks of my trade, and I'm proud of them! Then he realized what he had said and flushed like a guilty schoolboy. 'You'll think me blethering like a woman!'

'No, Mr Richards, I don't. I think you've every reason to be proud of those scars. I think you miners are among the really brave in this world. Most people can be brave under sudden pressure, but to keep it up every time you go or shift throughout your working-life takes the most tremendous guts.'

He scowled hideously. 'It's but a job!'

'Sure, but a very brave man's job. No use your denying that, Mr Richards, as your hands give it away. But if you d work up top, won't you be able to do a lot of good, what ever you're actually doing? As with your record and experience, the old hands'll listen to you, and you'll have s much to teach the new lads.'

'Maybe. If the laddies'll heed me.' He smiled very faintly 'I'd not in my day. Mind, the wife'll not be sorry, nor m daughter, Mary. She's living next door and has her ma working at the face. Aye, mining's hard on the women.' H sighed. 'The doctor says I've no choice, so small use greetin'

In the kitchen Mrs Richards was trying to take a splinter out of her finger. I did it for her with the very fine forceps that were my own property and lived permanently in my dress pocket along with matches for immediate sterilization if there was no other means available. 'Had he a wee chat with you, Nurse? That's good. Watch yourself on that bike! There's another drop of rain falling.'

The downpour lasted all day, drenching the rows of old grey and new orange-pink houses and flats; swirling off roof gutters, turning the endless flights of steps and steep closes and wynds into fast-running mountain streams. That evening I told Catriona I understood why the first city fathers had built Edinburgh high on the side of hills. 'Any lower and it'd be washed away.'

'Has today changed your mind about Edinburgh's charms?'

'Who minds a wee drop of rain? Even though somehow much wetter than any other rain?'

A girl in another set now had Sandra's former area and, as occasionally happened, a suddenly overloaded list. I was given three of her patients.

One was a Mrs Graham, a widow with a varicose ulcer on her right leg. She lived alone in her own detached bungalow. On my first visit I complimented her on the magnificent roses in her front garden.

'That's my son, Nurse. He tends my garden and my daughter, my home. My children know their duty. I saw to that when they were young.' She was white-haired, with good eyes, a neat nose, and small, tight mouth. 'Both bring their families to visit me once a week. As I've told them many a time, now their father's passed away, I'd be lost without them.' She showed me photos of her four grandchildren. 'Not married yet, I see, Nurse. Still, you're young, but youth doesn't last. Don't wait too long. All this talk of careers is all very well, but careers are for the men. A woman's place is in the home.'

I reminded myself I was her guest and didn't ask how she would get her leg dressed if all women felt as she did. I talked of Gemmie's wedding. Mrs Graham was nearly as interested as my favourite arthic, old Mrs Hunter.

Trousseau-making was occupying most of our evenings. Mrs Hunter took a vast and personal pleasure in every stitch, and now barely mentioned her neighbours' affairs during her blanket-baths. 'That'll be the third dress cut since last week—aye, the water's fine—but what of the going-away coat? The lassie'll need that.'

'We did the coat last weekend. I had the whole weekend off. The lining isn't quite finished, but that's all. Other hand, please, my dear.'

'It was you that cut it out?'

'Yes. We've a system. I cut after the bride has pinned, and then the third nurse collects up and sorts the pieces—careful!' I moved the basin out of range just in time. 'Tonight we have nervous breakdowns. Tonight's the wedding-dress.'

'Is that a fact?' Her old eyes lit up. 'What style has the lassie chosen? What material? And what'll she wear on her head?'

We were still thrashing out wedding-veils when her bed was done, her hair re-plaited, her many newpaper cuttings of unknown brides replaced in her plastic shopping-bag, and her crochet-needle working at the double. 'Could you maybe send me a wee snap later, Nurse?'

'With pleasure. I'll write and tell you every detail. Comfortable?'

'I'd like that, fine. And I'm fine, just now.' She stopped crocheting. 'Nurse, I've a wish to speak my mind. You'll no take offence?'

'Of course not.' I smiled, but braced myself inwardly. 'What is it, Mrs Hunter?'

'Lassie, you've a talent for this nursing work. Have you no thought to go into a hospital to learn to be a real nurse?'

I blushed. 'Thank you very much, Mrs Hunter. That's quite a thought, and one of the nicest things anyone's ever said to me.'

She moved her crippled arm awkwardly and patted my hand. 'You're welcome, lassie. You'll be telling about the wedding-dress the next time, eh? I'll be waiting on that.

Nylon lace? Aye, that'll be bonnie! Could you maybe bring me a wee bittie? You will?' She could have been fifty years younger from her enchanted smile. 'That'll be grand!'

Mrs Duncan was back from holiday. I met her coming away from headquarters when I returned early that afternoon for a lecture. 'All under control, Miss Hurst?'

'I think so, thanks.'

'As it should be.' She studied me keenly. 'You're looking a trifle peaky, but this third month can be tiring with the theoretical pressure building up and the practical side increasing as you're more experienced. And all this dressmaking can't be leaving you much rest off duty. Not that I disapprove of the young being kept hard at it! We all know what they say about Satan making work for idle hands,' she added with a smile, but uncharacteristically, as she was not given to clichés. 'Yet in my experience Satan is more concerned to set idle tongues wagging at both ends. Personally, few things annoy me more than tittle-tattle, though naturally I pay no attention to it, and nor does any sensible body. But this blethering'll make you late for your lecture! Cheerio!'

She was a kind, wise, and experienced woman. She hadn't said all that for nothing. I went in with the feeling of something like ice in my stomach.

A children's officer was lecturing another set as well as ours on the Children's Act, the schools' health service, and her work in general. She was very good. I forgot Mrs Duncan until I noticed the odd glances I was collecting from some of the girls. Catriona was concentrating on her notes, but I caught Gemmie's eye and raised an eyebrow. Instead of her usual wink, she replied with a positively reassuring smile.

I used the wedding-dress as an excuse for my silence when the three of us walked home. During the cutting-out Gemmie was reduced to breathless grunts and Catriona mangled her hands about a yard from the sitting-room table until the dress was cut, pinned, and tacked. She then carried it away like the holy grail to her bedroom to try on over a long white evening slip. Gemmie collapsed on the sofa. 'I've sweated off six pounds! Thanks, love. Do the same for you some time. Hey—I tell you Miss Bruce says she'll recommend me for Glasgow if I pass? And have you heard there's a district vacancy coming up in Caithness? Suit you?'

'If I hadn't a yen for the one going in Inverness.' I sorted aside enough scraps of material for the buttons we were getting professionally covered. 'Can I have this spare bit for one of my old girls?'

'Help yourself.' She got off the sofa and began folding away the pieces of pattern Catriona had been too fraught to touch. 'You don't fancy Caithness? What's up between you and Robbie, then?'

I looked at her. 'Nothing. Why?'

She was avoiding my eye. 'Just that he's not been round lately.'

'Lots of women having lots of babies.'

'Oh, aye. Reckon you're right.'

'Do you?' She looked at me then. She looked upset. 'Gem, what's going on?' She didn't answer, so I told her what Mrs Duncan had said. 'You been hearing idle tongues?'

She hesitated, and normally she weighed in like a force-ten gale. 'You know me, Alix. My Mam says I was born leaning on fence chatting up the neighbours. Get to hear all the muck that way, but that doesn't mean you've to pass it on.'

'Give, Gem,' I said tensely, 'give!'

'I don't fancy this.' She looked round and lowered her voice, though the door was shut and we were alone. 'Reckon I'll have to tell you, as Catriona'll not do the job, and, anyroad, she's likely not heard. She never chats. But the girls are saying—and not just our lot—that you fancy our Charlie.'

'Do I?' There was clearly more. 'And?'

'They're saying you used to chase him round on district and chat him up, and that's why you've chucked Robbie.' She jerked a thumb up. 'They're saying that's why you got yourself up there, but Charlie doesn't fancy you and slung you out on your ear, and that's why Bassy blew his top. I've tried to stop 'em—I've blown my top more times than I've had Sunday dinners—but I've got to say as it's still all round the shop. They just shut up when I come along. And you know the set that's coming after us isn't coming here?

We've all known that from start, as the new place'll be ready for them, time they arrive. But now they're making out Charlie's refused to have any more nurses as tenants—that's what comes when muck starts piling up. Just gets muckier. I'm sorry, love.' She was very red and very miserable. 'I've told 'em it's a right load of bloody codswallop and just hoped you'd not hear.'

I was too angry for speech. I sat down.

'Girls! How's this?'

Catriona looked breathtakingly lovely, and the perfect fit of her slip made the barely hanging-together dress seem almost finished. Momentarily even I forgot what had gone before. 'Don't you dare marry in anything but white lace, Catriona! Ideal with your hair!'

Gemmie walked round Catriona congratulating me. 'You're in the wrong trade, Alix! Your cutting's got real class! Get the fall of that skirt! Hey—you reckon a flower up here?'

'Hold still, Catriona.' I gathered lace scraps into a flower and pinned it on top of her head. 'A short veil from something like this, Gem?'

'I want to see! Let's go back to the hall mirror,' insisted Catriona.

The front-door bell rang about five minutes later. Gemmie was nearest and opened the door without looking round. As I was standing at an angle to face both door and mirror, I caught Robbie's immediate and unguarded expression as he saw Catriona, and hers in the mirror.

Robbie recovered first. 'Getting married, Catriona?'

Gemmie spun round. 'Great daft ha'porth! As if we'd let any lad see her in that dress if she were! Give us the lad's-eye view, Robbie! Reckon my Wilf'll fancy it?'

'It's beautiful, Gemmie. Beautiful.' Robbie sat on the one hall chair as if it were a choice between that and the floor. 'Been a tough day,' he remarked to no one in particular.

Catriona said, 'Every pin is now sticking straight into me. I'll get this off.'

'I'll give you a hand. You watch my lovely, lovely dress . . .' Gemmie disappeared with her.

I watched Robbie still breathing as if he had run up the stairs. 'Want some coffee, Robbie?'

'I've just eaten, thanks, and can see you girls are busy. I only dropped over for a few minutes to remind you what I look like. How's life?'

'Full of little surprises. Really not stopping? Then come out here.' On the landing I fixed the door-lock, closed the door, checked over the landing, above and below. He had followed me reluctantly. 'Is this something new, or a hangover from Glasgow?'

'It isn't what you think, Alix.'

'I don't know what I think. I do know seeing her in that dress threw you like a kick from a horse.'

'Maybe.' He took a long time to ask simply, 'Do you mind?'

'If this has just happened—and these things do just happen—no, I don't think I mind.' I looked up at him. 'But I like Catriona, even if her right touch of the Emily Posts sometimes has me wanting to scream. So if you've been using me to get at her I mind like hell!'

He turned very angry. 'Not that at all!'

'Then what is it?'

'The only girl I've been trying to get at in this flat is you! Is it my fault you're sharing with her? Or that the after-effects of some hangovers take longer than others to get out of the system? And if you're about to object to that, just let me remind you of yourself! Do you think I enjoy waiting in the queue for you to get over this John?'

That jolted me into the realization that I had wholly forgotten John. I did not tell him so. 'You had an affair with her?'

'We did not!' He was ready to throttle me. 'I asked her to have me. She turned me down—flat! That was bad enough, but the way she did it was worse! It takes top-class breeding and impeccable manners to be capable of the ultimate in rudeness,' he said savagely, 'and Catriona Ferguson has both qualities!'

I glanced up the stairs behind him. 'That's true.'

'Here's some more truth! No gurrrl gets the opportunity to slap me down in that way twice! I'd not have her now if she handed herself to me gift-wrapped—and I'd take great pleasure in telling her so! If that does me no credit in your

114

eyes, that's just too bad, as that's the man I am! I have my pride.'

'So does she. She's never breathed a word about this. It was her face that gave me the picture just now.'

'Then see it clear. That was shame on her face. Not that she's cause to be ashamed of our relationship—or what her maiden aunt, if she had one, would consider cause!'

'I see.'

He said, 'I hope you do. This is the first and last time I'll be exhibiting my scars for your benefit. Two-year-old scars. When can I see you again?' He glanced up the stairs. 'Or have I lost my place in the queue?'

'Oh, God!' I rubbed my eyes, but that didn't make it look better. 'You've heard too?'

'You know what hospital grapevines are like. As I do too, anything I catch goes through one ear and out the other.' He flushed almost guiltily. 'You know my views on Charlie Linsey.'

'Do I? Or do I,' I asked deliberately, 'only know some?'

'You've had all I care to give you. If you've since filled in some gaps for yourself, that's your business and his business, not mine! When I can see you again is mine. When?'

'Sure you still want to?'

'Don't be such a bloody wee daftie! What am I doing here, now?' He reached for me with both hands and kissed me firmly. 'Nothing like a shot of adrenalin to cure a hangover.'

Catriona was alone in the sitting-room when I got in. I straightened my hair, and asked if she had heard of the vacancy going in Caithness. 'Take your fancy? It's not for me. I want Inverness unless I can fix one in the Outer Hebrides. You haven't heard if one's going there?'

She dropped her lecture notes. 'Why the Outer Hebrides?'

I picked up her pad. 'Just a sudden urge to do my own thing far, far away.'

She accepted the pad absently. 'I know just how you feel, Alix.'

As I was out for a man's blood, that time she very probably did.

CHAPTER TEN

Mrs Graham had attended the same varicose-vein clinic for three years and had the same G.P. for the last twenty-eight. She rated her doctor just one step below the Almighty, and her son-in-law, a physicist, two steps down. 'His mother was English and second cousin to an Earl. Such a nice family—very nice people. One can't deny that makes a difference, Nurse. Of course, he attended a nice public school.'

I unwound her bandage. 'Really?'

'Indeed, yes. And then down to Cambridge to take his degree.'

I sat on my heels to rewind. 'Which college?'

She tightened her invisible lips as if she considered that an impertinence, then recalled I was English. 'You've nursed in Cambridge?'

'No. That's where my parents met when my mother was in her third year and my father doing post-graduate research.'

'Indeed?' From her expression I'd shot into the ranks of nice people. 'Your parents don't object to your doing this work?'

My parents wouldn't have taken serious objection had I chosen to be a stripper, providing I enjoyed the work and kept union rules. 'They're all for it. They know I love nursing.'

'How much nursing experience have you actually had, my dear?'

I wondered if I had imagined that note of appeal in her prim, plushy voice. Then I saw the anxiety at the back of her rather vacant pale-blue eyes. I gave her my professional history in detail.

'Then you'll know a little about'—she looked away—

'women's troubles.'

'A little.' I watched her closely. 'Are you having a little trouble, Mrs Graham?'

She smoothed her skirt. 'I don't really care to talk about it, Nurse. It's—not nice.'

I guessed, and correctly. 'Have you told your doctor? Mrs Graham, you should.'

'I couldn't think of that! He's a man!'

I had heard that too often to underestimate the problem it seemed to her. 'Have you never thought of having a private talk with the clinic sister?'

'Nurse, it's a varicose-vein clinic—so busy—and it's not a subject I could bring myself to discuss with just anyone. The clinic sister is kind, but—from Yorkshire. Very brusque.'

'Some Yorkshirewomen can give that impression, though I've always found them wonderfully kind underneath. Have you ever had a cervical test?'

She blushed. 'Oh no, Nurse! It was mentioned, but I couldn't, at my age. I'm sixty-three.'

It took fifteen minutes to persuade her Martha's gynaecological department considered the test should be taken every two years by women over forty, married or single, and ideally over thirty-five. 'It only takes a few minutes. It does not hurt at all, and it can save lives. Can I get one fixed up for you? If not with your own doctor, I'm certain he'll be happy to have some lady doctor attend to you. I've never heard of a man doctor who didn't understand exactly how ladies like yourself feel about such matters. But you must have one, Mrs Graham. As you're over the change, this trouble must be looked into and cleared up.' A car had stopped outside. I stood up. 'Here's your daughter with the shopping. May I discuss this with her?'

'Would you? I couldn't—not with my children. It's not nice,' she repeated pathetically.

Mrs Allan, the daughter, was a younger, slimmer edition of her mother. Her mouth had not yet tightened to a trap, but, as she had the same mannerism of pressing her lips together, it would. We went into the kitchen, and I closed the door before we talked.

'Nurse, is it really necessary to submit a woman of my mother's age and fastidious temperament to such an experience?'

'Your mother bore two children, Mrs Allan. This is not so far removed from a normal antenatal examination.' She was only a couple of years older than myself, so I told her the truth without the tactful cotton wool. 'I'm not a doctor. I can't say how serious this discharge may prove. I can say it can't be left unchecked, as if it is serious, unchecked it could prove fatal. A hysterectomy, if necessary and done in time, can not only give your mother years more life, but a much more active life. I've lost count of the patients who've said to me afterwards, "Why didn't I have this done years ago? I'm a new woman!" '

'Would you give your own mother this advice?'

'I have.'

She nodded to herself. 'Oh dear. Always something, isn't there? Yes. We must do what's right.'

Miss Bruce sighed over my report. 'We're constantly coming up against this kind of reticence, and, though understandable, it can have tragic consequences. We've a dear old body on our books at this moment who's placed herself beyond hope because she was too shy to tell her doctor she'd a "wee pimple" on her left breast. She's another chronic varicose ulcer, and we've been attending her on and off for years, but only last month was she able to show her nurse that "pimple". She'd hoped if she just ignored it it would go away, but it wouldn't clear up.' She looked at me across the desk. 'By then it was an open carcinoma. Inoperable, with secondaries starting up everywhere. But taken in time she could almost certainly have been saved.' The expression in her eyes was the same as Dr MacDonald's with Mrs Thompson. 'I'm thankful Mrs Graham felt she could confide in you. No matter how excellent their medical attendant, so many women, and particularly older women, will only discuss their gynaecological problems with another woman and in the privacy of their own homes. We go into their homes. That gives us a great advantage and a great responsibility. A sympathetic ear is one of the most important qualities required in district work. Thank you, Miss Hurst.'

Mrs Graham's test was positive, plus. Within days her uterus and the entire growth were removed without complications.

I met Mrs Allan by chance one windy early evening in Princes Street. 'You'll be pleased to hear Mother is coming home at the end of this week. The surgeon is most satisfied, but told my brother; any real delay and he might have had a very different result. We are all most grateful to you, Nurse Hurst.'

I felt very pleased, rather guilty, and deeply thankful her husband and my parents had been at Cambridge.

It was Gemmie's day off, and she was trousseau-shopping. Catriona and I had arranged to meet her after work directly opposite the Scott Monument. I got there first, and being a few minutes early was crossing the road intending to look over the monument when a sudden squall drenched me as effectively as a bucket of water. I dashed back for the shelter of a shop doorway and was brushing rivulets off my coat when Catriona appeared with Sandra.

Catriona occasionally had maternally organizing moods. 'Alix, if you wait around so damp in this wind you'll end up with acute rheumatism. You need to go straight home and get in a hot bath. Don't argue! I'll explain to Gemmie, and she and I can perfectly well cope with her shopping between us! Do as Nursie says! Here comes the right bus, now!'

'I'll give you a hand with the parcels,' said Sandra. 'I've only got to book my reserved seat at Waverley, and there's no rush as my boyfriend isn't coming for me till seven. Got your key, Alix? Better make sure!' She smiled meaningly. 'Charlie mayn't be all that eager to rescue you this time!'

Catriona looked startled and then down her nose. Having discovered silence was the best answer to this from Sandra, and others, I just waved and got on the bus. It took me two-thirds of the way, but I did not bother to take another up the hill, as the squall-clouds had blown on, the wind was drying, and fighting the elements would use up some of the fury unleashed by that crack.

The wind there was very much stronger. My hat was anchored with two cap-pins, but I had to hang on to it and keep my head down. The passers-by were either, like me, doubled-up against the wind, or leaning back like skaters off balance, to prevent themselves from being hurled off, instead of merely down, the hill. All over the pavements and cobbles were bits of broken slates, and the window of a small dress-shop had been blown in. A woman was sweeping up heaps of glass. She leant on her broom to yell, 'Bit gusty!'

'A bit. Anyone hurt?'

'Just the boss's pocket!'

It took a lot of strength to open the front door of our house. It slammed itself shut so violently that I expected Mrs Kinloch to appear, then remembered the Kinlochs were away, visiting one of their married daughters. Mrs Kinloch had continued to be as pleasantly unobtrusive a neighbour as she had seemed from the start. Mr Kinloch and Mr and Mrs Dobie on the second floor were still only names to me.

Our flat front door slammed behind me. Gemmie had left her bedroom window open, and the gale was sweeping through the flat. The dressing-table was in front of the window, and the curtains had flung all her possessions round the room. None had broken, so I heaved the dressing-table aside to shut the window first. The bottom sash was right up and had jammed. I hauled on it carefully, and did not dare give the frame a thump in case there was a weakness in the glass, as the wind was blowing straight at my face. It began to shift an inch at a time.

The window overlooked the side-street where the car-owners kept their cars. I backed as Charles's car crawled round the corner and up to the kerb. But I was still facing the opposite roof. I saw the slate shooting off and across the road. It crashed and cracked as it hit the bonnet of Charles's car, and immediately there was a sound that could have been rifle-fire.

I looked down discreetly. I was certain his windscreen had gone, and no driver at this moment wasted energy on watchers from windows. I was at the wrong angle to see the screen, but not surprised by the lack of glass on the badly dented bonnet. Modern windscreens weren't easily penetrated, but, having worked in an accident unit, I knew that, along with just about anything else, could happen in any vehicle. So often simply a question of good or bad luck.

I wondered if Charles appreciated his good luck now. Or had he always had too much to get that in proportion? In traffic an opaque windscreen could be a major disaster; miles from anywhere, a wretched nuisance; in an empty side-street outside his own house, to him, no more than a minor inconvenience; to most others, an expensive inconvenience.

I now had the bottom sash moving freely, but kept it up. The street below was beginning to look unnaturally empty. Why wasn't he examining the glass and damaged bonnet from the outside? And if the windscreen hadn't gone, why hadn't he bounced out to look at that dent? A woman might take time off to powder her face before coping with a mechanical crisis, but in these circumstances a man generally leaps out like an enraged jack-in-a-box. Most men, I mused uneasily, cherished their car's paintwork as passionately as their own egos—what in hell was the man doing? Clearing up the mess inside? What mess, with safety-glass? Of course, if a chip had gone through above or below the special striped strip—and suddenly my stomach seemed to turn over. He was getting out of the car backwards, and very slowly. His face was soaked in blood, and he was holding one hand up to his right eye.

I slammed down the sash, and for around five of the most extraordinarily disturbing seconds of my life I had to hold on to the sill. Then I stopped thinking.

When I reached the front hall he was trying to fit his key into the side-door. He was having trouble, as he was only using his left hand. His right was holding his right eye open, and a smallish gash over the eyebrow was gently dripping dark blood into his left eye and down his face. The stains on his shirt were crimson.

I registered every one of these relatively trivial details

like a camera. 'I saw that slate hit your car, Dr Linsey,' I said casually. 'Got a bit of glass in that eye? I can't see as your hand's in the way.'

'Feels the size of the Castle Rock,' he said as casually, facing me. 'I haven't been able to have a proper look at it yet because of all this gore. Sorry to be in such a mess.'

'Spilt blood's like spilt milk—always looks more than it is.' That old placebo was all I could manage, as I had now seen his right eye. Only training stopped me vomiting. 'Not quite the Castle Rock, but it should come out, stat. I'll do it.'

'It's very good of you——'

'No trouble. No, don't bend your head—just hold still and, if possible, don't blink the left.' I had my fine forceps and throat-torch poised. 'I'm afraid it may hurt a bit. Light on now. Ready?' We were both holding our breath. 'That's out, but don't close that eye yet.' I checked again with the torch-light. 'I can't see any more on the surface—no—not in the lower lid. How does the upper feel?'

'A wee bit gritty. Thank you for shifting the main problem. I expect I've only dust under here.'

'I'll see if I can invert it.' I had to shake my head. 'Sorry. Not far enough. To do it properly I have to work from behind, and I want you sitting down. Have you got an ophthalmoscope in your car? That I'd like very much.'

'In my study. I could go up for it?' He hesitated. 'And a chair.'

My immediate professional reaction was 'Over my dead body'. Having seen the position of that splinter, I had no other. 'I don't think sailing up and down in your lift'll be a good idea.' I looked at his forehead. 'You've some superficial splinters in your face. I'm going to touch them. Don't blink, if you can help it. Yes. Superficial, but they shouldn't wait long either.' My third finger was on his temporal pulse. The rate was registering pain, not shock. 'Right eye still hurting a lot?'

'Just sore.'

Not according to his pulse. 'This standing isn't a good idea. I can take out the lot, but you must be sitting. Certainly the lift'll be better than the stairs.'

'You'll come up with me?'

'Yes, of course,' was the only possible answer, unless I was prepared to change jobs. I wasn't.

The study was across the hall from the drawing-room, and more like a well-equipped lab. Very briefly, as I stepped out of his lift, I remembered.

He said, 'I forget where I've put my ophthalmoscope. I think it's somewhere in the desk.'

'Can't I find it?' I pushed forward a deep-backed leather armchair. 'Could you sit here? The back's high enough to rest your head and low enough for me to work over. Can you sit down very gently—sort of all in one piece? That's fine!'

'Keeping this eye open?'

'Please. And as still as you can. Stare'—I looked round, then crouched by him to get our faces level—'at that microscope on the table over there. Isn't that your eye-level?'

'Exactly. Have you done much eye-work?'

'Two months in Cas. Eyes as a junior, and three in Acute Surgical Eyes as a fourth-year.' I was behind his chair. 'Now I'll invert that upper lid. I'll get my hand under yours, and when I've taken over you let go. About to touch you, now. Braced against blinking?'

He smiled. 'Braced.' He waited a few moments. 'Anything worth finding?'

'Just a little glass and a little grit.' I did another check. 'I think that really is clear, though it'll still feel gritty.'

'Much less so. Thank you very much. Do you now want the ophthalmoscope? Try the left-side drawers first.'

His face was in a horrible mess, but the gash had clotted. 'Yes. Ophthalmoscope next.'

The top-left drawer contained several rubber-banded notebooks, an old patella hammer, and a large framed photograph of Josephine Astley smiling. The ophthalmoscope was two drawers down.

I fitted it together, tested the light, then sat on the arm of his chair. 'Right eye, first. Light, now. Watch my hand, please.' I moved my hand slowly behind my head, right to left, then up and down. 'Good. And your left.' I repeated

123

the performance. 'That's splendid.'

'And the right?'

'A small scratch on the cornea. Hold it, please. Being one of Sir Jefferson's young ladies, I couldn't look the little man in the face if I skipped his double-check. Both, please.'

He waited until I switched off the light. 'Sir Jefferson Evans?'

'That's him. Evans the Eyes from Welsh Wales, and the pride of Martha's. No, no Doctor!' I caught his hand just before he touched his right eye. 'I'm sure you want to rub it, but please don't! Some dirt's bound to have got in, and touching it'll only shove in more.'

'I should've remembered. Sorry I didn't.'

'It's a reflex action in these circumstances. My fault for not warning you against it.'

'That another of Sir Jefferson's maxims for his young ladies?'

'Is it not!' I looked at the glass cupboard above the double-sink. 'I can see spirit, swabs, soap, and towels. Can I help myself for your face?' I had dressing-packs in my bag but, as the alternative was available, did not like to use them unnecessarily off my district.

'Please do, and many thanks.' He touched his face. 'Good God! Repulsive! I do apologize. Can't I just wash it off first?'

'Not just yet.' I put a hand on his shoulder very lightly, but it kept him in the chair. 'Only a little dried blood.'

His bloodshot eyes lit with laughter. He seemed about to say more, but changed his mind and did not talk until I had removed all his facial splinters and was dealing with the cut. 'I know more than one eye-man who considers Jefferson Evans the best in the western world. I've never seen him. What kind of man is he?'

'Fortyish, and so fat you wonder how he'll get near the table with his stomach, and then you see his hands. Six-and-a-half in theatre gloves. His touch is fantastically delicate. I don't like watching any ops., but to see him in action on the eyes is an—er—aesthetic experience.'

'If you don't like watching, how did you get on in the theatre?'

'By enduring it. You liked surgery?'

'Not much. I did the usual stint as a student, but without taking any satisfaction from the experience. Not surprisingly, I was never an h. s. I moved on to the medical side directly I qualified, and remained there until I specialized.' He smiled slightly. 'Thankfully.'

'Have you always wanted to be a pathologist?'

'Yes. I like bugs.'

'I guess you must.' I held poised a spirit-soaked swab. 'This is going to sting. Ready? Sorry.'

'No worse than after-shave. Is this early-warning system another maxim?'

'The top one. Whenever his ward nurses change the old boy rounds up the new girls in Sister Eyes' day-office. "There's welcome you are to my ward, young ladies, and there's welcome you'll remain so long as you recall the finest eye-surgery can be ruined by jerking and blinking. There's careful you must be to avoid the former and keep the latter to a minimum. If you are not you will not remain in my ward to repeat your mistake. My patients are most peculiar people. They have only two eyes. Close your eyes, young ladies. All closed and in the dark? Then you will be seeing why, in ophthalmic work, we can never make the same mistake twice." After which,' I said, 'one remembers.'

'I'm not surprised.'

I cut off some strapping. 'You'll need a stitch or two in this, so I won't stick this on too firmly, not to widen the gash when they take it off.'

He twisted his head round to look at me. 'I'm sure I'll heal without stitchery. I've always healed by first intention, and thanks to your good work I can't believe I need trouble anyone else.'

I walked round and sat on the chair-arm, much as I had sat on the end of Mr Richards' bed. 'I think it mightn't be a bad idea to let an eye registrar take a look at that right eye. The hospital's only a few blocks away. Why not take a taxi along there?'

He blinked as if having trouble focusing. 'Won't it be enough if I do that if I've any more bother with it? I don't care to bother any eye-department tonight. After the wind today half Edinburgh'll have been in with grit in the eye.'

'You didn't have grit. You'd glass. And you should have antibiotic cover against possible sepsis. Who wants a corneal ulcer?' I smiled as I would have to Mr Richards. 'I honestly think you should.'

He smiled back. We were buddies. In these circumstances we could not be anything else. 'Then naturally I'll take your advice. I'll ring for a taxi and go along now. Satisfied?'

'Yes, thanks.' I got off the arm and washed my hands.

He stood up and opened the study door. 'You did say you saw that slate fall?'

'Yes.' I explained how.

He said, 'Some chips came through my windscreen above the strip, like machine-gun bullets. For the first ugly minute I thought I'd got it in both eyes. I don't know what happened to the driving-mirror. It just vanished. To add to it all, my car had already let me down twice in traffic this evening. I was actually about to get out and look at the engine when that slate came down.'

'As well you didn't.'

'Yes.' He opened his front door. 'Thank you very much for all you've done for me. I'm sorry to have taken up so much of your time, but I have to say'—he hesitated—'I do appreciate your kindness very much in view of—er—our last meeting.'

He was right. He had to say that.

'That's all right. Take care of that eye.'

He had closed his door and I was still on the stairs when my legs turned into sawdust and I began to sweat. I sat down, put my head between my knees, and after a bit the world stopped revolving. Without that delay I would have missed Sandra. She appeared on the landing laden with parcels as I stood up.

'I don't believe it! I do not believe it! You haven't been chasing Charlie again?'

I unlocked our front door feeling too lousy for caution. 'He got something in his eye, and I took it out.'

'What a nice kind nursie to shift an itsy-bitsy bit of grit.'

'Expect me to leave it in?'

126

'Not you, dear! You never give up, do you? What's the poor man have to do? Slap your face? You really should lay off him, Alix! As I've just been telling Catriona, one really can't blame the Scots for thinking all English girls nymphomaniacs with girls like you around——' Her bell was ringing below. 'My date's early! Take these!' She rushed off.

I put the parcels on the floor and had to rush to the bathroom. I was very sick. Most nurses had their weak spots, and eyes were mine. In consequence Matron had moved me after only two months in Cas. Eyes as a junior. I had done the full period in Acute Surgical Eyes, as by the fourth year Martha's nurses were expected to have conquered their professional weak spots. If they had not authority no longer indulged them. In A.S.E. I had lost half a stone and drunk roughly a gallon of ammon. aromat. We had none in the flat, but there was some whisky someone had left behind at Catriona's party.

At first sight that slither seemed to be sticking straight into his iris. As far as I had been able to tell with the ophthalmoscope, he had got away with it. But I wasn't an eye specialist. It needed a specialized check. I did not have to be a specialist to know it had only needed one small jolt from bending his head, or the motion in any car or ambulance, to have that glass right in.

I sipped some neat whisky. 'There is much I can do to save the vision, young ladies, but once all vision in an eye has gone, as I cannot work bloody miracles, I cannot give it back. Would that I could! Indeed, yes.'

'Lucky,' I thought numbly, and remembered my thoughts when watching him from the window. And then I remembered those extraordinary seconds when I had to hang on to the sill. I had not seen the state of his eye then. It had not been the sight of blood. I got over that one by my second year.

'Oh no,' I thought, 'no! I can't go through it all again. Not yet. Not for a long, long time yet.'

I finished the rest of my whisky at a gulp.

CHAPTER ELEVEN

'I don't mind eyes.' Gemmie handed Catriona a whisky. 'Takes you like Alix?'

Catriona was pale green. 'Anything to do with the face.'

'Can't say I've ever fancied E.N.T.s,' mused Gemmie. 'Folk'll say casual, "My kid's having his tonsils out." They should take a look in an E.N.T. theatre on tonsil days. As much of a bloody shambles as in an accident unit after a multiple pile-up.'

'Gemmie, take five! My stomach's still very delicate.' I helped myself to milk. 'Let's see that going-away hat.'

Next morning old Mrs Hunter knocked her talcum powder onto the floor in her eagerness to produce the scrap of yellow silk. 'A wee straw bonnet this shade? And where did the lassie purchase it? There? Och, the best in Princes Street! It'll be a fine bonnet, no doubt of that!' Carefully she replaced the silk in the envelope with the bit of nylon lace. 'Is she a bonnie lassie? Aye, that's grand! Is he a braw laddie? And what's his work?'

She was only momentarily disappointed on one count. 'An Englishman? But a fitter?' She brightened. 'That's a fine trade for a man. If there's work to be had a good fitter can aye find it. The lassie shouldna go hungry, nor her bairns neither, with her man in that trade.' She was strangely quiet for a little while. 'My man didna have a trade, lassie.'

Her husband had died when a German P.O.W. in World War II. 'I didn't know, Mrs Hunter.'

She was not listening. She was thinking aloud, and her backward-looking eyes were glowing with an old bitterness. 'I'd been put to service as a young lassie. I couldna return for the five bairns. For years, aye, years, my man was idle.' She looked up at me then. 'It's a terrible sight for a wife to see her man with the wish to work and no work for him to put his hand to. First, he'd be away out each day with his head high—then he'd be back and couldna look a body in the face. He tried. He couldna get a job. And he was a good man, ye ken. Maybe he liked his wee dram and his fags when he could get 'em, but that wasna often, I tell you! For years he'd stand about the house or out the street. Just standing. Mind, he wasna alone. Many a man was idle those times. Lassie, you could see their spirits drain away. It was terrible. Ye ken what I'd do?'

I shook my head.

'I'd pick a fight with him. I'd never the wish for that, but I'd shout at him—terrible words I'd call him—to get his temper up. Then I'd have an eye shut the rest of the week, but it was worth it. He'd remembered he was a man. But times his spirits were that low. The War was a mercy.'

'It made jobs?'

She held out her stiff arms for me to ease on her warmed bedjacket. 'The War needed sodjers. He'd kept his health. He went for a sodjer. Lassie,' she added softly, 'you should've seen his face the day he was home for his first leaf. A fine uniform, cash in his pocket, the money regular for the bairns and maself. It wasna much, mind, but it was regular! I didna ken what the War was about, and I dinna ken now, but it seemed then from Providence. Maybe, though he didna return, it was that for him. For a wee whiles he lived, aye, and fought, and the fine letter I had said he died, like a man. The pneumonia. I was that grieved—but I'd not have him back to stand about more. Idleness destroys a man. He couldna have borne that again, nor me for him.' I replaced her glasses, and she saw my eyes clearly. 'Never greet for the dead, lassie. Greet for the living. It's them as needs the help. But no greetin' for me, as though I'd a hard time whiles back, I've it awful easy now! My bairns are that good to me, and my eldest laddie's wife in this house, as ye'll ken well, is like my own daughter! Maybe I canna get out, but I'm not so young as I was, and I like it fine having folks stop in and having a wee natter with my bath. Just tell me now, has the lassie settled what to wear on her hair?'

We returned to Gemmie's veil. As I was leaving I said,

'Mrs Hunter, you're a wonderful woman.'

'You're awful young, lassie! Away wi' you now, or you'll get the wrong edge of my tongue!' Beaming, she closed her swollen fingers into a fist. 'Cheerio!'

It was the most perfect day I had yet known in Edinburgh. The clear sky was a Mediterranean blue, the brilliant sun transformed the grey buildings to a delicate pink, and, in the narrow back streets between the old lands, the air was as fresh, sweet, and faintly salty as at the water's edge in Portobello. Mrs Hunter called it 'Pert-a-bellie'.

There was an old name back on my afternoon-list. Mr Richards had acute lumbago and was equally annoyed with himself and his doctor when I called. 'I'm not ill, Nurse! It's but my back. I'll be out this bed in the morn!'

'Your doctor probably asked me to call to make sure you're not, Mr Richards. If you get up before your muscles have had a chance to relax you'll only seize up again.'

His married daughter from next door, Mary Cameron, was sitting with him. 'Isn't that what I've been telling you, Dad?'

'You keep your lip for your man, my girl! I'll take none of that in my house! Away back to your duties!'

Mrs Cameron was unimpressed. She was a large-boned fair girl with a pleasant face, and very pregnant. 'What duties? With Ian on the night shift and sleeping and the three laddies not yet home from school, my house is awfu' quiet. What do you think I've in here, Nurse?' She slapped herself with an energy that alarmed her father. 'Say it's a girl! My Ian says, if it's another laddie Maternity can take it back. He's an awful hankering for a wee girl this time.'

'And what's wrong with four laddies?' demanded Mr Richards. 'Did I not have the four myself, and then you two girls? Will you watch how you treat that bairn, Mary! you've to hang about, away to your mother for a cup of tea while the Nurse attends to me. Easy, lass! Your time's that close!'

Mary Cameron had climbed over his bed rather than walk round to the door. 'The fuss men make! My Ian's the same, Nurse! You'd think this wee monster was my first. Do you know that great tall doctor up at Maternity?'

'Dr Ross? Yes.'

'I'm the pride of his life! I'm the pride of them all up at Maternity! Every one of my laddies was born on the right day, the right way, with no more than a few good twinges. I've never had a morn or night's sickness, and last time I'd have walked from the labour ward had they let me. But if I'm not wanted, Dad'—she pulled a face at him—'I can take a hint. I'll away out back to tell my mother you've been sorting me!'

Mr Richards stopped scowling when the door closed. 'You've not seen her laddies, Nurse? They're not so bad. I've the eight grandsons.'

'No granddaughters?' I shook out some tablets. 'You'd like one?'

It was not a question to be answered lightly. He swallowed the tablets, and I attended to his back and bed first. 'Maybe.'

'Nurse, I'm sorry——' Mrs Richards rushed in looking flustered. 'Mary's had but the one pain, and it's two weeks before her time and she's that regular—but could you come?'

I had seen dozens of babies delivered, and delivered my official number. I had never seen or, until it happened, believed it was possible to deliver any baby as easily as Mary Cameron's fourth. In all she had four pains in five minutes. Yet the baby's head was as round and unmarked as a Caesar baby's. She was a smallish baby, but with no apparent signs of prematurity, and outwardly perfect. She had a splendid head of fuzzy black hair.

Mary was only prevented from getting off the spareroom bed to make us all that cup of tea by the combined insistence of Mrs Richards and myself. 'I feel grand! I'm not sick. I've but had a bairn.' She grabbed her mother. 'Away and wake Ian. Or I'll go myself!'

Ian Cameron was a stocky, dark-haired young man with Mr Richards' shoulders, hands, and taciturnity. He sat on Mr Richards' bed with the baby in his arms. I said truthfully, 'She's an exceptionally pretty baby, Mr Cameron.'

'She'll do.'

'Aye,' said Mr Richards.

Mrs Richards had fetched the cot from next door. 'May I put her down now?'

Both men glared at me as if I had made an improper remark. I took the baby and all but slunk back to the spare room.

I rang Miss Bruce from a call-box.

'A nice healthy B.B.A., Miss Hurst? Good. Details?'

I enjoyed that afternoon so much I forgot it was Thursday until I got back much later than the others and heard voices in our sitting-room. Now our exams were just under four weeks off every Thursday evening our whole set met in our flat to go through old test-papers.

I grimaced at the sound of Sandra's voice. Another crack from her, and I'd start throwing things. I could only hope Gemmie had somehow talked sense into her today about last evening. It was in that hope that I had told the girls directly they got in. I knew Gemmie would do what she could, but I also knew Sandra. It did not look much of a hope as I changed quickly out of uniform and into a sweater and slacks.

When I joined the others Sandra was in the middle of a question. '... services provided by the local health authority?'

Catriona made room for me on the sofa. 'That comes under the National Health Service Act. Health centres, care of mothers and young children, including the unmarried mother and her child, midwifery——'

'Alix, is it right you'd another baby?' Gemmie looked up from the lining she was sewing into her going-away coat. 'How'd you fix it, then? Over 90 per cent of all babies born in Edinburgh are born in hospital, and you've had two!'

'Our Alix,' said Sandra sweetly, 'makes her own rules. Don't you, Alix?'

'As I was saying,' said Catriona, 'midwifery, health visiting, district nursing, vaccination, immunization, ambulance services, domestic-help services—I've dried up! What else—'

I spoke without thinking. 'You've got the lot.'

'She hasn't, love.' Gemmie stitched on as she talked. 'Regional hospital boards and executive councils.'

I made notes. 'Remind me to do more homework.'

'And who's that supposed to kid?' asked Sandra.

'Obviously you, love!' said Gemmie. 'There's masses more local authority services. School health service, children's officers, public-health inspectors——' The ringing telephone interrupted her. 'Daft bastard's forgotten it's Thursday!'

Catriona and I sat tight as Gemmie bundled her sewing into its protecting sheet. One of the Scottish girls from below asked, 'How can you be sure it's Wilf?'

Catriona and I chorused, 'It always is!' Catriona added, 'Next one, Sandra. Gemmie won't be back for a good ten minutes.'

Gemmie was back and looking dazed. She closed the door and looked at me. 'It's not Wilf. It's Charlie for you, Alix. He says not to disturb you if you're busy, but would I give you a message? He wants to know if it'll be convenient for him to come down here and see you in about fifteen minutes, or later if that suits better.' The room was as silent as if it were empty. 'What'll I tell him, or will you take it?'

'What's he want to see her for?' asked Catriona sharply.

'He didn't say.'

I said, 'I'd better find out.' I went out, closing the door after me and very conscious of our hall's peculiar acoustics. We had not heard Gemmie, as we had been talking. Then I heard Gemmie and Catriona talking together. I took a couple of breaths and raised the receiver. 'Dr Linsey? Alix Hurst. You want to see me?'

'If I may? There is a matter I would like to discuss with you, but not over the phone, as it is rather personal.'

I frowned at the wall. Sandra and others? With this man, God alone knew. I could say no. I said, 'Fifteen minutes time?'

'If that's convenient?'

'Hold on, please.' I put my head round the sitting-room door. 'Anyone object to a short break?' Everyone but Sandra shook their heads. I shut the door and went back to the phone. 'That'll be all right. How's that right eye?'

'Much better, thanks. I'll see you shortly. And thank you.'

I returned to the girls.

'Right, then! Teach-in's off till after supper. Everybody out!' Gemmie removed her dressmaking to her bedroom and rushed back. 'Get moving, Sandra! We've to get this room fit for company.'

'I'm not moving!' Sandra sat back in her armchair. 'Charlie calling on Alix I must see!'

'Then away with you to our kitchen and see it through the cracks round our kitchen door. They're big enough! Away with your books as well! Gem and I'll be with you directly we've this room straight! Or else get back to your own flat. This, I would remind you,' added Catriona awefully, 'is our flat!' From her manner, any further objection and she'd raise the clans. Sandra was sufficiently impressed to start moving. The other two loaded themselves with test-papers and books and vanished to our kitchen.

Gemmie attacked the furniture with an apron as a duster; Catriona straightened loose-covers and cushions; I stood around like a zombie.

Sandra sniffed. 'Anyone seeing you two now would think Charlie's gone on Alix. Of course, it's obvious why all this crawling, through I must say it makes me sick!'

'Who's crawling, then?' Gemmie was using her apron on the empty hearth. 'This room's not had a lick and a promise since Sunday. I'd not let ruddy cat's grandmother in without giving it the once over.' She threw me that day's paper. 'Shove it safe, as I've not yet seen it.'

Sandra rounded on Catriona. 'Haven't you told Gem that item I'd from a patient about Charlie's mother?'

Catriona looked down her nose. 'No.'

'Whyever not?' Catriona did not bother to reply. 'Covering up for Alix, obviously! Alix knows, even if she's never told us. Why pass on the big attraction, eh, Alix? Get this, Gem!' She went on to endow Charles more generously than Pete and name his mother incorrectly as Mrs Linsey. 'If you want my opinion as to why he's decided to come slumming——'

'When we want your opinion, Sandra, we'll ask for it!'

Catriona gestured magnificently at the open door. 'Close that door and the kitchen door after you, please!'

Gemmie dipped a corner of her apron into the flowers' water to rub out an inkstain on the mantelpiece. She looked round as Sandra slammed the door. 'She right about Charlie?'

Catriona and I exchanged glances. I said, 'Roughly, from what someone told me and asked me to keep quiet.'

'Oh, aye? That's all right for him then, isn't it? Not that I'd fancy it myself.'

Catriona slapped a cushion. 'Why not, Gem?'

'For starters, as my Wilf'd not be wedding me four weeks Saturday if I'd that lot stashed away. Nor me him, t'other way round. Wouldn't work in a month of Sundays. Getting wed's a hell of a gamble, but Wilf and me'll at least start level. Cinderella's grandkids' stuff, but I don't fancy saying ta-very-much until death us do part. Nor having a hubby thinking, she's wed me for my lot—and stands to reason he must unless he weds a lass with her own lot, and I reckon ninety-nine point nine he'll be dead right. Hey, Alix!' She chucked me a comb. 'Stop brooding like a nervous rice-pudding and fix your hair. Bad enough having you looking like a refugee from one of Bassy's sit-ins in that clobber, but you don't have to make like you've been mixing it in Grosvenor Square.'

'Here.' Catriona had fielded the comb. She took the paper I was still clutching in exchange, glanced at the date, then opened it to show me a picture on the front page. 'Seen this?'

'This' was a small wedding photograph beneath the caption, 'Edinburgh man marries financier's daughter in London.' Josephine Astley made a very pretty bride, and her husband had a nice face.

'Daft ha-porth!' Gemmie whisked away the paper and stuck it among a pile of nursing magazines on the bookshelf. 'This is no time for a quiet bloody read. That's more like it.' She could now afford to look worried. 'Why's he coming? His eye? Our Sandra?' I shrugged. 'She doesn't mean to make trouble. I know that sounds right odd, but she doesn't.'

Catriona said, 'If that's so I should hate to be around when she puts her mind to the job.' She smoothed her hair. 'Particularly after hearing her at lunch today.'

I had been late for lunch. 'I missed her.'

'Just as well,' said Gemmie. 'She and I'd a set-to after you'd gone to ring your auntie, Catriona. She kept trying to tell me summat, but as I kept shouting her down, didn't get a chance. I get that now, but not that it's any of that that's really bugging her. You know her trouble, don't you?' I nodded. 'I'm quite sorry for her.'

Catriona said coldly, 'Then you are much more charitable than I am, Gem.'

'Not her fault she's in a right state at being a virgin at twenty-five. Gets some that way, and they all talk like every lad that looks at 'em can't wait to lay 'em. I've told her straight, doesn't have to mean she's sick, but I've not got through.'

Catriona gasped. 'All just blether?'

I said, 'Sure. Sticks out a mile. I just wish—do you think Charlie could've heard? If he has, what's the point of coming here? What can he do about it?'

They could not answer as the door-bell was ringing. 'I'll let him in,' said Catriona. 'You keep Sandra under control in the kitchen, Gem. If necessary, use violence, and if she's too much for you don't worry. I'll handle her. In the sixth at my school we could do fencing or judo. I did judo.'

Gemmie and I gasped, 'You never told us!'

'The occasion never arose.' Catriona propelled Gemmie into the hall. I heard her opening the front door. 'Dr Linsey? Good evening. Come in, please.' She ushered him into the sitting-room with her most social smile, then removed herself and closed the door.

CHAPTER TWELVE

I barely recognized Charles.

He could have stepped out of an advertisement in one of the classier colour supplements. He was wearing a darkish light-weight suit with an 'into-the-seventies' cut, a white silk shirt I coveted, a French-blue tie that matched his socks, and dark glasses. The strapping on his forehead added the right gimmicky touch, and even his short hair fitted. 'Only the man who dares to be different should use DEADLY so-and-so.'

We exchanged stilted formalities. He apologized for disturbing the girls as well as myself. I said they were revising in the kitchen. 'Our exams. are looming.'

'So Miss Bruce mentioned when I met her as I was leaving the hospital this morning.'

'This morning?' I wished I could see his eyes. 'They kept you in overnight?'

'More for general convenience than necessity. They'd several empty beds. The registrar wanted his chief to look at me, and he was away last night but expected in early this morning. He'd a list at nine-thirty and fitted me in before he started in the theatre. I was home by ten.'

'Good.' I would have liked the specialist's verdict. I waited, but, as he did not volunteer it asked about antibiotics.

'They've put me on the usual course, and I'd four stitches in my forehead. Away with these damned things!' He pushed the glasses up on the top of his head. 'They told me to wear them for a day or two to keep out dirt and draughts, but I think I'd prefer both to perpetual shadow.'

I agreed, but did not say so. This was being even more difficult than I had expected. I wished I had had the moral courage to say no, then realized I couldn't have said that now I had had him, if only very briefly, as a patient. The nurse–patient relationship is a very odd thing, and perhaps the oddest thing about it is its strength.

I tried to prompt him. 'What's the specialist's name?'

He told me and fell silent.

I folded my hands in my lap and went on waiting.

'May I stand? I think better on my feet.'

'Do.'

He stood with his back to the hearth, his hands in his pockets and the glasses perched on his head. He sought and apparently found inspiration from the carpet. 'I very much want to talk to you, but I don't see that we can talk anything but shop until we've got, if not out of the way, into the open the subject we'd both prefer to avoid.' He glanced up. 'May I go on?'

His left eye, in sympathy, was nearly as inflamed as the right. 'Sure,' I said mechanically.

'Now, listen,' he said, 'to this first. I realize I've a psychological advantage as an ex-patient, but there's a limit to how far I'm prepared to use it. You don't have to hear me out.'

I gave him my full attention. 'Sorry. Go on.'

'Thank you.' He breathed deeply. 'I've thought on this a great deal. I think what actually happened with such lamentable consequences was simply a total breakdown in communication between us. I must add that's no excuse for my behaviour—merely an explanation. Do you agree at all?'

'Yes. Completely.'

'You're very generous. I take it we're now in communication?'

I spelt it out without saying how I knew. He didn't like it, nor did he correct me. I said, 'I heard afterwards.'

He removed his glasses and fiddled with them. 'I'm in a dilemma. This is one of those occasions when any apology can seem to add insult to insult. Yet to leave it unspoken— what do I do?'

I wished he would stop being so understanding. It was making me nervous. 'I'd much rather you let it drop and talked about something else.'

'If you wish. Have you the same vision in both eyes?'

I blinked at the speed of that switch. 'Yes. I'm such a norm the students used me as a control during slack moments in Cas. Eyes. Why?'

'I'm the reverse. One very good and one lazy eye. In the glasses I use for close work the right lens is plain glass. My left eye's not too bad on long sight, but even with a very strong lens blurs anything close to.'

I had to look at the floor. 'I see.'

'Could've been a problem,' he said mildly. 'Which reminds me—I've a message for you from the eye pundit.'

I looked up swiftly. 'What?'

'He asked me to say to you, "Precisely what I would have expected from one of Sir Jefferson's young ladies." '

I had not been so pleased by a professional compliment since Mrs Hunter suggested I did a general training. 'How very sweet of him! Thanks for telling me.'

'He said a wee bit more.' He came a little closer and stood facing me. 'Again, I quote: "From the position of that scratch there's no doubt in my mind that even had you been driven to us immediately or gone up to your flat via lift or stairs the inevitable minor jolting plus gravity would have caused that slither to slip in too deep for any of us here to do more than greatly regret our own helplessness. In short"—I'm still quoting—"you owe the sight of that eye to the providential arrival, cool head, and steady hand of that English lassie." But this you knew yesterday.'

My temporal pulses were thundering. 'I couldn't be sure. It was just obvious it had to come out.'

'So you took it out, and in consequence saved my eye and my job. Without the right, I'd have to give up pathology. No matter how powerful the microscope, my left eye stays out of focus.' He had tensed up. 'Naturally I'm aware being forced to change jobs would present me with none of the usual and formidable financial and domestic problems. I'm aware that no man with my undeserved advantages has any right to complain when life appears to treat him with a little less than her usual generosity. I'm aware that if I had to switch off my microscope other doors would open, in or out of medicine.' His brief smile was both derisive and self-derisive. 'I just happen to like my work. If I had to give it up I'd miss it—quite considerably.' His expression now had much in common with Messrs Richards and Cameron with that new baby. 'These last twenty-four hours have illustrated that rather clearly. You'll understand from this how grateful I am to you. I wish there was some way of thanking——'

'I was only doing my job. I don't need thanks for that. I'll tell you something.' I hurried on as he was about to interrupt. 'Our Sister P.T.S. said long ago in her final lecture to my set, "Never expect a pat on the back for doing your jobs properly, Nurses. May God have mercy on you if you don't, as neither this hospital nor the great British public will show you any!"'

'That may well be, but it doesn't alter the fact that I owe you a debt I can't repay.' I was shaking my head. 'I can? Right! You've worked with one of the world's great eye men. You'll know roughly what Sir Jefferson charges his private patients. What'd it cost me to get him to repair my eye after all vision had gone? Give me a figure?'

'You know I can't.'

'Precisely.' He was smiling. 'Sorry, Alix, this one's to me—oh, I hope you don't object?'

This was like a see-saw. Being up, I smiled. 'I prefer it.'

'Good. I can't say I'm keen on first names at first meetings, though naturally one gets accustomed to that. But as it's three months since our first meeting we could scarcely be accused of shedding formality with undue haste. By the by, I'm Charles.'

'I know. Like you said—three months.'

He nodded as if I had reminded him of an important point and gave the carpet another thorough inspection. 'I'm glad our relationship has progressed to this stage,' he said without looking up, 'as I now want to move on to that more personal matter. It's one I've been turning over in my mind for several days, and, having had so much time for thought today, by this evening I decided I must talk it over with you.' He looked at me now, and his face had gone rigid. 'I do realize you may find my timing as misplaced as my conceit in raising this particular matter at this particular moment. If you'll forgive the obvious it seems the right moment to me.'

My end of the see-saw came down with an ugly jolt. Sandra, and others? I sat upright. 'What's the problem?'

'I'd like to get married. Would you care to marry me?'

I sat back as carefully and stiffly as he had in his study chair yesterday evening. 'Why *me*?'

His eyes suddenly looked much redder and the bit of strapping much more noticeable. 'For the obvious reason that I believe you'll make me a good wife.'

I glanced at the pile of magazines, then back at his set face. He wouldn't be the first or last man who had decided to marry the nearest vaguely suitable girl within twenty-four hours of his ex-girlfriend's wedding. Had I been a man the day after John's I might have been fool enough to do the same. Nor was it always foolish. I had known two separate occasions when it had worked out very well. And he was no fool, though on this occasion his judgment could not have been helped by the physical and mental shock of his eye injury.

Yet the 'Why *me*?' did add up. I was Josephine's physical type, unattached, and living only one floor down and instantly available, which was probably more import-ant than he realized. Pre-breakdown, we had seemed to get along rather well, and whatever guilt he felt about the breakdown had been enlarged out of all proportion by that slither still in my match-box. He could settle up a lot by marrying me, and if it did not work divorce was something else that wouldn't present him with a financial problem. If I played along he would undoubtedly make me a very gener-ous settlement. Even if I didn't he would make it fair be-cause of his right eye. He was being fair now. No pretence about love on either side. 'A marriage has been arranged.' The French did it all the time. Some people thought the French approach to marriage the most civilized in the world. Some people might be right—only I wasn't French. And irrationally or otherwise, I was angrier than I had ever been with him. My previous fury had been red-hot. Now it was white. I had to remind myself his eyes were hurting and he patently had a crashing headache before I risked

141

saying a word. 'I'm sorry,' I said, 'to take so long.'

'You're very sensible. Marriage is a serious business.'

As he would have said, 'Precisely'. I got out of my chair. 'Thanks for asking me, and I'm sorry, but I'm afraid it's not for me. And just to prevent any more communications breakdowns, nor's the alternative.'

He said coolly, 'The alternative never entered my mind. For clarity's sake, I'll enlarge on that. I don't want you as a mistress. I want you for my wife.'

That figured too. 'I'm sorry. No.'

'I'm sorry too, though if you'd care to think it over——'

'No, thanks.'

'Your mind's made up?' He answered himself. 'I'm being inexcusably obtuse! Naturally there's some other man in your life.'

I was trying to keep my temper, but that well-worn bit of masculine reasoning was no help. 'Why do men automatically assume another man can be the only possible reason for a girl not wanting to marry them? Why can't a girl just not want to get married yet? I don't. I enjoy my job and life very much, and am in no hurry to change either. Maybe I'll think differently at thirty-three, but at twenty-three what's the rush?' The smile that produced in his eyes was even less help. 'I should've said "think differently about marriage in general", as that's what I meant. I'm afraid I'd still give the same answer to any man who offered me marriage as a straight business deal. No, please let me finish!' I held up a hand as he opened his mouth. 'I'd rather we had this one out in the open too. One can dress it up, but that's what it is basically. We may've met three months ago, but we don't know each other at all, and we both know it. We only got to first names five seconds before you asked me to share your name, bed, board, and far from trivial worldly goods. Marry you and I live, if not happily, well-heeled ever after. Marry me and you get a chance to work off that imaginary debt that's weighing you down—plus me. Looked at academically, it's a deal heavily in my favour, and I do appreciate you meant it as a compliment. Only I don't feel complimented. I feel—well, it's hard to say as this is something I've never felt before. Then

142

never before has any man in cold, or come to that hot, blood—tried to buy me.'

'No question of that! This you must believe!'

'Must I?' I looked very deliberately at his right eye. That's much more sore than this time last night, though one would expect that. Will you do something for me, Charles?'

'If I can, of course.'

'You can. Just tell me, honestly, if you hadn't all your wordly goods, would you have asked me to marry you tonight?'

His face tightened, but he met my eyes. 'No.'

I wasn't surprised, but I had to look away. I felt even sicker than last night, and mostly sick with myself. I sat on the nearest chair-arm and examined my hands as if I were Catriona. The room was very quiet, but not peaceful.

'I'm sorry to have taken up so much of your time and kept your two friends out of their sitting-room, but thank you for listening.'

'Not two—five,' I corrected absently. 'The girls from downstairs are up here.'

'All in the kitchen? They're very quiet.'

'That's because the doors are shut and they're in the kitchen.' As he had replaced his glasses and was making civilized smalltalk, I forced myself into the act and told him about the hall's acoustics. 'Did you know they're so odd?'

'Now you mention it I recall some tenant——' He snapped his fingers. 'Central-heating pipes are empty! I expect they carry the sound. I'll have this looked into.'

If an extraordinary note on which to end, it was no more so than what had gone before. 'Can that wait till we do?'

'You'd prefer that?'

'Much. These last four weeks are going to be sufficiently action-packed without added domestic upheavals. We haven't nearly finished our book-work or Gemmie's trousseau, and any time now Catriona and I are going off to get a few days' special rural experience, as we've both worked exclusively in cities. Catriona let you in.'

He nodded. 'Where do you go?'

'We haven't been told yet. This isn't the routine here, though I think it is in England and Wales. Miss Bruce is fixing it up for us, as we both want to move to rural areas.'

'Seems a sensible arrangement.' He moved to the door and waited for me. 'We'll probably run into each other before then, but if not, good luck with the exams.'

'Thank you.' We were so civilized I wanted to scream. 'I hope that conjuctivitis clears up soon.'

'I'm sure it will.' He opened the door and followed me into the hall. 'Before I go, Alix,' he said very slowly and very clearly, 'I want to ask you to do something for me. Even if you won't marry me don't forget I only live one flight up, and if at any time in these next four weeks there's anything I can do for you, just pick up that phone. You do that, and I'll be very grateful.' He shoved up his glasses again and tapped his right cheekbone. 'You may wish to forget I owe you the sight of this eye, but I neither can nor will. I'm sure you understand that.'

I understood so much I was speechless. He thanked me some more, said goodnight, let himself out, went up the stairs, and I went on staring at the open front door.

At supper Gemmie said, 'The only chat now'll be folk asking if you're out of your bloody mind, turning down all that lovely lolly. Didn't you even reckon he fancied you?' I shook my head. 'Must say you could've knocked the lot of us down in there with that one feather! And what's all this you've been giving us from start about his clobber? He looked right dolly—hey—tell you what I do fancy—his voice. Lovely voice!'

'Yes, I like his voice, even when he's being pompous.'

Catriona had been very quiet. 'I feel rather sorry for Charlie. He not only suffers the crushing disadvantage of being that quaint, olde-worlde creature, a gentleman, but he lacks a Glaswegian accent.'

From scratch I went to flash-point. 'Don't be such a bloody hypocrite and a bloody snob, Catriona! I've heard Robbie being as pompous in Glaswegian as Charlie in Edinburgh-gentry. Bassy in his cherished London-grammar twinge, or John in Oxbridge English! Ever met the man

144

under forty who doesn't wallow in pomposity from time to time?' I turned on Gemmie. 'Doesn't Wilf?'

'Oh, aye. When he gets the chance to open his mouth wide enough.'

I returned to an astonished Catriona. 'For God's sake stop trying to make out that Robbie's my own thing! I like him, but no more want to marry him than I do Charlie! Believe it or not, I came to Edinburgh to get myself a district training and away from a man—not to lumber myself with a husband! But if I had to have one of those two men and they paid the same income-tax, I'd have Charlie! As his ex-girlfriend's now married, even if he is still in love with her, that problem could be cut down to size. And he's not carrying a chip big as Edinburgh Castle. Poor old Robbie is, and if you're the sort of thing up with which he's had to put, I'm not at all surprised!' I glared at her. 'I'm only surprised he manages to be such a good-natured, hard-working sweetie, plus—to use another quaint, olde-worlde expression—so loyal to his old and new pals!' Our telephone was ringing. 'If that's anyone for me say I'm dead!'

'If it's not my Wilf the bastard'll wish he were!' Gemmie rushed out.

It was Wilf.

Catriona said, 'The one certain factor in an uncertain world.'

I was back to scratch and thinking my own thoughts. 'Precisely,' I said vaguely.

CHAPTER THIRTEEN

Bassy had a temporary job as a night porter in one of the hotels. He had worked there as lift porter last summer, so the manager let him keep his beard trimmed to an imperial and his hair to an old-fashioned beatle-cut. This made him look so exactly like any medieval portrait of any young English Crusader that Gemmie offered to embroider the Cross of St George on his sweat-shirt when her wedding-dress was finished.

He stopped in on his way to work the evening she and I were working on it. We were sitting on the sofa draped in clean sheets, with open textbooks and test-papers spread out on the coffee-table in front of us. Catriona was away on her rural crash course.

Bassy sat on the windowsill with his own pile of books. He said he was getting a lot of reading done in the small hours. 'The manager's a good guy. He draws the line at his temps. bringing in birds, but doesn't mind the homework when we're slack. With his staff problem, the poor guy needs us as much as we need him. Seems to me, what it really takes to get into the hotel business this time of the year is an Ucca form. The other guy on shift with me is doing Eng. at Sussex, the second lift-boy's Maths. at Southampton, the wine-waiter's Mod. Lang. at Cambridge, the deputy hotel-porter's at L.S.E.' He glanced round. 'Catriona chez Auntie?'

Gemmie explained. 'Alix told you Catriona's decided she fancies that Caithness vacancy?'

'Yes. Handy for her folks as her home's in Sutherland.'

'And how'd you have fancied our Charlie as brother-in-law?'

Bassy shuddered extravagantly. 'It's not that I'm pre-judiced, Gemmie, or would ever hold the colour of his bank balance against any man, but let's face facts! If you'd my image, would you like your sister to marry one of "them"?'

After he had gone I tried to get her back to the test-papers. 'What are the responsibilities of the district sister as teacher?'

'Shove me those fine scissors! Sister—hey! We pass, and this time next month we'll be sisters. I'll be Mrs Wilf—and you could be Mrs Charlie and we could be making you a dress.'

'In the time we've got left? Get thinking, Gem! Responsibilities?'

'I am thinking.' She looked upwards. 'Seen him since?'

'No.' I re-threaded my needle with rather more concentration than it required.

'Two weeks back. Rum do. Responsibilities? I'll do headings first, then break 'em down. To the patient, the family, disabled patients, home-helps, ancilliary workers, students—can you see us teaching students?'

Suddenly it was one o'clock in the morning, but the dress was ready. We packed it between folds of tissue and fell into bed.

In the morning I was off on my own rural project. I only caught my train because of a taxi-driver and a station porter.

I missed the bus I wanted as I could not get across the road in time. A taxi-driver in the wrong lane and going in the wrong direction saw my frantic waves. There was a scream of brakes as he swung round. I shut my eyes waiting for the crash.

'You'll be in a hurry, Nurse? Where to?'

'Waverley, please! I want the seven-fifty!' I fell into the back. 'How did you do it? I've been dithering for a break in the traffic for ages!'

'You'll be from England? Small wonder you couldna cross! A body's to be born this side to get away to the other this hour the morn. Seven-fifty? That's four minutes! I'll get you there!' He revved his engine painfully, swerved widely round a bus, and nipped backwards and forwards from lane to lane with superb, if unnerving, precision. By the final swoop down into the station yard my eyes were closed again. He drew up shouting the name of my destination to the air, and at the first sign of a porter said, 'The Nurse is wanting the seven-fifty! Is it away?'

The porter grabbed my suitcase and nursing-bag and ran for the ticket-office as I paid my taxi. I reached the booth in time to pay for my ticket. 'After me, Nurse!' bellowed the porter, charging on. I charged after him up steps, over a bridge, down steps, along yards of platform, then round a curve to another as gates closed and the smallish train was about to pull out. The porter's stentorian 'Can you no be holding that for the Nurse!' worked. Two seconds later he bundled me in at the first carriage door, slung in my possessions, and waved his cap triumphantly. 'We made it, Nurse!'

'Bless you and thanks.' I chucked out two bob, and he fielded it neatly in his cap.

I had the carriage to myself and had barely drawn breath when the guard came along to see if I was all right. 'The way you took that platform, Nurse, you'll have no trouble with a three-minute mile! Off to an urgent case?'

'Just overslept.' I explained my journey.

He was a short man with thick grey hair and a sensible, fresh-complexioned face. He was from Edinburgh, his wife from Kirkcudbright. His two sons were still at school, and his only daughter had married an Englishman eighteen months ago and lived near Tonbridge. He had taken his wife down to see their daughter last autumn. 'Beautiful countryside,' he said, 'with the fruit then abounding and the leaves turning.' He was glad I had enjoyed working in Edinburgh, but, though not ashamed to say there was no wee spot in the world to touch it for him, he'd to admit Edinburgh folk were that stiff with strangers. 'There's no doubt in my mind we could be more helpful.'

I had the impression only my uniform saved his taking my truthful answer as a send-up. When my shortish journey ended he returned to carry out my bags, shake my hand, wish me well. 'I'll be looking out for you on your return, Nurse.'

The sun was shining and a very stiff breeze was blowing over the empty country platform. The little town lay directly ahead between low green hills that reminded me faintly of East Sussex. Then a plump, middle-aged woman in a shapeless uniform coat, battered uniform hat, and carrying an aged handbag large enough to hold a dozen spare nappies, two tins of dried milk, and a pair of bedroom slippers in addition to the usual contents, jog-trotted out of the booking-office.

Walking towards her, for one desperate moment I thought seriously of marrying Charles, Robbie—any man! Any marriage must be preferable to the prospect of my turning into such a tatty old bag in twenty years' time!

I only thought that once—and ever after was deeply ashamed of that once.

She was a Miss Robertson, and she had worked on the district for thirty-three years. Miss Robertson was midwife and health visitor, as well as 'the Nurse' to her patients. She had an unpowdered, weather-beaten face, long grey hair skewered into a tight bun with massive hairpins that were constantly falling out, and a voice as soft as Edinburgh rain. She never stopped talking, or, while I was with her, working. By nursing standards her official free time and rest days were good, even if one week on her official working rota would probably have every factory and bank throughout the United Kingdom out on strike.

I asked her once, 'Sister, do you ever take your off-duty?'

'Lassie, that'll depend. Have we time now for a wee cup before we start out again?'

Her district covered a considerable area. Daily we drove through miles of gentle green country. If the road ran in the wrong direction sometimes we walked up tracks and over a field to some isolated cottage she called 'a wee butt and ben'. In actual fact, we didn't walk: we jog-trotted, as she had worked in a hurry for too many years to slow down even when returning up her own small garden path at the end of the day. We jog-trotted in and out of solid little and not-so-little farmhouses, in and out of the grey boxlike houses on the new estates with their unexpectedly and delightfully gay, bright green, blue, red, and yellow front doors. As in Edinburgh, she nursed the chronic sick of all ages, the accidents, the returns from hospital, but, being also the midwife, a large number of home deliveries. She was the best midwife I had seen anywhere, and the kindest. She said she'd a weakness for bairns and a good cup of tea. The patients loved her. Never, ever, had I drunk so much tea. I once asked how many babies she had delivered.

She laughed. 'I need my records. I lost count after the first thousand. Look where you will, lassie'—we were driving out of town—'you'll see my bairns, and many more than a few pushing the prams with my second generation. The lassies in these parts marry young, so it'll not be long before I'm well into my third. And when I look back to my own student days, times they'll seem like yesterday, and times a hundred years back.' She drew up briefly in front of a 'road closed' sign. 'Have they not finished the work yet?' She hooted to get the attention of the man guiding a reversing steam-roller taking up the entire narrow road. 'Can you not get that wee monster out the way, Donal?'

Donal and mate obligingly inched the roller aside sufficiently for us to scrape by, and on our return moved the 'road closed' sign as well. They replaced it after us.

'Have you seen true puerperal sepsis, lassie?'

'Not true, Sister. Only incipient.'

'Imagine! And thirty-five years back when I took my midwifery as a lassie of twenty-two it was our constant dread. That was before the old M. and B. 693, which you'll not have used. Have you so much as heard of it?'

'Yes, Sister.'

'Along with Lister's carbolic spray, I've no doubt! Aye, but we thought it wonderful, for all we'd to be that careful our patients took no eggs or onions. It turned them blue.'

'Truly?'

'Aye! We'd to watch for that! But then we'd the full range of the sulfa drugs and then penicillin.' Her voice softened. 'You'll take it and the antibiotics for granted, lassie. I was too old when it started for that. The dying I've seen turn to the living from that wee drug. Mind, first we could but give it in injection, and each time we'd to make it up fresh from the wee crystals and sterilized water. No disposable syringes then, lassie. We'd to boil the lot, and we all but boiled ourselves! Yet, and heed this well, even before we'd the grand weapons we've now to help us fight sepsis we fought it, and well, with just nursing. Many's the day now we'll read of a ward here, maybe a hospital there, being closed for sepsis. I'll tell you this, Lassie, in the days when there was no antibiotic shield to protect the nursing few wards were closed for sepsis. We cleaned—aye, maybe too much—we scrubbed, we boiled, and the wee bugs didn't have a chance! I'd my midwifery training in a large city hospital and large city district in hard times, but I didn't see the one bairn or the one mother die. I did two years' midwifery. Mind, I'd not wish to go through that training again. We thought it good to have one day off a week. Many had less. We worked from seven in the morn to nine at night with two hours off in which we'd to have our meals and lectures. And if your bairns came at night—and you'll recall seventy-five per cent are born at night—that was your bad luck. Seven next morning you were on.'

'Sister, how—why—did you stick it?'

She said, 'I've wondered that myself. I think, maybe, as we were too busy to have time to think of anything but the next job. Mind, it wasn't right to work lassies like that, and it's no surprise to me there's now a shortage of nurses. My generation,' she added thoughtfully, 'are now the mothers, and some the grandmothers. If you've remained in the profession and seen it change—aye, slowly—but it has changed, and for the better for nurses, then maybe had I a daughter I'd say, "Aye, lassie, you take up nursing." Had I left the profession twenty years or more back'—she shook her head—'and had a daughter with nursing in mind, I'd do my best to talk her into medicine, physiotherapy, or one of the other sidelines. The generation gap's not so wide as folks make out. Times change, not human nature. The lassie in the new housing estate having her first bairn remains as brave, or as feared, as her mother in the two-up, two-down or her grannie in a wee butt and ben. The first question she'll ask will be theirs: "Nurse, is the bairn all right?" And then, "Nurse, did you ever see the like of my bonnie bairn?" And hers will be the first voice the bairn heeds, and her ideas will be the first in that bairn's wee head. Would you have your daughter a nurse?' She shot the question at me as we drew up outside her house.

'If she liked working with people and didn't kid herself she was dedicated or going to spend her life laying cool hands on fevered brows, I'd be all for it.'

'With a mother a trained nurse, she'll harbour no romantic illusions about the work. It's the outsiders that see the romance. We just do the hard work, and if we like the work, we like it fine, or fine enough. But it's the work that'll aye keep out the wrong sort. All this fine talk about paying too much money, and you'll get the wrong type nursing. Lassie! Can you see the wrong type lasting one week in a normal heavy hospital ward? But as you're here for your own future and not the future of our profession, tell me this, now—you're away on your own with no phone, no sensible body to send for medical aid, and after an apparently normal delivery the mother starts to haemorrhage just as her new-born bairn stops breathing. What would be the first thing you'd do? Don't think it over, lassie. Tell me! You'll have no time for stopping to think. Well?'

'Raise the foot of the mother's bed as high as possible as fast as possible——' I stopped. 'The baby?'

She said very seriously, 'You've but one pair of hands. Times, they can do the two jobs, times, one job has to wait. You'll know your training, you'll know the established procedure for such emergencies, but when they arise yours will be the responsibility. So be sure you'd make the right choice. You'd save the mother first?'

'I—I haven't thought out that one, Sister.'

'You have, lassie. You mayn't be aware of it, but you have, as your immediate reaction showed. If ever you've doubts about your true thoughts take a good look at your own actions. They'll tell you best of all the way your thoughts and your heart lie. Now, think. Why'd you, as an individual, save the mother first?'

I said, 'She might have other children?'

'Very probably.'

'Or more later.'

'Aye.'

'And—her death could destroy a family.'

'That's a fact. The death of a bairn can be a terrible grief, but the death of a healthy young mother can be a terrible grief with many a tragic consequence. And you'll have to live with the knowledge of those consequences. Turn this over in your mind. There's no easy way out. Let's away out ourselves! I could do with a good cup of tea before we start out again!'

I remembered my first impression with despair as well as shame when I watched her jog-trotting away from my train the following afternoon. Despair that my conventionally brainwashed and blinkered mind had so instantly seized on her shapeless uniform and roughened complexion, and ignored the lines of her face and the expression in her eyes. I thought of her face as the train speeded up, and then of the faces of other women in their late fifties, friends of my parents or mothers of my friends. They were women with husbands, children, often grandchildren, apparently comfortable homes, apparently fulfilled lives. None of their faces had Miss Robertson's serenity, and she was the first woman in that age-group I had ever known to radiate not just content, but happiness. I found that as thought-provoking as the many professional problems she had intentionally planted in my mind.

I did not see the guard on my outward journey on that train, and, while I had enjoyed his company, I was grateful for my first period of thinking time since I had left Edinburgh. Tea never kept me awake, and after the massive suppers Miss Robertson termed 'wee snacks' every night I had been asleep before turning over twice.

Last week Robbie had taken me to a hospital party. Hospital parties generally went well, and that one had, but by mutual consent we had left early. Robbie said, 'I used to think there was nothing to touch a good party.'

'Me too. Outgrown it, I guess.'

'Just how I feel.'

It had still been early when he took me home, and we both agreed there was nothing like an occasional early night. He expected to be free this evening, and had asked me to ring him if I was back in time and felt like a date. There would be time, but I wouldn't ring him. I didn't think he would mind, though he might try very hard to persuade himself he did. He gave himself a rough time, did Robbie. He had to keep telling himself exactly what he wanted, to make dead sure he stifled any heretical thought to the contrary. He should, I reflected, have worked a few days with Miss Robertson: 'Take a good look at your own actions.'

I had believed him when he had said he'd been visiting me and not Catriona. I still believed he wanted to believe that. Catriona was another matter, and, possibly as we were the same sex, much easier for me to fathom. Whatever had happened in Glasgow, her opting for Caithness proved, if only to me, that she had decided to do something tangible about her second thoughts. I had not known this when I last saw Robbie, and wondered how he would react. Then I started wondering how I would get on in Inverness, and, beautiful though the place sounded, why I had been so eager to take that particular leap into the unknown. There were a few Edinburgh vacancies going, and as I had done so much city nursing one more year before turning rural would not make much difference.

Miss Robertson had left her mark. I had wanted to move out to avoid drifting into a marriage with Robbie that neither of us fundamentally wanted, but might well have settled for had we seen too much more of each other and too little of other people.

Miss Robertson and John. I was still such a coward that I flatly refused to let myself think of Charles. When he came unasked into my thoughts I threw him out, consciously. I was very glad he was so rich, as that helped. King Cophetua never had been my favourite character, and I fancied myself as the beggar-maid still less.

The train slowed to run into Edinburgh. The Castle was pale sepia on a green, sepia, and grey rock. The old city was celebrating high summer in one of its pink moods, and the sky, for the moment, was a clear and gentle blue. From the dampness of the near-by buildings and the puddles in the station-yard it had rained heavily in the last half-hour. I caught myself smiling foolishly at a puddle and thinking even more foolishly, 'Good, I'm home.'

I walked the whole way back to try and walk that off. I dwelt intentionally on the more obvious differences—the staggering number of banks and bookshops, the far greater number of physically small men than in any comparable southern English crowd, the occasional drunk reeling between friends or against a wall, alone. I could not remember when I had last seen a drunk in the West End of London at this hour on a week-day—but I could remember the sad, ageless young meths-drinkers round Covent Garden, morning, afternoon, and evening.

I stopped looking, merely to absorb the varying greys that so entranced me, the constantly changing sky, the jostling crowds, amiably ignoring alike the traffic cops, the little red men in the traffic-lights, the wild gaiety of the rush-hour traffic. The clatter of hurrying footsteps on stone flags seemed clearer than the noise of the traffic. To me the sound of London was a mechanical roar, the sound of Edinburgh, human footsteps.

I thought of Beethoven and how impossible it was now going to be for me to disassociate his seventh from the view from the North Bridge—and Charles. Then I turned the last corner, and he came out of our front door. He had seen me, so I couldn't run. We walked equally slowly towards each other. 'Back from your journey into the interior? Let's have that case. No taxis at the station?' His manner was as pleasant and as polite as I would have expected. And very sensible. This was our first meeting since I realized the calculated risk he had taken on my behalf and what it must have cost a man of his temperament to so publicize his supposed personal emotions. I suspected he would rather be burnt at the stake than have me thank him, though if at the stake he would undoubtedly politely offer me a match to get the bonfire going. That would be sensible too. If there's no alternative to burning, the sooner the better.

'I felt like walking.' I held on to my things, assured him they were not heavy, told him a little about Miss Robertson, noticed his eyes were back to normal, but did not ask about the right one. Once a debt has been paid, who wants to remember it?

He held open the front door. 'If you're sure I can't help you up with those? As I have to go out, I'll get on. Good luck again for next week.'

I went up the first flight quickly, and then on very slowly. I wished to God he hadn't chosen this specific moment to go out for the evening. I didn't have to see him to remember what he looked like—and just now I'd even thought his short hair looked cute. Hell, I thought, hell, hell, hell! Were it not bound to involve me in an unwanted date I'd ring Robbie to thank him. Inverness was just what I needed as John o' Groats was out. Or could I try for a last-minute switch to the Outer Hebrides? Take up nursing and see the world. Fall in love with the wrong men and see Scotland. I couldn't be seriously in love with him? I couldn't be that much of a fool? It must be a passing infatuation. I breathed carefully. I could only hope it would pass on, soon.

Catriona was back and having a bath. Gemmie had gone home for the night and her last day off before her wedding. There was a little pile of post for me on the hall table. I read my mother's postcard and the note from Robbie saying he was working this evening before opening the thick envelope addressed to me in a handwriting I did not recognize. It had an Edinburgh postmark.

It was a letter from Mrs Brown. Archie had died in his sleep the first night I was away. She was giving up their flat and moving in with the married brother who had lent them his van for their Cornish honeymoon. She was changing jobs, though her boss had offered her a raise.

She wrote: 'My Archie planned all this and made me promise to follow his wishes. He said, then he would not feel he had failed me in everything. As if my Archie failed me in any way, Nurse Hurst. He said, if he passed away while you were still up here, I must write this to you as he knew I would not find it easy to speak these words, but you would be concerned for my welfare. He greatly appreciated your kindness, and so do I. He said you would not wish to be thanked, but would I be sure to remember him to you kindly.'

Catriona came out of the bathroom. 'How was—Alix! What's wrong?'

I was sitting on the hall chair. I mopped my eyes with the back of my hand and gave her the letter. Her hand shook as she lowered it. 'How could she find the courage to write this?'

'She's got tremendous guts, and these few months—God, has she needed them! So had he. Poor Archie!' I put away the letter. 'I hope that poor girl gets a good rest before she starts any new job. I've never heard her complain, or even act as if she'd cause for complaint, but lately she's looked ready to drop.'

'Didn't you say he seemed better again, just before I went away? Do you think he suddenly realized it was too much for her and just let go?'

I thought of Archie's hollow face and blazingly aware blue eyes. 'Won't be on the death certificate, but, yes.'

Dr MacDonald said it in other words. 'He was a brave laddie. The time had come, so he went in peace.'

CHAPTER FOURTEEN

Mrs Duncan waited in her car outside headquarters.
'Nervous?'

'Hollow!'

'Great! Confidence in any candidate the night before a
exam. is a very disturbing symptom!'

Sandra, Catriona, and I walked home together. The plac
was swarming with sailors from some ship in at Rosyth
Their uniforms and cap-ribbons were foreign and the
colouring was Scandinavian. Several posses made politel
determined efforts to pick us up.

Sandra snorted. 'Bloody Huns! My dad'd go spare if h
could see this lot!'

'They're not German,' explained Catriona. 'They're No
wegian.'

Sandra was unimpressed and uninterested. 'All blood
wogs after the same thing! Industrial injuries come und
the National Insurance Act, don't they? Or do they?'

We decorated our sitting-room with the good-luck card
silver-paper horseshoes, and white heather loaded upon
by our patients. Gemmie and I were in the middle of
blazing row over the iron when Catriona stormed in wi
the bread-knife. 'Some vandal has wrecked this edge! I car
get a decent point on my pencil!'

'That's out for cutting our throats, then! You can ha
the iron first, Alix! I'm going to have a bubble-bath a
read a lovely slushy story for the next two hours.' Gemm
retreated to the bathroom, and shortly after Catriona
Aunt Elspeth. I had just finished unnecessarily ironing n
freshly laundered best uniform dress and apron when Bas
arrived. 'It's my night off. I've borrowed Hamish's car
run Melly home to Dunfermline. How about you gi
coming along for the ride?'

I banged on the bathroom door. 'Coming, Gem?'

'Ta, love, no! The hero's just told the heroine she's too pure to be sullied by his touch. He's a lovely lad! I'm not out this bath till he sorts that one.'

I couldn't be bothered to change. I put on my old grey school mac which I still kept as it was the one outer garment I possessed long enough to cover a uniform dress skirt. 'I didn't know Hamish had a car, Bassy.'

'He only got her last week. Wonderful old bird! Cost him all of thirty quid.'

When Charles drove up twenty minutes later Melly and I were getting our breath back on the pavement and Bassy was inside the old car's bonnet. Charles seemed to hesitate, then drove past the side-turning to the parking-lot and drew up ahead. He came towards us. 'Having trouble?'

'May the Lord preserve us,' muttered Melly. 'With two men on the job we'll be here all night.'

Bassy emerged streaked with oil. 'I don't know what ails her. Starter's working, lights are working, so it can't be the battery. She got us up here like a dream. Then she stopped.'

Charles dived into the bonnet. 'What did she sound like when she stopped? Normal?'

'Yes—no! She did give a sort of splutter.'

'That could be the petrol-pump.' They had both disappeared. 'Yes, I think that's it.'

Melly stopped tying her hair in knots under her chin. 'Isn't that a long job *if* you know what you're doing *and* have the right tools?'

Bassy popped up, scowling. 'Hamish is washing up till midnight. I can't abandon his old bird here. Sorry, but you'll have to get yourself back to Dunfermline, and as Flix has waited four months to see the not-so-new bridge he'll have to wait a little longer.'

Charles glanced my way as if he had only then realized I was there. 'You've not seen the new Forth Road Bridge?'

'Isn't it disgraceful?' Melly answered. 'And just the job for her this evening when she's utterly disorientated with exam-nerves.'

I said, 'Actually, I should be working.'

'You won't remember a thing you do tonight!' Three

voices shouted me down. Charles added, 'Can I run you all over?' He was addressing Bassy. 'And then bring you back here with your sister? Your car can stay round the corner for the night.'

Melly said firmly, 'How very kind of you, Dr Linsey! Thank you.'

Bassy gave me a cursory glance, wiped his hands on his pants, and closed the bonnet. 'Yes, thanks very much. If we can just shove the old bird out of the light—come on, women! Get shoving some more!'

Charles said, 'Surely you and I can manage her alone?'

'Fair enough. Give the girls a break as they've been shoving up and down for the last fifteen minutes.'

Melly backed to lean against the wall of the house. 'If there's one spectacle I enjoy in this man's world,' she murmured, 'it's the sight of intelligent men resorting to brute force to prove their virility to the little women. You think they'll do themselves a mischief?'

'Doubt it. Too young for coronaries, too thin and in too good shape for slipped discs or herniae.'

She turned her serious goggled gaze on me. 'You can formulate that on observation alone?'

'Not all that hard when you know what you're looking for.' Charles was back in the heirloom tweeds. It was a relief to discover I still thought it a terrible suit, even if it did not worry me nearly as much as my old school mac.

On the outward drive I sat in the front with him. Melly and Bassy entwined themselves in the back and nibbled each other's ears without interrupting the flow of exam nerve horror stories and university 'in' talk they were swopping with Charles. They didn't bother to include me in the conversation, and after three civil attempts he gave up.

I didn't bother to listen. This was an unexpected bonus and even if I later regretted it I wanted to watch him without distraction. What had happened to me now was like a dam bursting. I suspected the pressure had begun to build up imperceptibly from the night Mrs Thompson died. Certainly I hadn't been aware of it that night in his flat, but with his eye injury the first crack had let the first trickle through. I recognized disturbingly well so many of my present emotions, but one great difference did puzzle me. From first to last being with John had left me literally breathless. With Charles I breathed more easily.

The Forth was calm and slowly darkening. The lights on the new bridge glowed palely and the old bridge was a series of deep-red curves painted against the blue–mauve sky. On our return, on both land sides the lights were coming on. The twilight softened green grass, green trees, dark water, and white houses into a gentle pastel world lit with land-based yellow stars. The colours had the haunting quality of colours in a dream.

I said, 'I'm glad I've seen this.'

'Quite pleasant in this light,' said Charles.

We said goodbye in the hall. I hoped I had remembered to thank him for the drive. I wasn't sure, and only realized he had wanted to shake hands when I saw his hand go down.

Bassy's manners were in better shape. 'Thanks a lot for this. I'll get the old bird shifted in the morning. See you round.'

Charles smiled his polite smile. 'I hope so, if only on opposite sides of the barricades.'

Bassy saw me up, but did not come in. 'Tell the girls the usual from me, and tell Gem I've fixed a spot for Wilf's car and he can have his pick of the other three beds. See you at the farewell rave. And, Alix——'

'Yes?'

'There are some things a guy can't help. You don't have to love MacGalahad for it, but do you have to spit in his eye?' He did not wait for an answer, which was as well since I hadn't one.

The starch in our best uniforms crackled ominously as we waited for the practical. The three-hour paper stretched into eternity.

'You may now read your papers, Nurses.'

It seemed ten minutes later: 'Last five minutes, Nurses.' And then, 'Stop writing, please, Nurses. Thank you.'

Gemmie had insisted on our farewell party originally,

against the combined opposition of our entire set. But for her determination our last day would have been even more unbearable than it was. We had all finished work, were leaving the following morning, meeting briefly at Gemmie's wedding on Saturday before scattering to our separate lives. The girls from downstairs came up to help us with the party preparations, and the mutual strain of awaiting results and the coming break-up transformed us into a slightly hysterical and passionately devoted band of sisters.

Sandra and I took over the kitchen, and as we turned out sausage rolls, cheese straws, and vol-au-vents, we commiserated with each other on the hideous reception awaiting us when we returned to our training hospitals as jobless Scottish rejects.

I was half dressed when Gemmie called me to the hall to zip her up. 'Alix, I do feel bloody mean! We've asked everyone but our Charlie. Why not ring him and tell him come on down? He can say no.'

Catriona had joined us. 'Do you think he'd like that?'

I said, 'That means you don't.'

'I was only thinking how I'd take a last-minute invitation if I were him. Either as pity, which I'd loathe, or second thoughts. Are you having them?'

'Don't be daft!' Gemmie hitched her bra-straps out of sight. 'If she were she'd not be wasting ruddy time now. She'd be asking him!'

'But she's asked Robbie.'

'She did not!' I protested peevishly. 'I told you, Robbie asked himself when he rang to wish us all luck, and said if we were having a farewell gathering there were two chums as well as himself who'd like to come.'

'I'd forgotten.' Catriona examined her reflection in the mirror. She was wearing a long, sleeveless black lace dress with a pie-crust neckline and looked a knockout. That did not appear to give her any joy. 'Well, Charlie's up to you, Alix.'

'Too late. I've got to get a dress and my eyelashes on.'

She came into my room a few minutes later to say Wilf, Bassy, and Melly had arrived, and hung around. 'Gemmie's right. This is so mean to Charlie.'

'Hell!' I had to strip off my eyelashes. 'Take five, Catriona, or I'll never get these right!'

'Don't you think it's mean?'

I spun round. 'Use your IQ, Catriona! Think what that man's got, and then tell me you honestly believe he'll give a damn at missing one crummy knees-up!'

'Use your IQ, Alix!' she retorted with rare vehemence. 'He mayn't give a damn about the crummy knees-up, but this is your last night here. Or have you forgotten he asked you to marry him?'

'No. Nor that he took the biggest god-awful calculated risk when he did! It's all right'—I waved down her unspoken protest—'I know he'd 've married me if I'd said yes. But he'd also have got one hell of an ugly shock!'

'Why? Alix, this I don't understand. You must explain.'

'Understanding can wait. My eyelashes can't.'

'Alix, you in there?' It was Robbie's voice. He thudded on my door. 'Come on out and look after your guests!'

'Give me strength!' I put on my dressing-gown, opened the door, and swept Catriona out and at Robbie. 'Talk about the good old days in Glasgow, duckies! I've got to finish dressing!'

It was hours later before Robbie cornered me alone in the kitchen. I was making more coffee. 'And what was the purpose of that unpleasant little exhibition?'

'Self-preservation.'

He said grimly, 'I don't get you.'

'No, you don't, but as neither of us really wants each other, isn't that a good thing?' I put on more milk. 'When you two meet up in Caithness you can talk about the good old days in Edinburgh.'

He had gone wooden. 'Wilf's a decent laddie.'

'Very. Why did you come to Edinburgh?'

'As you very well know, to obtain first-rate obstetrical experience in a first-rate obstetrical hospital.'

I sat on the kitchen table. 'The maternity services are excellent here, but I've heard they're very good in Glasgow.'

His colour and temper were rising. 'You're not suggesting I'd stoop to running away from a woman?'

'Just running after her in a rather strange circle. As she, you.'

'She didn't come here for me! She's got her family——' He broke off abruptly. 'Friends,' he added oddly.

'She's got dear old Aunt Elspeth—but friends? Then why not one date? Not one in four months? Not one grotty coffee with one local lad! With her looks, going to tell me no one's asked her?' He did not answer. 'Or that you're not still hung-up on her? And if you're not, why do you get such an erotic thrill from making her squirm? Are you too sloshed, or have you any idea how often tonight you've just had to manhandle me when she's just happening to be watching?'

'I'm not at all sloshed, and you know I find you sexually exciting——'

'Come off it, Robbie! No audience now! After four months you don't have to tell me you're a frustrated heterosexual, so on occasions any woman's better than no woman! But you're no exhibitionist unless Catriona' around. I'm not saying she didn't maybe rate that and do you dirt, once. Maybe, as I've only heard your side. But that she's as hung-up on you I haven't the slightest doubt!'

'If she's never talked to you about me, how can you possibly make an absurd statement of that nature?'

'Because I know my own sex. I don't pretend I've the faintest notion how men's minds work, but another girl can read. I know when a girl's in love and in hate, and I've known Catriona in both with you. I've shared this flat with her four months, and if I haven't all the details of her past know one hell of a lot about her present. In the present she's a very nice girl, if a surprisingly tough cookie.'

There was a chilly little smile on his face. 'Not surprisingly to me.'

'Then take my tip, and if you meet up in Caithness—and no matter how big it is, I'm sure you will—don't try and make her squirm more. There's a limit to how much she take, even from you. Not all women appreciate the Marquis de Sade's technique as much as a lot of men seem to think'

He was livid. 'I will not be called a sadist!'

'Didn't you tell me you'd take great pleasure in slapping

her down? What's the term for a perverted pleasure in cruelty?'

'You know bloody well that was but hot air! Not that she'll ask me in a thousand years!'

'Then it's eternal chastity for you, dear. You've tried to make yourself love me. I guess you'll try again, elsewhere, with the same result. But if that's the way you want it—coffee's ready. Hand me that tray, please.'

'It's not what I want, Alix. It's what I've got.' He passed the tray, and then he said very quietly, 'I'm glad you think she loves me, even if there's nothing I can do about it.'

'Of course there is!'

'By God, gurrrl!' His voice shook. 'Do you think if there was I wouldn't have done it?' He looked over his shoulder as the door opened. 'Wanting this coffee, Wilf? Coming up!'

The party ended in the inevitable orgy of kissing and handshaking after Auld Lang Syne. 'Always makes me weep,' I explained to Mrs Duncan.

'Me, too, dearie.' She dried her eyes cheerfully and drew me aside. 'Don't ask me which wee bird from high places has whispered in my ear, as this is strictly off the record. You can take it from me you can all stop worrying. I'm very pleased as you've all worked hard. I'll not say good-bye, as it's a word I dislike, but if you ever think to work in Edinburgh again I'll be glad to see you back. Now, where's my good man? Ah, there you are, my dear! Thank you all for a grand party, and the best of luck in your future. Cheerio just now!'

I had to wait till all the guests had gone. The six of us then had another party. And then we had to clean up the flat and get our final packing done. Wilf was calling for Gemmie at eight, and I had reserved a seat on a morning inter-city train. I could as easily and more cheaply have stayed with Bassy and travelled with him to Liverpool on Saturday, but that last drive with Charles had clinched things for me. I wanted out as soon as possible. I had fallen in love with Edinburgh first, but now the man and the city were all wrapped up together, the only way I could go was out. I had been rather afraid I might have to explain this to

Bassy, but directly I told him I wanted to get home he said he always felt suicidal after exams. too.

It was five before we got to bed. When Wilf arrived with his car at ten to eight Catriona was dressing and Gemmie and I at breakfast. We had loaded the car when Catriona came down looking as if she had been put through a mangle.

It was a chilly, misty morning. The mist dripped off the tall houses like slow tears as Catriona and I walked back alone from the end of the road. 'I can't believe it's all over,' she said.

I talked of Gemmie and Wilf and did not look at the side-door as we went back into the house. If experience had taught me nothing else it had taught me how to deal with this stage. 'I think those two stand a better chance than most. They're crazy about each other without being at all crazy. Ten, twenty, thirty years from now they'll be the same. Gem'll still be saying, "Daft bastard! Why'd I wed you, then?" and Wilf, "You fancied me from start, luv. Same as me you." ' I watched her pale, composed profile as we went upstairs, and for a very good reason was reminded of Charles. He was so present in my mind he could have been with us. There was nothing I could do about that, but there was something else I could do—or attempt. 'Was it from the start, between you and Robbie? And what went wrong? Or is it still none of my damned business?'

She looked almost ill. 'Are you all ready?'

'Just have to ring for a taxi.'

She was coming with me to the station, then returning to move her luggage to her aunt's before taking all our keys to Miss Bruce. She was staying in Edinburgh till Saturday and going to Liverpool with Bassy. 'Come into the kitchen, Alix. I must talk to you.'

We sat on the table. The kitchen was cold and unnatur ally clean and tidy. I said, 'Still smells like a bar-parlour the morning after.'

She was working on her finger-joints. 'There's so much should've told you. I've kept putting it off. And there' always been so little time—but I feel so awful about i now. I thought I was being prudent, keeping it to my self——' and she dried up.

'About Robbie?'

'Not merely Robbie.' She put a hand over her eyes. 'I don't know how to start.'

'Maybe I can help. Robbie'll want to kill me for this, but I won't be around to collect.' I told her what he had said last night. 'Why all this sturm and drang when a few choice words like "I'm sorry" could sort it out.'

'Och, it's not as simple as that!'

'I am! Give it to me in simple English.'

'Nigel was English,' she said, and then her dam burst.

She had been at school with one of his sisters. 'That's how we met. A very good family, not much money, but enough, or so I thought. He was the youngest son. A good job, I thought. Public relations. He travelled a lot. He talked of marriage constantly. He left out one wee detail.'

'His wife?'

'Yes.' Her face was haunted. 'She was English—was—is! They'd met and married in the States. She came from a different background. She came to see me. Alix, I could have died of shame!'

'She wanted a divorce?'

'Not really. Just money. Nigel had—had given her some of my letters. She said I could buy them back, but if not she would divorce him, but he'd fight it and then she'd use my letters. You understand?'

I was wondering what I had missed. 'No! This doesn't make sense! Even if Nigel was in on this with her, where's the point? What were you then? Third-year? What could they hope to squeeze out of your pay? Or, at the very worst, what could they gain from involving your name in a mucky defended divorce case?'

She swallowed visibly. 'I've never told you, but my father is a very wealthy man. He—both my parents— would be so hurt if I involved them in any scandal.'

I nodded. 'Which Nigel would know from his sister?'

'Yes.'

'What did you do?'

'I didn't dare tell my parents. I told my brother. He— er—fixed things. He told me after they'd done it before.'

I said, 'That figures, though not Robbie's part.'

'His mother comes from near my home. She used to work in the house for my father's family before she moved to Glasgow and married. My first two years in Glasgow I saw Robbie around and knew who he was, but we didn't meet.'

'That figures, too. Go on.'

'Somehow Robbie heard I was seeing a lot of Nigel. He asked me out to supper and told me I was being used.'

'And you told him to go jump in the Clyde?'

She said, 'This'll sound so stupid. But I loved Nigel. I'd never loved any man before, but I loved him. I know he wasn't worth it, I know he didn't love me at all. I just thought he did. I was sure of it when Robbie tried to make me see sense. You see, I thought knowing his sister and family—people like that wouldn't behave like that.'

'You didn't say all this to Robbie? You did? Oh, blimey! And this was when he asked you to marry him?'

'No, no! That was afterwards.' Her face tensed at the memory. 'Alix, maybe I'm super-sensitive, but it was horrible for quite a long time. The girls in my set were sweet, but—er—not everyone else. Not that they knew the truth, thank God! But everyone I met seemed to know Nigel had dropped me. It seemed quite a good joke.'

I thought aloud, 'Such chicken-feed is always news.' I blinked. 'You'd get the works far worse than me as you're so much better-looking and there's your father. Not all ward sisters love a pretty face or a debbie-type even when she's trying to do a decent job of work. Not all nurses are bitches, but those that are are queen bitches. No wonder you've an anti-gossip fixation. And this was when Robbie weighed in like an outsize bull in a china-shop? And you thought he was trying to save your face and took um?'

'Much worse. I didn't trust anyone then. In fact, I've only begun trusting people again since I've lived with you and Gem. And that time Robbie told me he'd guessed the exact truth, and I thought, as he knew I'd do anything to keep it from my parents—they'd been so against my leaving home and nursing, and without my brother coming down on my side, I'd never have got away—well——'

'You didn't think Robbie was doing another Nigel on you?'

'I knew he intended marrying me——'

'But as your father's daughter? Oh, God! You told him so? Baby!'

'He's only told you I turned him down?'

'None too tactfully. Yes. Did you think he'd told me more?'

She said honestly, 'I didn't know what to think. Once I met him by chance down the road from here. This was one evening about two months ago. I asked him to promise not to tell you. I begged him, Alix! I really did. He wouldn't promise. He just walked off.'

I remembered filling in my second monthly report. 'And arrived here spitting blood. You didn't by any hideous mischance ask him to behave like a gentleman in so many words.'

'I meant it as a compliment.' I had closed my eyes. 'I know now that was a red rag. Living with you and Gem has taught me a lot. I wish I'd shared with girls like you both before.'

'Who did you share with? And how did you manage to survive a general training without the other girls, medics., patients, straightening you out on things like this?'

'I've never shared. Even at school we'd our own rooms, and it was the same the year I spent in Switzerland.'

'Finishing school? Then hospital? You lived in?'

'All my training. My parents insisted. We'd nice recreation rooms, but I didn't use them much. I liked the girls in my set, but I didn't have any particular friends. I expect that was my fault. I'm not a good mixer.'

I said, 'As you've gone from one all-girlie institution to another, I'm not really surprised. I've known one or two girls at Martha's go through an entire training without one date or close chum, either as they lived near and went home whenever free or were too shy to take the first plunge into the social scene. Then that gets a habit. They end up knowing a hell of a lot about birth and death and damn all about what comes in between. Like you.'

'No, not quite. Yes, there's a lot I don't know, but there's quite a bit I know that you don't. Have you ever walked into a party and had people fall over themselves to make a fuss of you, not for what you are, but for what they hope to get out of you? Have you ever seen the kind of people you'd like to meet taking one look and running? Or had the mothers of impossible sons drooling over you. "I'm sure you and I can be great friends, dear Catriona!"' She smiled ironically. 'Mothers of many sons love me. They think I'm so noble to be doing a worthwhile job for a few years before—well—naturally, a suitable marriage. Even my parents still think I'm playing at nursing. "Get it out of your system," they say. Aunt Elspeth understands I'm not playing. I'm nursing. That's why I like visiting her so much.'

My mind had gone off on a private track. I had to recall it and my train. 'It all figures now, but as I must move in a few minutes, skip the past and tell me this—do you now want to marry Robbie? Not today, tomorrow, but some time?'

She shrugged helplessly. 'He'll never ask me again.'

'No,' I said, 'I don't think he will. You'll have to ask him.'

'I can't——'

'For God's sake, no more codswallop about pride! If you love the man, swallow yours if it chokes you!'

'I'd do that gladly,' she replied quietly, 'if it didn't mean asking him to choke on his. Two years ago he was willing to do that to save my face. He's a lot more than two years older now, my face doesn't want saving, and he doesn't want a wife much richer than himself. What decent man does? And even though it's easier for a girl, think of Gem's and your reaction to Charlie——' She stopped appalled as our front-door bell rang. 'Oh no! I meant to tell you before he arrived—I had to tell him the time of your train—I felt so dreadful last night!' She was in a terrible tiz. 'Alix, don't be mad—it was my own idea—he's going to offer you a lift—it's not his fault.'

She was not alone in her tiz. 'Whose fault?'

'Charlie's.' She leapt off the table. 'I'll answer him.'

I followed her into the hall and saw the fleeting but

deeply personal glance she exchanged with Charles as she opened the door. 'I've just told Alix you've offered to run her to the station.'

'Good.' He looked at me over her head. 'If that suits you, Alix. It won't be out of my way. I've a meeting in the West End shortly.'

I glanced at Catriona, then back at him. 'Thanks. It'll save me a taxi.'

Catriona backed towards the kitchen. 'Alix, do you mind if I don't come? I detest stations. Have a good journey—I'll make sure Bassy doesn't miss the train on Saturday—see you in Liverpool.' She turned to Charles as he picked up my suitcases. 'I'm sorry. I couldn't. Will you?'

He was wearing his light-weight suit and looking very nice. Suddenly he looked as rigid as when Meggy press-ganged him into offering me that other lift. 'Yes. Alix, as time's getting on, I'll get these down.'

'Thanks.' I didn't follow him down. I stayed in the hall and looked at Catriona as if I had never seen her before. In a way, I hadn't.

She said nervously, 'You'd better go.'

'Yes, I must. See you Saturday. We'll carry on the conversation then.'

I went down so slowly Charles had my luggage in the boot and was waiting by the front door. When we were in the car he didn't switch on. He twisted to face me, looking, if possible, even more rigid. 'We haven't much time, but as I'm about to deliver what I suspect'll be an unpleasant shock, I'll do it while you're sitting down. Being up to the neck in it myself, I've no excuses, and I won't insult you with an apology. Catriona's the elder of my two half-sisters.'

I scrutinized his face as I had Catriona's. They hadn't a feature in common, but the family resemblance was something else that was clear enough if one knew what one was looking for. 'I've thought she might be for the last few minutes. So that's why I noticed you at the station our first day.' He was hating this so much I had to look away. I looked at my watch. 'Shouldn't we move? I don't want to miss my train.'

'No. You wouldn't want that.' He switched on. 'Let's hope the lights are kind.'

They were all green.

CHAPTER FIFTEEN

The only other occupants of my carriage were two elderly women sitting on opposite sides of the corridor door. They watched Charles stack my luggage over my reserved seat by the exit door without interrupting their conversation on grandchildren. 'Personally, I blame Dr Spock, but dare I say as much ...'

Charles stepped back onto the platform. I nerved myself for my most disturbing moment in Edinburgh, if not my life.

'Is that your brother, Alix?'

Any excuse was golden. I dropped my bag and gloves on my seat and went out. 'Where? I'm not expecting him.'

'I'm sorry, I was mistaken.' He glanced casually at the clock. Less than five minutes left. 'You saw me here the day you arrived?'

It was his first reference to it since telling me. We had driven down in silence, and I had been as oblivious to the Edinburgh scene as on my first drive along Princes Street. There'd been another difference. Then I hadn't bothered to look; now I hadn't dared.

'Yes. I didn't see you meeting Catriona, though I could've. Risky, wasn't it?'

'Possibly,' he agreed evenly.

That wretched clock was mesmerizing me. 'Or didn't you then know she wanted to disown you? She said something just now about it being her fault. She spring it on you here? That why she got in such a tiz over my meeting you?' He nodded. 'Did you sent her those roses on her birthday? She got in a tiz over them, too.'

'So I gathered. I—er—also gather congratulations are unofficially in order. May I offer mine?'

That was when it properly sank in. I felt quite horribly

173

exposed and hurt. I had to hit back. 'Very efficient, your hot line. Do tell me, are you Aunt Elspeth as well as most literally Big Brother?' I smiled nastily. 'I know I've spoken to a Mrs Ferguson on the phone, but I guess that could've been just another smoke-screen.'

A muscle in his left cheek was tying knots. 'Elspeth Ferguson is the widow of my stepfather's youngest brother.' He added her address. 'We've tried to keep to the truth, if not all the truth.'

'What do I keep to on Saturday? Is the privilege of illumination reserved for me, or, now it's safe, for all—no, enjoy's hardly the word—to share?'

'Please do as you wish. I'm sorry,' he said, 'but not surprised you're so angry. As you're incapable of dissembling, this'll hit you harder than most—and God knows most'd be angry enough. I should've been.' He watched the porters shutting doors for a couple of seconds, then turned back to me. 'I wish we'd more time for this, Alix. I wish you weren't leaving on this note, but as you have to go, you'd better get back on.'

Suddenly I surfaced. 'I don't like parting in hate either. And it's most unfair to hit at you for only doing what Bassy would've done had I asked him, and even if he thought me a bloody moron for asking. Not that Catriona was such a moron. She didn't know us, and after the talk we've just had I can see—oh, blimey! Robbie! Is he hung-up on that girl! He could've bust this wide open any time these last four months—and I could've spent them in plaster if you hadn't saved me a few busted bones!' I was smiling. 'So why am I griping at you?'

'Alix, I must tell you——' he began urgently, then stopped as if he'd forgotten what he wanted to say. 'I must tell you,' he repeated in his most precise voice, 'you're the most generous person I've ever had the pleasure of knowing. Have you forgotten what I owe you?'

I daren't even think of his eye. Not now. 'As we're having this mutual-admiration society, how about the four quid, or whatever it was, you saved me?'

'And fifteen shillings.' From his smile he was recalling the laugh of his year. 'I'm sorry I gave you that shock when woke you.'

'I don't suppose it was half as bad as the shock I gave you and poor Catriona. "You kissed him?" Oh, baby! She nearly had a coronary. I'm sorry about that.'

'You've no occasion to be as I enjoyed it,' he said pleasantly. 'So much so that as this is where we say goodbye, I'd like to return it. May I?'

Civilized to the last, that was us, and it was hell. 'Why not?' I increased the voltage of my idiot grin and braced myself for a social peck.

He took my shoulders lightly and brushed his lips against my face. And then it was as if a tidal-wave had hit me. Simultaneously his mouth covered mine and his arms held me clamped against him as he kissed me more passionately than I had ever been, or imagined I could be, kissed. I was too astounded, too enchanted, as well as too overwhelmed physically, to do anything but drift gloriously with the wave.

I felt his whole body give a kind of shudder as he drew away. 'Alix, I'm sorry, very sorry about this,' he murmured. 'I didn't mean this to happen, and though I love you very much, that's no excuse.' He practically lifted me into the train and hung on to the open door as if he needed the support. 'Enjoy your journey and future. I wish we could've shared—pity—I'll miss you. Goodbye.' He shut the door, walked off as rapidly as he had spoken, and was through the gates before I had time to take in more than the expression in his eyes. He had managed to keep it out of his face, but I had seen that expression in my own eyes the first time I looked in a mirror after John's final phone-call.

The train gave that slight backward jerk before starting. I jumped out just before it moved forward.

'You'll miss it dear!' The elderly ladies gasped in unison.

A guard yelled from a van, 'We're away, miss!'

'I'll catch another, thanks!' I tore through the gates too fast for any ticket collector as my train moved out for its slow run through the city.

Charles had left his car across the yard and facing the exit. He was standing by it lighting a cigarette when he saw me. He did drop that cigarette, but otherwise he looked

175

neither happy, unhappy, or even mildly surprised as he came towards me. He just looked at me.

'Charles, what time's your meeting?'

He blinked. 'I've time in hand if you want me to drive you back to Catriona?' He glanced at my ungloved hands. 'Left your handbag with your luggage on the train?'

I looked down absently. 'Yes. Doesn't matter. Those two old girls'll hand the lot over to a guard. I'll borrow from Bassy.'

'We'd better have an immediate word with the station-master.'

'Not yet.' I knew what I wanted to say, but I would have to say it before my nerve ran out. 'Masses of time before the train gets to London, and I want to talk to you.'

He considered this and my face unemotionally as he stepped aside to let a porter trundle by with luggage. 'Before you see Catriona?'

'Yes.' I had to dodge another porter.

He moved closer. 'Let's go and have some coffee. This mist is thickening and very chilly.'

'No.' I looked round the busy yard. 'I don't want coffee. I just want to talk, and we can't talk here. Can't we drive somewhere—like up the hill?' I saw his brief frown. 'Haven't you time for that?'

'Time enough, but I think we should first attend to your luggage. The train stops at Berwick——'

'Why waste energy getting it taken off at Berwick when I'll want it in London. And though I did book the seat I've just wasted, that obviously wasn't necessary.'

'It's generally necessary to reserve a seat at weekends.' He paused expectantly, but I did not answer as I didn't know that answer, yet. He turned his attention to the mist. 'This'll blot out the view from the hill and is going to turn to rain shortly.'

I was too on edge for civility. 'I didn't get off that train in a Scotch mist for a bloody sightseeing kick! Nor, after four months on the Edinburgh district, does my blood run cold at the prospect of Edinburgh rain.'

'Come to the car.' When we were seated he addressed the windscreen. 'You got off to talk to me?'

176

'First.'

'Then Catriona? Then, I would say, Robert Ross?'

I watched his profile. Catriona had never looked more composed. Very, very alike. 'Roughly.'

'I see.' He did not say anything more until he had driven us up the hill. He parked on the flattened plateau, got out rather quickly, walked round, and opened my door. 'I expect you'd prefer to stroll as it's not raining yet. Have you seen the view from here by day?'

'I've only been here that night you brought me up.'

'Pity,' he said politely. 'The view's worth seeing by day. I wish this mist would clear.'

The mist was showing as little sign of clearing as he was of belonging to the human race. It was very much thicker up there and swirled round and between us as we walked a foot or so apart and transformed the pillars of the old, unfinished war-memorial into ghostly fingers pointing at the invisible sky. The noise of the traffic below was as silenced as the surrounding city was hidden. I said, 'If this was my first visit I'd never guess it was there.'

'One wouldn't.'

I stopped on the path. 'Charles, this is impossible.'

He stopped and turned, but stayed where he was. 'You're finding it too chilly?'

The dampness glistened on his hair and eyebrows, and made his eyes seem greener. His collar and tie were as limp as my hair felt. It was down and kept falling in heavy strands in front of my face. I pushed it back in near desperation. I still knew what I wanted to say, but in his present mood I could have said it more easily and hoped for a better response from one of those barely discernible pillars. With every passing second it seemed more incredible that he should have kissed me as he had. As he had, I had to start somewhere. 'Not the weather. You. After you kissed me you said you loved me. Do you?'

Momentarily he looked down his nose exactly as Catriona when confronted by a solecism. 'Yes, though it's scarcely surprising you should now doubt my word.'

'I don't.' But I could have said that to one of those pillars. 'It's like this,' I began again, and rather desperately. 'After

177

you said that and vanished, as I thought you did mean it—I—well—it struck me I'd probably given you the wrong impression, and I couldn't leave——'

'You most certainly did not!'

That made me blink. 'I didn't?'

'Of course not!'

'Charles, are you sure?'

'Of course I'm sure!' He was adamant. 'Alix, I may be in love with you and want to marry you, but though that's had such a lamentable effect on my self-control, it has not, to the best of my knowledge, softened my brain. In consequence, I now see very clearly why you'd no alternative to getting off that train or to insisting on privacy for this conversation. This is not one for a crowded station, or any other restaurant. But you want to get this matter straightened out between us before seeing Catriona either today or Saturday. Right?'

'Well, yes, though I still don't think you understand——'

'If you'll forgive my saying this, Alix, don't be absurd!' He was off again. 'Have you forgotten I've personal experience of your refusal to allow anyone whom you suspect of forming the wrong impression from your actions to linger under that impression one unnecessary second? Do you think I wasn't conscious of your wholly uncharacteristic passivity in my arms? And don't understand why you're now afraid that may have misled me into hoping you less unattracted to me than you've previously given me to believe! And, in consequence, as distances these days can be measured by one's income, starting to make a bloody nuisance of myself? I said "may",' he snapped, as I tried to break in, 'for the very simple reason that I know precisely why you let me kiss you as I did. I left you no alternative— and that, I don't mind telling you, now appals me! Never in my life, until today, have I used or wanted to use force to kiss a woman. I thought I'd more self-control. Admittedly, it was the thought of losing you that triggered it off, but that's no excuse for releasing one's most primitive instincts.' He bristled visibly as I smiled. 'If that amuses you I can only regret my failure to appreciate your sense of humour.'

'Give me strength!' I moved closer and flattened my hands on his chest. 'This is worse than impossible! If your money didn't rule it out we'd still be freaky to marry! We just don't communicate!'

He covered my hands with his and tried to push all four through his chest-wall. 'There's some question of us marrying?' He sounded as dazed as he looked.

'No! And as neither of us fancies living in S.I.N., maybe I should've stayed on that train though you love me and I love you—like crazy. That's why I couldn't leave you looking so unhappy, and to go through it all over again. I remember what hell it was, and even if I'm just your rebound, rebounds can open up new as well as old scars. I had to explain I'm not running out because I don't love you, but because I do. And what's happened? Every time I've opened my mouth you've shoved your consequences and hang-ups down my throat! You had me in your arms, but could you tell I was loving it? Oh, no! Crushed into submission! Helpless victim of your primitive passion! Duckie, my clumpy heels are very solid. Had I wanted to resist and all else failed you'd now have some very nasty bruises on your shins. Understand?'

He swallowed. 'Alix, I am most delightfully but utterly confused——'

'Maybe this'll communicate better.' I kissed his lips.

The second tidal-wave was more wonderful than the first. The mist turned to a drizzle and then a downpour before we noticed it had started to rain. We ran laughing to the car. He unlocked the front passenger door and followed me in.

I flicked back my wet hair. 'You want me to drive?'

'I want you back in my arms without that damned wheel in the way. That's better.' He draped my hair carefully over his left shoulder and forearm. 'After four months without being able to touch you, now I have five seconds without and I feel incomplete.' He kissed me as for the first time. 'So you love me like crazy?'

'Yes. No wait!' I held his face a little away. 'What about your meeting?'

He looked younger, incredibly happy, and even more incredibly gay. 'A convenient myth. Seeing your brother at the station was another. I had to get you out of that train, if only for the last few minutes.'

'You did a great job on that one.'

'Did I?' His arms tightened. 'Tell me again why you came back.'

That took some time as my explanation had to include John and Josephine Astley. He looked so troubled that I wished both could have been avoided. 'I had to give you the lot or this wouldn't make sense. Get the picture now?'

'Very clearly. You don't, as there's something I've still to tell you which I'm afraid you won't like——'

'You haven't got a wife somewhere?' I tried to sit forward, without success.

'I have not! Nor have I ever wanted any girl but yourself as my wife. Yes, that's what I've to tell you. I wasn't engaged to Josephine, though I knew that impression prevailed——'

'What?'

'No. Never.' He was very upset. 'Did—er—Catriona tell you I was?'

'I think—no! Now I think back—not in so many words. Nor did she set it up. We did. She just let it ride.' I relaxed and thought it over. 'I can see why. Five single girls all unknown quantities downstairs, brother Charlie loaded and single above. Next to a wife, what better cover than a loaded fiancée? Not that we then knew you were loaded, but we might've. And if she wanted to remain incog she couldn't risk us seeing much of you, and certainly not you two together. You don't look alike, but you are in lots of ways. Also,' I added, 'she probably wanted to protect you as much as herself. Don't look so grim, love! Could've been a wild scene—five eager birdies on your own doorstep.'

His mouth twitched upwards at the corners. 'A trifle alarming. You're not angry?'

'Just shaken. So much wouldn't have happened if I'd known this earlier. We wouldn't have had our sturm und drang—oh, God! And I wouldn't be here now.'

'Both those agonizing thoughts occurred to me while you were so sweetly explaining. I've got to kiss you.'

Some minutes later he said, 'We haven't always communicated as badly as recently. Without knowing anything about John when we first met, I was convinced you'd just been through some emotional trauma of that nature. You didn't know, or want to know, I was a man. Isn't that so?'

'Yes. Exactly. It was like a wall.'

'Exactly. It saddened me for you, but eased the problem of my arrangement with Catriona. I'd have regretted my promise to stay out of her way much more had I not been certain that to try and force matters with you at that stage would have been disastrous. Then,' he said bleakly, 'I had to create my own disaster——'

'Let it go and tell me something much more vital!' I took us firmly back to Josephine and asked about the photo in his study desk. 'Why's it there, if you weren't engaged?'

'That's where it is? I wasted an hour looking for it last night. She left it with me for my mother. Mother's her godmother. I thought I'd take it up this weekend, not much caring for the idea of spending it over your empty flat.'

I stroked his hair. 'Last night seems centuries back. Gemmie wanted me to invite you.'

'Catriona told me.'

'Do you mind?'

'Not now.' His smile was a caress. 'Not that I normally enjoy parties, but then I've never taken you to one. My normal aversion to parties was a cause of much displeasure to Josephine.'

'Parties her own thing?'

'Very much so. Fortunately, Ian, her husband, is equally sociable. I'm not, but as he's one of my oldest friends and I've known Josephine since were children, when he asked me to take her around while she was up here with her father, I did. Ian got up from London most weekends. Poor Josephine!' His eyes danced. 'I'm sure it was absence and not my taste in music that finally persuaded her to ring the wedding-bells after keeping Ian dithering for years. But there's no question that after our third Beethoven concert the poor girl was near screaming. Ian wisely chose the next day to fly up with the ring. He'd been dangling that for years, but she's always refused to contemplate a long official engagement. On that I agree with her. Do you?'

I nodded vaguely and changed the subject. 'You like Beethoven?'

'Very much. So do you. When we're married, if all other lines fail, I'll re-establish communications with a record of his Seventh.'

I watched the rain turning the plateau into a fast-running, shallow lake. 'It was this kind of a day. Did I give you any fleas?'

'No more than six of such a singularly tenacious strain that I was spraying the inside of this car for a good two weeks after. And since tenacity is a Scottish trait—why won't you even discuss marrying me? Too much deception on my part? Unhappily, I can well understand that.'

'It's not that! The first was Catriona's idea and the second—well—she did try to straighten me out by showing me the wedding announcement and photo in the paper.'

'I know.'

I felt the new tension in his arms and saw it in his face. 'Did you ask her to?' He nodded. 'Why? To see how I'd react?'

'To let you know I was free.'

'Were you in love with me then?'

'A little, from the beginning. Very much, from the last time we were up here.'

Happiness lent its own detachment. It was some second before I caught on. 'As you didn't then know why all the sweetness and light, no wonder you were so foul-tempered. That night I was sitting on the stairs, did you think I was waiting for you? Didn't you meet Robbie? Think he'd told me about your cash?'

'Yes, to all three. Also—hadn't he just been kissing you?

'I don't think so—not then. Earlier, yes. You weren't seriously jealous of Robbie.'

'I was jealous of his kissing you, but—er—as you seemed so friendly, I didn't think you could be too interested in him.'

'As you thought I'd decided to land you, that figures.' I smiled quickly. 'Did you really think I'd take off my bra

He flushed. 'No. I'd realized what I'd done before you admitted to being England's secret answer to the S.N.P.'

I ran a finger over his set jaw. 'And you're still a little mad at me for sending you up.'

'Not with you. Never with you.' He caught my hand and kissed it. 'With myself, and not a little. Very mad. The damage I did that night was irrevocable and unforgivable. And why you won't marry me.'

'Rubbish! On the face of it I must've looked on the make. And you must've met that before. As Bassy said, "One doesn't have to love the bastard to see he's a sitting duck." Anyway, you more than straightened that one out the night you asked me to marry you. I suppose Catriona told you what was going on? I would like to thank you——'

'You try that, Alix, and I'll be bloody mad with you! Incidentally, though a god-awful calculated risk, it wasn't the one you assumed. The one risk worrying me was that you would ask the one question you did. For your information,' he said unsteadily, 'neither then—or now in cold blood. As it's miraculously not what I thought, why won't you marry me?'

It had to be said, 'Because I won't make you a good wife. I'll make you a lousy wife. I can't do that to you.'

'No,' he said, 'you couldn't. May I ask, why will you make me a lousy wife?'

I hesitated, 'You won't like this——'

'Go on, my darling.'

'Charles, you've got too much money. As you'll take that for granted, having always had it, I can't expect you to understand the kind of pulverizing effect it has on me.'

'As you take for granted hair like gold silk, indescribably beautiful dark-blue eyes, a skin as disturbingly soft as I've long suspected, and the most exquisite pair of female legs I've ever seen. I take your point. And——'

I blushed. 'Charles, I'm serious.'

'So am I, Alix. You were saying?'

'Having all this money, your wife'll have it easy. Dandy, for the right girl. Not me. If I don't work, if I've to chuck five and a half years' training, even for you, I'll go crazy with frustration and resentment. It's no use kidding you, and would be downright criminal to try, that I'll settle gracefully for being a decorative little woman among the fleshpots. Or that I'm the type to suffer in silence. Or that you, darling, are the type to put up with my nagging. Yes, it'll work for a month or so,' I added unhappily, 'and then we'll clash morning, noon, and night, until I walk out leaving you thanking heaven, fasting. I hate saying this, and I'll hate leaving you, but I'd rather leave you this way, with love, than with a "Praise the Lord, it's over" syndrome.'

'That last would be unpleasant,' he agreed mildly. 'There's just one wee detail I'd like to draw to your attention. I'm asking you to form a contract, not break one. Or are you under the erroneous impression I want to marry you after you've worked this contracted year in Inverness?'

'But you don't want a working wife!'

'By your reasoning, do I want a job? Does Catriona? Should we both ask for our cards?'

'No, but——'

'We don't work for the pay-packets, and you do?'

'Obviously.'

'You nurse for the pay? It's so good?'

'You know it's lousy!'

'Then, as money's so important to you, what are you doing in the nursing profession? As it is so important, I'd better warn you, as my wife your salary will vanish in my tax-bill. You wouldn't consider working for love of the job?'

'You really wouldn't mind?'

'I not only wouldn't mind your carrying on nursing as long as you wish, I'd be very worried if you gave it up. I know some nurses regard training as a useful but temporary occupation before marriage, but those are seldom the real professionals. Catriona and you are, and being professionals you'll both object strongly to the word "dedicated". But since that's precisely what you are, any man who disregards that is asking for trouble from both of you.'

'You do understand! I didn't think you could.' I thought of Catriona this morning. 'She said she couldn't have got her parents' original consent without you. I wish to God Robbie had your attitude.'

'Could you marry those two off this afternoon, Alix?'
I smiled slightly. 'So sorry.'

'Not at all. I hope that's now disposed of the nauseating prospect of my having to return to a home presided over by a decorative little woman among the fleshpots? But in case you're still perturbed over these clashes—morning and noon we'll be working. We should get the occasional weekend together, and of course the nights.' The expression in his eyes was in direct contrast with his prosaic tone. 'Admittedly, we've had difficulty in communicating with words, but after this past hour do you seriously fear we'll clash at night?'

My heart was behaving as oddly as his. 'Dr Linsey, you're making verbal rings round me.'

'Miss Hurst, I haven't finished. A rather pleasant idea has occurred to me. I'd like your opinion. If you were to ask Miss Bruce if she could arrange for you to work this contracted year in Edinburgh instead of Inverness, you'd only then have to make the minor adjustment of living one floor up. Naturally, if Miss Bruce can't, we'll still marry as soon as suits yourself and your parents, and I'll commute to Inverness at the weekends. But—er—don't you rather like Edinburgh?'

'You know I love it and you! You're making it all sound so wonderful and so simple. Only, it's not. That's why I'm scared. You'll do all the giving and me all the taking. Too one-sided.'

'Like this?' He picked up my hand and held it over his right eye. 'Yes, I'd have had a one-sided vision for life had you not shifted that glass.'

'Don't, please!' I snatched away my hand and covered my face. 'I can still see it. I've got a photographic memory for injuries——'

'And eye injuries literally revolt you. That's why I've not messed mine since Catriona told me. She said you were really ill that evening. What that did to me I can't describe.'

'I'd much rather you didn't!' I shuddered violently. 'Not just an eye, but your eye. Don't ever talk about it again, please.'

'I'm sorry to upset you, darling, but I most certainly will

and in great detail—now and when we're married—every time you mention this one-sided nonsense. If necessary, if we have sons, I'll insist the first is Jefferson and the second Evan. Don't worry, I'll carry an ample supply of paper-bags.'

I dropped my hands from my face. 'Charles, how can you be such a sod!'

'Because you have to be reminded my offer includes myself and I owe you an unrepayable debt.' He waited a few seconds, then said very gently, 'Or won't your pride let you contemplate that one either?'

I caught my breath. 'Hoist!'

'Precisely.'

I had to think without confusion. I moved out of his arms, and he made no attempt to stop me. I sat in the driving-seat, leant both arms on the wheel, and gazed unseeingly through the curtain of water. I felt him watching me as he waited in silence.

When I discovered what I was thinking I knew why, and what to do. I turned to him. 'Charles, I've just had an idea. I've got awfully fond of a cute old arthritic called Mrs Hunter. She's hung-up on weddings, and a pretty wonderful woman. Tell you about her some time. I hated saying goodbye to her, and she vowed she wasna greetin'! Just a wee bit water in the eyes, ye ken, Nurse. I'm going to ask Miss Bruce if I can have her back.'

I never knew how I got there, but I was back in his arms. It was a long time before he looked reluctantly at his watch. 'If we move now we can get your things put off and returned from Newcastle. And if we stay much longer the deluge'll wash us off. It hasn't let up once.'

'Och, it's but a wee drop!'

He laughed. 'Edinburgh's your scene, Alix!'

It was about an hour later that Catriona had her second near-coronary of that morning. 'You can't ring him, Alix! Won't be any use! I've told you, he doesn't want to know me now! Charlie, stop her!'

Charles folded his arms as he leant against the edge of the flat-topped rosewood desk in his drawing-room. 'I want marry the girl, Catriona. If I knock her cold she may change her mind. Nothing less'll stop her when she decides to take action—and I think she's right. You and I owe Robbie Ross far more than we gave him credit for, which does *us* no credit. If I tried to thank him he'd be grossly, and rightly, offended. But I think he'd appreciate thanks from you.'

'He won't even talk to me! You'll see!'

I was through to the hospital. 'Is Dr Ross available to take a private call! Miss Hurst. Thanks. I'll hold on.' Charles had moved off the desk. 'You don't have to go, Charles. This isn't a deathly secret—Oh, Robbie? Yes, Alix. No,' I said, before Robbie asked the obvious, 'I haven't gone. I've been getting engaged.'

'You've been doing *what*?'

'Getting engaged. But that's not why I've rung you. I've rung to tell you you are one two-timing, thick-headed sod! I know you're in love with Catriona. Why couldn't you have known I was in love with her brother? Luckily Charles told me, and a good thing he did as a girl likes to know who her in-laws'll be. What if I didn't like Catriona? And then found myself saddled with her as a sister-in-law? Think of all those future family feuds and my poor kids having to console each other every Christmas with "It's not us that's making Mum do her nut—it's Aunty Catriona. When's she going?" All very well for you to gasp like a landed fish the other end, and I know you only wanted to protect Catriona, but *hell*——'

'Alix Hurrrst, will you stop that blethering, gurrrl! What the devil,' bellowed Robbie, 'is all this about?'

'Just letting you know chivalry isn't dead; it's taken refuge north of the Border. Place is lousy with MacGala-ads! Keep in the groove, lad! Catriona's right beside me and going into an acute anxiety state as she wants to talk to you. By the way, I'd better tell you—I told her what you said to me last night.'

'Alix, if I could get my hands on you——'

'You can't, duckie. Charles wouldn't like it.'

There was a small silence. 'I'd like a word with Catriona, please, Alix.'

I held out the receiver. 'Robbie would like a word with you, Catriona.' Charles grabbed my other hand, and we belted for the hall. 'Think it'll work?'

'Come into the study.' He was shaking with laughter. 'I don't think you'll marry them off this afternoon, though I'd say you've given them—how shall I put it—a wee push in the right direction. I could add, God help them if they try and push back! Come here, please. What wouldn't I like?' I told him. 'Most certainly not! My prerogative.'

We were in the leather armchair when Catriona came in looking very pink and slightly bored. 'You don't mind if I leave my luggage here till later, Charlie. I've rung Aunt Elspeth. She doesn't mind if I don't lunch with her.'

Charles said, 'I don't mind.'

I said nothing.

Catriona looked at us, and then her hands. 'One can't talk on the phone. He's on wagon call. I—I asked if he'd stand me lunch in the canteen. I'm going over now.'

I said, 'You'll need a mac.'

Charles added, 'And umbrella.'

'Thank you,' said Catriona politely.

It was still pelting when we drove down to Bassy's. He had just got up and was cooking his breakfast. He gave us tea with powdered milk and added more sausages to the frying-pan. 'So you didn't go, Alix?'

I explained one half, Charles, the other.

'Christ,' said Bassy, 'I hope you know what you're doing taking that bird on. She's going to set you back a packet in lost-property fees.'

'I believe you,' said Charles.

Bassy turned over the sausages. 'Something else I'd better warn you. Don't take her near Greece. She's too like our old man. Know what happened first time he hit Athens?'

'Lost his passport? Travellers' cheques?'

'Not only the whole bloody lot, but the ship. It was eight weeks before Mum could get him back on another. You told Mum and Dad yet, Alix?'

'No. I thought I'd ring them this evening. I didn't tell 'em I was coming today. Did you?'

'I sent 'em a card. I said you might show up this evening, ᵇut I thought you might wait till after Gem's wedding.' He ᵖoked at us over his shoulder. 'I figured this might happen.'

'How?' I demanded. 'We didn't.'

'Ah well,' said Bassy. 'It's a question of experience. When ⁱou've seen as many of the old "Make love, not war" ᵖlacards as I have you get to read the message three miles ᵒff.'

Charles's mouth was twitching wildly at the corners.

I said, 'That's why you said I didn't have to spit in his ᵉʸe?'

'Natch. More tea?'

'Thank you.' Charles held out his mug. 'I hope you ᵃpprove?'

'Sure. As a private citizen I'm all for it. Not that I could ᵒᵇject in any other capacity. I don't hold with any form of ᵈiscrimination. Not that I approve of your being over-privi-ᵍed, but as you're neither responsible for the laws of ᵖrimogeniture nor heredity, be bloody unfair to blame you ᵇᵉcause our freaky but democratically elected legislators ᵃllow said laws to stand. Of course, it won't help my image ᵃny, but who minds the odd sacrifice?'

'Thank you,' said Charles, 'thank you very much. I must ˢᵃy, Bassy, I do appreciate your tolerant attitude.'

'Only intelligent attitude.' Bassy turned with the frying-ᵖᵃn in one hand and fork in the other. 'I'll tell you this, ᶜharles, if there's one thing I can't something tolerate, it's ⁱntolerance. I say—the old bird's petrol-pump had gone. Do ʸᵒu know anything about wiring?'

Charles was with me when I rang Gemmie that night. Her 'Get away!' nearly wrecked the line from Liverpool. ᵒur Catriona's brother? The right bastard! Hey, Alix—you ʳeckon he'd fancy our knees-up, Saturday? You do? *What's ⁱt*? You fancy him after all. Going to wed him? Seen ᵃˢ Bruce? She's fixing for you to stay on in Edinburgh? ˣait till I tell my Wilf! You must bring him, Saturday— ᵃⁿᵈ my Mam can't wait to thank you. She's dead chuffed ʷⁱth my lovely, lovely dress and all! Come again? Don't be ᵇloody daft, lass! When'll you have time to say ta-very-much every five minutes, seeing you'll be out on district? So he's got more than most stashed away? So who's bloody perfect?'

After we had rung off Charles asked, 'Why are yo looking at me so thoughtfully, Alix?'

'Just thinking how your short hair has hooked me. I looks cute.'

He blushed faintly. 'Thank you. I'm glad you now thin that, as to grow it long is about the one thing I won't do fo you.'

I smiled. 'That, I do know.'

He locked his hands behind my waist and leant back little to look at me. 'Do you know what I'm hooked on That typical English phlegm in the face of defeat.'

'I don't feel defeated. I feel'—I linked my hands behin his neck—'this is my world!'

He smiled quite wonderfully. 'Precisely, my darling. Pr cisely!'

— THE END

HE HEALING TIME *by* LUCILLA ANDREWS

'hen, after a gap of six years, Pippa Holtsmoor returned to
. Martha's as Staff Nurse on the Transition Unit, it was
om necessity and not from choice. Widowed and with a
'ung daughter to support, Pippa had to earn a living as
iickly as she could.

ie hardly expected her life to be easy—but the situation
is not helped when she discovered that Dr. Joel Kirby held
senior post at the hospital—Joel, who six years before
d been her closest friend and had tried to prevent her
sastrous marriage to a racing driver.

it now it seemed there was nothing left of their old friend-
p and, indeed, there were times when Dr. Kirby made it
iin that he thoroughly disliked Pippa . . .

2 09502 8—**30p**   T134

IE FIRST YEAR *by* LUCILLA ANDREWS

young probationer nurse at a large teaching hospital
·sn't have much time for leisure—let alone romance.
ung Rose Standing learned what it was like to work under
exacting sister, to be so busy that she lost count of the
·s in the hectic routine.

then came an emotion she was unable to deal with—a
, frustrated love for a senior member of the medical staff
love which hospital etiquette quickly tried to stamp
· . . .

09503 6—**30p**   T135

A SELECTED LIST OF CORGI ROMANCE
FOR YOUR READING PLEASURE

All these books are available at your bookshop or newsagent: or can be ordered direct f
the publisher. Just tick the titles you want and fill in the form below.

CORGI BOOKS, Cash Sales Department, P.O. Box 11, Falmouth, Cornwall.
Please send cheque or postal order. No currency, and allow 10p per book to cover
cost of postage and packing (plus 5p each for additional copies)

NAME (block letters) ....

ADDRESS ....

(JUNE 74) ....

While every effort is made to keep prices low, it is sometimes necessary to inc
prices at short notice. Corgi Books reserve the right to show new retail prices on ce
which may differ from those previously advertised in the text or elsewhere.